Afterwards

Also by Rachel Seiffert

THE DARK ROOM
FIELD STUDY

AFTERWARDS

Rachel Seiffert

WILLIAM HEINEMANN: LONDON

Published by William Heinemann 2007

2 4 6 8 10 9 7 5 3 1

Copyright © Pfefferberg Ltd, 2007

The author has asserted her right under the Copyright, Designs
and Patents Act 1988 to be identified as the author of this work

First published in Great Britain in 2007 by
William Heinemann
Random House, 20 Vauxhall Bridge Road,
London SW1V 2SA

www.randomhouse.co.uk

Addresses for companies within The Random House Group Limited
can be found at: www.randomhouse.co.uk/offices.htm

The Random House Group Limited Reg. No. 954009

A CIP catalogue record for this book is available from the British Library

HARDBACK ISBN 978 0 434 01186 5
TRADE PAPERBACK ISBN 978 0 434 01551 1

The Random House Group Limited makes every effort to ensure that the
papers used in its books are made from trees that have been legally sourced
from well-managed and credibly certified forests. Our paper procurement
policy can be found at www.randomhouse.co.uk/paper.htm

Typeset by Palimpsest Book Production Limited, Grangemouth, Stirlingshire
Printed and bound in Great Britain by Mackays of Chatham plc, Chatham, Kent

For Willy

Again. As always, again. Why does this persist? What more do we have to tell each other? I remember nothing today. Absolutely nothing.

Frank McGuinness, *Observe the Sons of Ulster Marching Towards the Somme*

One

Winter afternoon, five hours patrolling, seventeen minutes on the vehicle checkpoint and counting. Rain. Two cars, two drivers: one man, one woman. She was in the white car, three children with her. One adult passenger, male, in the other car, the red one. One multiple: four men on the rise, four in the fields, and four on the road. Two of us by the first car, two by the second. One round fired.

There were reports to do, days afterwards when Joseph had to be interviewed. RUC and army. Debriefing, the doctor, the welfare officer. He vomited before the first one, with the police. It was the same afternoon, after they got back to the base. Joseph didn't tell anybody about being sick, thought they'd smell it anyway, anyone who went near the bogs.

Still had the sweat on his back and his hands when he was marched in to go over and over what happened. Six faces in the room, RUC and Red Caps, nobody Joseph recognised. There was the army solicitor too, who sat to one side of him and wrote things down while the others did the asking. Only two hours since Joseph was out on the road, maybe three, but it was still hard to get it all in the right order. MPs sitting back and watching, RUC wanting to hear it from him again and again, checking and checking, with the same and then with different questions.

– What colour was the Astra?
– Red.

He'd said that before.

– It was red.
– Do you know how long it was there?

No.

– Before we started checking it?
–Yes, you said it stopped a few metres away and waited.
How long?

He didn't know.

– They stopped too far back from us. Had the engine
running. The whole time we were checking the car in
front.

Sounded stupid, everything he said made him sound like
he was slow or something. It didn't make much sense
to Joseph either, now he tried to explain it.

– Wasn't safe to have the checkpoint up that long, you
know? Had us all on edge, the last car hanging back
when we should have been packing up.

It was Armagh, it was getting dark and they'd been
patrolling for hours, fields and roads. No buzz, no fuss.
He hadn't been expecting anything to happen, not until
he saw that car waiting for them. Joseph tried again. To
find the best place to start.

– There were two cars. The one we'd stopped and then the Astra.

– Yes, right. The first car, the white Escort, had stalled you say.

– We'd finished checking her and then she stalled when she was driving away.

– Draw it. Bird's-eye view.

Pencil and paper pushed across the desk, Joseph made his lines. Drew a box for the Astra, then the Escort, with an arrow showing the direction it was going when the engine cut out. But once that was in, he saw he'd drawn the Astra too close: looked like it was at the checkpoint already. So he re-drew that box, further back, and then asked if they had a rubber, explaining:

– I've not drawn it right. It's that one, see? Further back along the road.

He scribbled over the first box and they gave him more paper so he could draw it all again, and then they asked more questions. About what happened next, when the Astra pulled up to the checkpoint, and Joseph drew some new boxes for them, on another bit of paper.

– He opened his door, but he didn't get out. Not at first.

– The driver or the passenger?

– Driver. The Lieutenant was talking to him. We were all watching, you know?

The whole patrol, thinking something was about to kick off, or why was the driver not getting out like he was meant to? Joseph looked at the men across the table: they must know what he meant, surely. But if they did, they didn't show it, they just wanted to know where everyone was standing, and Joseph marked the patrol onto his plan with crosses. Drew ones for the Lieutenant, and for Townsend, they were both by the Astra. Then the man he shot, because he was standing by the car with them. But that was after he got out of the driver's seat to answer the Lieutenant's questions. Maybe he should start on a new sheet, but no one said anything, so Joseph drew a cross for his Corporal, Jarvis, by the other car, the Escort: he'd gone to talk to the woman after she'd stalled. And he must have put one for himself somewhere around there too, because if he hadn't they would have asked him. Questions were coming all the time: about how long it took before the driver got out of the Astra. And about the other man, still in the car, in the passenger seat, wouldn't wind his window down, even after Townsend kept knocking.

– Corporal told me to keep an eye on what was happening. We didn't know if he was hurt or sick or what. Hiding something.
– What gave you that suspicion?

Joseph didn't have a ready answer. Felt like that the whole time he was in there. Being asked about the order of things and about the warnings: if any were shouted, how many and when. He tried to keep it all together, one eye on the bin by the desk in case he had to puke again.

He kept reaching behind him. Why would he do that if he wasn't carrying something? Don't remember thinking about it. Just wasn't a risk worth taking.

Mostly we flew at dawn. It was often very misty up there over the forests. Pale sunrises and cool, a lot of moisture in the air. Best to get out before the heat had built up and the cloud, and you still had a chance of spotting something, usually it was smoke from their cooking fires. The Mau Mau had been flushed out of Nairobi by this stage, but they were holding out up in the Aberdares. The army was fighting them on the ground, Royal Inniskillings, if I remember rightly, and King's African Rifles, but it was very difficult terrain. Mountainous, dense forest. We were there to provide support from the air.

The spotter would be in a Piper Pacer, or a Harvard, something light. He'd send down a flare to mark the target, and then we'd go in. Sometimes just one Lincoln, sometimes as many as four or five. Each of us would be carrying five five-hundred-pound and five one-thousand-pound bombs. Something in that order. We'd follow these visual attacks with low-level strafing runs: had gunners in the front and rear turrets and, cloud permitting, we'd use both. At around five hundred feet, banking steeply over the canopy.

Most mornings that was the routine. About an hour all in. I was there for seven months and later on our strikes were stepped up, eight in one day was the most I remember. They lasted almost two years, the air operations. Best part of a decade in all, the whole Emergency, and the insurgents were up in those mountains right to the end.

I can't say what effect we had. It was too dense to see much, the forest. The white spotter's flare I can remember. Sometimes a darker grey cloud thrown up by one of our bombs, but nothing much else. No real indication of what might have been happening underneath. They seemed to swallow everything, those trees.

Two

Alice saw him twice before they slept together, and it was exciting, that waiting and seeing. Three times really, if you count the first evening: in the pub for Stan's birthday, everyone sitting around the big tables at the back, and Alice didn't even know his name then. They were all playing cards, and Clare had gone round the table before she started dealing, so everyone would know who everyone was, but there were so many of them: Friday night noise, and everyone leaning into each other to get heard. Alice was on her second pint by then, and she'd forgotten most of their names before the first hand was played. Blokes from Stan's poker night; his brother and sister, come over from Poland to celebrate; the rest were men who worked with him, plus wives and girl-friends. Alice had met a couple before, she was sure, but she found it hard to keep track, and in any case, she didn't remember him from before. He was sitting next to her and he could see her cards, because she was too busy watching what was being laid, thinking she might have enough to win this hand. Alice only ever played if she was out with Clare and Stan and the idea of winning was enough of a novelty to have her preoccupied. He leaned over halfway through, curled his fingers round hers, tucked her little fan of suits together and smiled.

It wasn't much, that small gesture, but it was enough for them to say hello to each other a couple of weeks later. Same pub, and out with Stan again, but just for a weekend drink this time, no special occasion. She was glad and surprised to see him, because he wasn't one of Stan's regular crowd. Surprised that she was glad too, but that wasn't such a bad way to be feeling. They ended up standing together in the crush at the bar and got talking. *Alright, Alice*: he said it like they knew each other already, smiling. And then she had to spend the rest of the evening waiting for someone to say his name. Joseph.

He wasn't tall: they were shoulder to shoulder at the bar, just about. He rolled a cigarette while they were waiting, and she watched his bony knuckles, long fingers, noticed the small gap in his teeth at one side, and that she could see the pink of his tongue when he smiled. She couldn't remember his eyes, just the feel of them on her every so often, even when they were back at the tables and talking to other people. It was a good night: Clare was at home with the kids, but Stan was on form. His brother had stayed on, and a few other friends were there that Alice always enjoyed seeing. She didn't speak directly to Joseph again, but was aware of him all evening. Skinny frame, the frayed collar of his T-shirt, work dust on his arms and trousers. Had to ask him to throw her jacket across the table when she was leaving. Joseph stood up and passed it to her, started chatting while she was pulling it on.

– Where do you know Stan from?
– Clare. I've known her years.
– She's a nurse, isn't she?
– Physio. We both are. We were at college together, a while ago now.
– How old are you, then?
– Thirty-one.

Alice looked at him, at his smile.

– Why?
– Too young for you.

Clare told her he was lovely. Thirty next birthday, as far as she knew. It was a Friday morning, and they were sitting on one of the benches in the hospital courtyard, drinking coffee. Willing summer to start early, their legs stretched out in front of them, faces turned to the sun. Alice had been at Clare's house on Wednesday, after work, when Joseph came round to pick up the keys for a job he was doing with Stan. He was a plasterer, and Clare said they were glad to have him on their books: the best one they'd found this side of the river, and a useful painter and decorator too. He'd been working on and off for Stan for a while.

– It would be more on than off if we had our way, but Joseph's in demand.

Stan did extensions for people, lofts too. He was from Wroslaw: Stanislaus. He'd been in London fifteen years, the last ten of them legal, after he got married to Clare. She took care of the books for him, and the business was doing well enough for her to go part-time at the hospital. They had two kids, and once they were both at school, Clare had done a couple of accountancy courses. She was the one who paid the wages, told Alice that Joseph was good about it if they ever had to be late, for whatever reason.

– He's not a pushover or anything. He'll always call you. But he's not an arsehole about it like some of them can be.

Alice knew Clare was getting curious, had felt it earlier in the week too: that Clare was amused at how familiar she'd been with Joseph. But Alice didn't bite, just sat and sipped her coffee, eyes shut against the sun, waited for Clare's question to come.

— Why you asking, anyway?
— No reason.
— I've seen you talking.

Clare was smiling, Alice too: she still had her eyes closed, but she could hear it in her friend's voice.

— Stan says he's smart. A good finisher. I reckon he'd be nice to have around.

Alice knew Joseph liked her, but that didn't mean anything would happen. *Will we, won't we?* Go to bed together, like each other enough to keep going to bed together? It made Alice smile at herself: the way it distracted her, how much she was enjoying it. Days drifting at work, her head busy with what her body wanted.

It was easy when it happened. Quiet and clumsy, but effortless too. Afternoon, not drunk. Curtains closed against the day, but her bedroom was still light. The first time with clothes still on, the second without. Joseph took them off: smiling, self-conscious, intent. His bed-warm hands on her belly, between her thighs.

Alice liked the awkwardness of those first few times: the quiet and the question of what was going on between them. When he left, Joseph would just say he'd see her soon, and Alice liked that too: the way he wasn't asking or presuming, and how they managed neither to force nor avoid the question. She didn't tell anyone for a while, not even Clare, and this made her laugh, because she was too old for that, surely: *can't put a jinx on things by talking about them, can you?* She was enjoying all of it. The sex and the uncertainty, the finding out about someone and liking him, the phone messages on the fridge when she got home in the evening. Martha in the front room, buried in marking, calling through to her while she made some tea.

– Joseph rang. About half an hour ago.
– I saw, thanks.

Alice took the milk out and closed the fridge door. Looked at the scrap of paper stuck there, and the number that she still hadn't written in her book.

– Should I be setting his place for breakfast, do you think?

Her flatmate was in the doorway, teasing. Alice waved her away, but she was aware she was smiling. Whatever came of it, she was glad it was happening. Her friends were too, the ones who guessed or got it out of her. Clare said:

– Good for you. You've had a rough time of it lately.

Joseph went round the back of his sister's house to the kitchen door, found her standing by the sink holding a plate, hurrying a sandwich. She kissed him hello with her cheeks full of bread.

– Sorry, Joey. It's a bit mad today.

He filled the kettle and Eve started on the dishes, talking to him over her shoulder.

– Ben's still asleep, I'll get him up in a minute. He's due at nursery at two. I've got the buggy ready, his drink and that. You could just play with him in the garden or something till then.
– No problem.

Joseph yawned, hard, his eyes tearing up. He'd slept in until gone eleven that morning, could have stayed in bed all day. His first off in a couple of weeks, he'd been working straight through on two different jobs, and he stayed over at Alice's last night: it ended up being a late one again. She didn't wake him when she left for work, and the flat was empty when he got up. Felt weird to be helping himself to breakfast in her kitchen, so he went home. Found a message from Eve on the answerphone.

– You hungry, Joey? You had some lunch?

Eve had started on the surfaces, emptying her handful of crumbs into the bin as she was passing, the crusts of her sandwich she didn't have time to be finishing.

– Haven't managed breakfast yet. Do you want a cup?
– Can't. Meant to be there for half one. The minister couldn't make it any later.

Eve was doing the flowers for a wedding, a bigger job than her usual ones. Normally she managed to fit things around Ben, just about, because Arthur drove a cab and his shifts were flexible, only there were two drivers sick today, so he was covering and she had to meet the people up at the church. Joseph made tea for himself while his sister swept the floor around him, patting his legs to move him out of the way.

– Eve, come on, leave it. I'll do it after you've gone.

She sat down and watched him rubbing his face.

– Haven't seen much of you lately, brother.
– No. There's been a lot of work going. Got a job up in Hackney starting next week, but it'll slack off a bit after that, I reckon.

Eve looked at him a couple of seconds longer than usual. She wasn't smiling, not exactly, but there was something in her face. Never asked him where he was this morning when she'd phoned. Joseph couldn't tell if she was winding him up. She grabbed a gulp of his tea on her way out of the kitchen.

– I'll go and get the little one up.

Joseph carried Ben out to the van to say goodbye to his
mum, sat him up on his shoulders, so he could see her
through the glass. Eve rolled down the window and blew
a kiss at them, asked Joseph to make sure he locked the
back door before he took Ben up the road.

– Don't worry.
– Make yourself something to eat, skinny malink.
– I will.

She started winding the window up again, with that
same look on her face from back in the kitchen. Hard
not to smile. Joseph said:

– Her name's Alice.

Eve laughed.

– About time, Joey.

She stuck her hand out of the window and waved at
him and Ben as she drove away.

The Saturday traffic moved fast, dispersed, the South Circular was clear and Alice arrived sooner than she expected. Earlier than arranged with her grandfather and he wasn't at home. She rang the bell a second time, just to be sure, before she let herself in.

Three letters lay unopened on the side table in the porch, one for her gran. The house was cool, dim, although the day outside was bright spring. The tiled hall was swept, the carpet runner clean, but surprisingly threadbare: there all her life and Alice had never noticed it before, that the red–green pattern had worn brown in places, marking the path of feet over years and decades. Two weeks since she was last here, and not quite four months since the funeral. When the house had been full of quiet guests holding plates of uneaten sandwiches, and her grandfather paced between them, shaking hands and saying thanks for coming, as if he wanted them all gone as soon as possible.

Alice didn't like to go further inside the empty house, stepped out again through the porch, past the roses along the short gravel path to the gate. She looked up and down the street, but there was no sign of him, just pillar-box and lamp-post, bay windows. Parked cars and bedding plants. He didn't say he had anything planned, but then why should he tell her his business? More empty hours to fill each day, more chores to do now he's on his own.

Alice went inside and put the kettle on. In the kitchen, she noticed it too: everything clean and in its place, but somehow sparse and worn. Colours faded, numbers rubbed off the cooker dials over the years. The cupboards mostly empty, a few tins and jars, and though they were all spotless, they still smelled of crumbs.

The kettle roared and Alice pulled out mugs, teapot, a spoon from the drawer. Didn't hear the key in the door.

– Hello hello. You're early, dear. Or is it me? Late I mean?

Her grandfather called from the hallway and Alice stepped out to meet him. A quiet smile, smart in his blue blazer and tie. Pressed and trimmed and groomed. That familiar smell, as though he were freshly shaven, which he carried with him through the day.

– Hello, Grandad. Traffic was better than I thought.
– You came by car?
– I borrowed Martha's. Easier than getting the train.
– Yes. We suburbanites are not well served these days.

Alice smiled at him: the usual pragmatics, the usual opening gambits. Her grandfather squeezed her shoulder in silent greeting. He looked well, she thought. A bit tired maybe.

– I put the kettle on.
– Yes, you're a good girl.

He walked ahead of her back to the kitchen and Alice saw he was carrying her grandmother's shopping bag. Carton of milk, tealeaves, newspaper, visible through the string weave. He lifted it onto the worktop and started unpacking. Shopping seemed such an unlikely activity for him: he'd been doing it for a while, at least since Gran got ill, but Alice still wasn't used to the idea.

– Shall I put these away?
– No, no, I'll take care of things in here. You go and get some china for us to drink from.

He pushed her gently back out into the corridor. Alice could hear him working while she collected cups and saucers, the good spoons from the sideboard. There were a few cards on the shelf above, lilies and remembrance: most Alice had seen already and all from people she knew, family friends and neighbours, a modest circle of familiar names. Above them, at eye level, were the photos of her grandparents' life together, their small family. Alice's primary school photo, gappy teeth and bunches, her eighteenth birthday and her mum's graduation. Mum and Alan walking in the Dales: Alice remembered taking that one, on holiday with them while she was still studying, not long after they got married. Her grandfather had been rearranging the pictures since the last time she saw them, and it made her pause. Touched her when she realised his wedding photo was now in the middle: he and Gran holding hands outside the old registry office in Lewisham. On either side were the portraits they gave each other while they were courting. Those pictures used to be in an album, Alice could remember which one, so he must have been out and bought frames for them: Gran in a silk blouse and Grandad in uniform, both taken in a studio, somewhere in Nairobi. The most recent photo had been moved: it stood on top of her grandmother's piano now, opposite the chair her grandfather sat in when reading. It was of the five of them, all together on their anniversary, their forty-fourth, and it was taken here, out on the patio. Alice, her mum and Alan, flanking the still-happy couple, holding their champagne glasses up to the camera. That was before Gran got ill and was still plump, her hair still curly, done every other Monday in the salon on the Sydenham Road, opposite the post office. Only four years ago, but it seemed a different time, a different woman. Alice wondered how long it would be before the image in the photo took over in her memory again. Her grandad called from the kitchen:

– It's brewed, Alice. I'll pour when you're ready.

They took their teacups out into the garden and did the crossword together, sitting on the plastic chairs on the patio. They couldn't finish it and fell silent over the last two clues. Five across and eight down. Alice followed her grandfather's eyeline over the trim borders of the garden, couldn't see what he was looking at, something in the middle distance. The cakes he bought this morning sat untouched on the table between them, iced fingers sweating in the sun.

– Did we have a reason for you coming?

Alice blinked.

– No, I just wanted to see how you were. Keep you company for a bit.
– Yes. Only this morning I couldn't remember. Thought there might have been something to sign, but then I was sure I'd done all that.

The sun was strong on the back of her neck and her hair had grown hot. Alice sat up. She could see the kitchen clock through the open door: nearly five, and she'd been here longer than planned. She was seeing Joseph later, and had promised Martha the car would be back before dinner. Her grandad looked tired, eyes elsewhere, squinting against the sun. Alice started clearing the table, told him she'd wash up and then get going. Watched his face, but she got no response. Afterwards, in the car on the way home, she thought he couldn't have heard her, because when she stood to take their plates inside he'd looked surprised, had pushed himself up out of his chair.

– Oh. You're off. But you'll come again soon, won't you, Alice dear?

Been a while. It had been a while since there was anyone interested, anyone interesting. Alice hadn't been looking. She hadn't felt the need, so Joseph was unexpected. Came at a time when she was still caught up in her grandmother's illness and passing.

Nineteen months, Alice counted them, *from diagnosis*. Plus the weeks before, made it almost two years. She'd always been regular about seeing her grandparents, and spent a lot more time with them after the treatment started. Helping her grandad with the chores, driving Gran to the hairdresser's once a fortnight, while she could still manage the time under the dryers, before the chemo robbed her of her hair. Her grandmother kept up her music as long as she could, and Alice would sit next to her at the piano on free afternoons, following the notes and turning the pages. Gran started repeating and then missing phrases, more so as the months went on, and she was aware of it too, but she still wanted to play. Missed it when she went into the hospice. That was during her last weeks, over the winter. It was only two stops on the train from work, and Alice visited her daily. Brought her sheet music, read the interesting bits of the newspaper out loud to her: she always wanted the letters to the editor and the leader column first, the gardening articles at weekends. Alice carried on, even after Gran stopped asking. Talked to her quietly about work and the weather and what was happening on the ward

around them. Visitors coming and going and snow that
wouldn't settle. Anything really. Watching her grandmother's half-closed eyes, her thin fingers dance and tug
along the edges of the sheet.

Alice had been seeing Joseph a month or two when she
told him about her gran. They were both up early: it
was a midweek morning and she had to go to work,
Joseph was meeting Stan. He left the flat with her,
carried her bike down the stairs while she locked up,
and then they walked together as far as his bus stop.
Long morning shadows and the streets were peaceful,
they turned the corner by the station in sleepy silence.
Alice hadn't seen Joseph over the weekend. He'd been
away, on a job in Brighton for a friend of his dad's: Clive
was renovating a house down there for his retirement,
weekends usually, whenever he had time, and Joseph
went every few months to plaster the rooms as they got
done. He'd phoned Saturday lunchtime to see if she
wanted to come down, said his dad's friend had a tent
they could borrow. He had Sunday off, and did she want
to spend the day together, at the coast maybe. Alice had
already arranged to see her grandad and Joseph didn't
make anything of it when she said she couldn't come:
she saw her grandfather every couple of weeks, he knew
that by now. But he did sound disappointed and, after
she'd hung up, Alice didn't think she'd given him enough
of an explanation: saying her gran had died recently just
didn't seem to cover it. So she tried again, while they
were walking to work.

– I always used to go and see them together. I've been
every other Sunday, just about, since I left college.

Alice wheeled her bike while she talked to him, tried to describe why the visits were important, for her as well as her grandad.

— For months there was always something to do, you know? While Gran was ill. It's not been easy to get used to, since she died. Like I'm out of practice.

Days off came with nowhere to drive, nothing to fetch, no one to sit with or bathe. Or sheets to change, or nails to cut, or cream to rub into old hands to keep them soft. Alice had known her grandmother was dying, so it was hard, but she'd loved it too.

— All of that to be missing now, as well as the person.

Joseph didn't know what to say, Alice could see that, and she felt uneasy, hadn't wanted to make him uncomfortable. But then he slowed down as they got nearer his stop, as though he wanted to give her more time, and he kissed her goodbye when his bus came. They hadn't done that before and, in the minutes after he'd gone, it was tempting to see it as some kind of affirmation. The idea brought a strange, lurching feeling with it, and Alice wasn't sure if this was pleasure or pressure. She had to smile at herself again, cycling to work: she looked for the significance in every gesture these days, and she'd forgotten that about these early stages. When you don't know yet, whether you are in love. If you want to be, if he does. Perhaps she'd told him a bit too much, but it had felt like a good moment, and she didn't want to question that now. *You can pick things to pieces if you're not careful.*

Joseph hadn't said a great deal about his family yet. When he did, a few evenings later, Alice felt as though he were returning a compliment. He'd been at his sister's, and she lived not far from Alice, so he came round on his way home. Alice was in the bath when she heard the buzzer go under the noise of the taps. Martha was on her way out, and called down the hall that she would get it. Alice turned the water off and listened to the exchange in the hallway.

– Is she busy?

That was Joseph. Another first: an unannounced visit.

– I'll be out in a second.

Alice's voice was loud against the tiles. The talking continued in the hallway, and she looked around her for a towel, but didn't move to get it yet. She'd been out late two nights in a row, catching up with friends she'd not seen while gran was ill. Both were good nights, and they'd filled her up with wine and smoke and conversation. It wasn't long after nine, but bath and bed had been her only evening plans. She listened again, still lying in the warm water. Could hear Martha in and out of the living room, her bedroom, looking for her keys or her bag. Alice couldn't hear Joseph, thought he must be in the kitchen or on the sofa, and she thought how much she'd like to spend the rest of the evening lying down there with him, but then he put his head round the door.

– Just here on the off-chance. I can get lost again.

Alice hadn't realised it was ajar. She looked up at him: half in, half out of the room.

– Don't be silly.
– Don't get out then.

Alice heard Martha call goodbye and the front door closing, and then Joseph sat down. On the floor, his back against the radiator, forearms resting on his knees. Left alone, they smiled at each other across the rim of the bath.

Alice had opened the window earlier; it was the first warm evening of the year, and a few doors down someone had done the same, pushed their speakers round to face the street. Joseph had spent the afternoon with his family, she'd heard him telling Martha, and Alice was curious about them, so she asked him who'd been there.

– Mum and Dad, Eve and Arthur, my sister and brother-in-law. Well, they're not married, but you know.
– They've got a little boy, haven't they?
– Ben, yeah. He just turned three. We blew out some candles for him today.

He was pulling tobacco and papers out of his jacket, and Alice thought about standing up, the towel, getting out, but then Joseph said:

– Any room in there for me?

The water was loud as Alice sat up. Cooled on her back in the silence while Joseph undressed. Made her aware of the damp hair at the back of her neck and her temples. Her pale breasts, hidden now by her knees, and the sweat on the skin beneath them. It was strange to feel so shy, and Alice tried to remember the last thing Joseph had said, a thread to pick up. Felt the warm bath rise around her thighs as he climbed in to sit behind her, legs on either side of hers. The overflow slopped, and outside there were summer noises: thudding bass and people talking. It was her turn in the conversation, Alice was certain. Seconds passed and then she felt a palmful of water, poured between her shoulder blades, sliding down to her hips, joined by another, then another, and then his fingertips. It was gentle, and she stayed where she was, not wanting it to stop, until Joseph's fingers came to rest, and he rubbed his unshaven chin against her neck.

– What do you want to know then?

He was smiling. About her curiosity, maybe: how obvious it was. Or about how shy she was being.

– I don't know.

Alice leant back a little, against his chest.

– You could tell me a bit about your mum and dad. Are they still working?

Joseph folded his arms around her.

– My mum's a hairdresser. My dad's retired, he took redundancy a few years back.

He let her settle between his legs, told her that his parents still lived in the house he grew up in, bought it from the council with his dad's severance pay. Joseph carried a photo in his wallet. Alice had caught sight of it before, when he was paying for drinks or cabs, and she'd wondered about it, who it was of. His jeans were on the mat, in easy reach, and he folded his wallet open with wet hands to show her: a family of four, out in front of a red-brick box.

– That was thirty years ago or something. Will be soon.

Alice shook her fingers free of drops before she took it from him. The grass on the picture was yellow, dusty, and they were all wearing summer clothes, pink cheeks and squinting. Joseph's chest was bare and skinny, and you could see where the tan line stopped at his neck, his upper arms, where his T-shirt would normally have been.

– It was that hot summer.
– I remember. My Gran used to make me have a sleep after lunch. Because she wanted one, probably. Seventy-seven, wasn't it?
– Seventy-six. Southampton won the Cup.
– You remember that? How old were you, four?
– They were underdogs, you know. My Dad was a fan. Just one of those stupid things that stick in your mind.
– Yours, maybe.

Alice looked at his family, all standing by their car. It was new second-hand, Joseph said, and they'd never had one before.

– My Dad just bought it, so we had to get a photo.
– What's your sister's name again?
– Eve. Evelyn, after my Nana. My Dad's mum. She says people always expect her to be an old woman.
– You look alike.
– I know. Everyone says that. Take after our Mum.

Eve was in her pushchair in the photo, with Joseph behind, holding onto it with his big brother's hands. They had the same sandy hair, and there was something cheeky, quick about both their faces. It looked to Alice like there was only about a year between them. Joseph was grinning, standing on the low brick wall that marked out their patch of dry grass from the neighbours'. Alice thought the camera had caught him talking, head tilted towards his mum in the foreground, who looked so young. Ten years younger than Alice was now, probably. With two kids and an uncertain expression: arms folded, face somewhere between a smile and a show of defiance.

– She looks proud of you all.
– My Mum?

Alice held up the photo so Joseph could see for himself. He took it from her and she sat up, shifting round in the water a little, so she could watch him looking at his mother's face. Joseph shrugged, but not like he disagreed: maybe he just didn't need her to tell him. He said his mum always worked hard for them and he passed the picture back to her. Alice took it, but stayed where she was, sitting between his knees, facing him while he spoke. He told her his mum used to clean a pub when he was small, an hour or two every morning, and if his nana was busy she had to take him and Eve with her. The publican used to sit them up on a bar stool together, in front of the fruit machine, let them bash the buttons.

– No money or anything, you know, just flashing lights. We thought it was great, but I remember my Mum saying she didn't want to see us playing them when we got older.
– Do you? Or were you properly corrupted?
– I've got it under control.

He smiled and Alice looked down at the photo again, his parents. Joseph said his mum learned to cut hair later: after Eve started school and she had more time, could earn them a bit more money. It had got darker while they were talking, harder for Alice to see the faces in the photo with just the street lamps and the light coming in from the hallway. Joseph's father had one arm around his wife, the other hand resting on the new car bonnet. Joseph said he worked nights at the car plant back then, came home before they left for school so they had to be quiet about breakfast and dressing. Alice couldn't tell if his dad was smiling, what he was thinking, she leaned in closer to the photo.

– Looks like a miserable sod, but he's not.

Joseph was smiling at her and she handed the wallet back.

– Our school was just down the road. I used to go home at lunchtime some days, because my Dad got out of bed then. I stirred the sugars into his tea, two of them: that was my job. Then I went back to school again.

He looked at the photo once more before he put it on the edge of the sink. Said his dad was a fat man, you could always hear him breathing, especially when he'd just got up, and he'd liked that noise when he was a kid: it was reassuring. Alice liked the way Joseph laughed after he said it, as though he was embarrassed to be telling her, but didn't mind if she knew it. They smiled at one another then, their wet faces, awkward limbs pressed against each other, held by the high sides of the bath. Water cooling off, but neither of them moving to get out. Funny how it was easy to talk once they were both undressed. And then easy to get into bed with him too, before they were dry. Hadn't told each other much yet, but it was starting. Joseph was unexpected, but he was welcome.

Three

Alice invited Joseph to have a proper dinner, or rather Martha did. It was Martha's flat, and she rented out the spare room because her lecturer's salary didn't cover the mortgage. Alice moved in three years ago, not long after she'd started at the hospital. It was affordable, handy for work, and she thought it would just be until she got a place of her own. Whenever she talked about leaving now, Martha told her to stop.

– You can't, no one else would put up with us.

Martha had been with her boyfriend for years, on and off, and Keith lived there too, while things were on between them. Alice kept clear when they argued, but they weren't hard to live with. They were always good to her, even when they couldn't be good to each other, had been especially so during her grandmother's illness. She was pleased when Martha suggested inviting Joseph, because he'd been staying over quite a bit, and she had started to worry about it. He always brought something with him, a few cans or bottles, and he went out to the shop in the mornings sometimes too, got bread and milk so no one would be short for breakfast. But still, it was a small flat for four of them to be sharing, even on a part-time basis, and Alice didn't want Martha getting annoyed. She liked living here, and having Joseph over. Didn't want either of those things to end in a hurry.

They started cooking late, and were only halfway through when Joseph arrived. Keith had bumped into him at the off-licence and they'd come up the street together. Between them, they'd bought far too much to drink. The first few minutes in the kitchen together were mainly spent getting in each other's way. Joseph stood by the door, smiling at Alice and rubbing his face after she gestured to him to sit down. He put a few beers in the freezer and then as many as he could in the fridge, and after that Martha said he could slice some tomatoes too, if he wanted to feel useful. He smiled, kissed Alice first and then picked up the chopping board.

The phone went just after they sat down, and Martha waved a hand, said the answerphone could get it. Alice was spooning rice onto plates when she heard her grand-father's voice, the tinny speaker emphasising his proper vowels. He hated talking to machines, she knew that, so she felt embarrassed for him, stopping and starting again with everyone listening from the kitchen.

– This is David Bell. Would Alice Bell call me, please? It's concerning tomorrow. I'd like to know if she'll be coming as usual. I'll need to go shopping for lunch in the morning.

If Alice picked up now, he'd be offended. She'd done it before and he'd been confused at first and then very curt. He finished his message with a pause and then a thank you.

– I'll call him after we've finished.
– Is this your weekend to see him?

Martha was holding her plate out. Alice shook her head and carried on serving. It had bothered her too, that he'd got the weeks confused, but she didn't want to think about that now. Two beers on an empty stomach, plus nerves: Alice thought the evening might be getting ahead of her before it had even begun. Joseph got another bottle out of the fridge and held it up like a question.

– I'll wait a bit, thanks.
– I'll have it.

Keith reached for the beer, and turned to Alice while he was opening it.

– You grew up with your grandparents, didn't you?
– Partly. We lived with them until I finished primary school.
– Oh yeah, okay. I think Martha might have told me once.

Alice had talked about this with Keith before, she could remember it quite clearly, and thought Keith probably could as well. He was just moving the conversation on, or maybe he thought Joseph would be interested: she looked across the table and saw he was waiting for her to go on.

– Mum got pregnant when she was at university. A first-term fling with someone in the year above, medical student. When she found out I was on the way, she went home to live with her parents.

When Alice started nursery, her mother went back to university and trained to be a teacher. She found them

a flat on their own once she started earning enough. It
only had one bedroom, but the kitchen was big, the best
room in the place, so they put the sofa in there and her
mum slept in what would otherwise have been the living
room. It was only five minutes on her bike to her grandparents' house.

– I still went there most days after school, until I was
well into my teens.

Did her homework at the kitchen table while Gran
supplied her with juice and toast. They used to play
piano as well: her grandmother disapproved of how little
music Alice had in her timetable. So they played duets,
perched on the stool together, one pedal each, once Alice
could reach, the other foot planted on the ground. Her
mum would pick her up when she finished work, put
her marking in the basket on Alice's bike, and they would
take turns wheeling it home along the evening streets,
talking about what to cook for tea, what to watch on
telly.

Martha said she envied Alice, never got to know her
grandparents properly, not her grandfathers anyway, and
Joseph agreed:

– My Nana lived round the corner when I was little,
but both my Grandads died before I came along.

He'd been very quiet until now, and Alice was glad he
felt like joining in the conversation. She smiled at him:

– David's a bit like my Dad, really. Or the closest I've
got.

Joseph had asked about her father once, when she was talking about her mum and Alan: *what about your Dad dad then?* Alice had been half expecting the question, and she'd started to tell him: that she never knew her father while she was growing up, just his name and what he'd been studying and where his parents lived. Her mum had always kept the address in case Alice ever wanted to look him up. She'd got that far talking to Joseph about it, but then she felt herself stop. Hadn't known him long enough yet, maybe. She'd had friends for years and never told them: Martha was the only person outside her family who knew about the letters she'd sent him. Her dad had been the one who stopped writing, and that just wasn't something she liked people knowing. Too recent, still too confusing. So Alice had stopped talking, shrugged and smiled at Joseph for hesitating, but she couldn't continue, and she'd liked the fact that Joseph accepted it: hadn't asked more questions, or changed the subject for her, just let her be quiet about it. He nodded at her now over the plates and bottles, and Martha picked slices of cucumber out of the salad bowl.

— What's he like then, your Grandad? We met your Gran a few times, but I've only ever spoken to him on the phone.

Alice smiled. She wanted to say that she loved her grandfather, but she was too aware of Joseph, sitting across the table from her. She didn't think she'd be like this if he weren't there.

— You heard him on the phone. He can be funny like that sometimes. A bit formal. Mum says he's not very good at being sociable. Gran always took care of that side of things. They were married forty-odd years, so I expect he's forgotten how.

Joseph was smiling at her now, probably at the colour in her cheeks. Alice thought of how her mum planned to stay the whole week after the funeral, but Grandad had started getting impatient with her after only three days.

– I'm making him sound awful, aren't I? Best not to crowd him, that's all. He was crowded by the three of us for years. Me, Mum and Gran. 'House full of blessed women!'

Alice laughed. A refrain from her childhood. Bellowed from the corridor in the weekday morning bathroom rush.

– I never knew if he was angry or happy when he said that. Both, I imagine. But I should go and call him anyway. Is there a bottle open?

Joseph and Martha were stacking the dishwasher when Alice came back from the phone with her empty glass. Keith was at the table, shuffling a pack of cards.

– Joseph's going to teach us Brag.

The early awkwardness had gone, and Alice was happy to have them all together, filling the kitchen with their wandering about, nicely drunk. Her grandfather had been fine on the phone: she'd heard him smiling when he said he'd looked at the calendar already, realised his mistake.

– I can come this week anyway, I don't mind at all.
– No, no. I've got plenty to be getting on with in the garden.

Joseph took them through a couple of hands, explaining the game as they went, patient and amused at Martha's mock ill-humour about rules she didn't understand. Keith ran out and bought more wine from the off-licence before it closed, and they all stayed up too late, playing cards until there was nothing left to drink and Keith got his pipe out. Alice groaned and pushed back her chair.

– Not for me.
– Ten more minutes. One more hand.

Martha passed the cards to Alice to deal and Keith told her it was unfair on them for her to leave while she was winning. Joseph laughed:

– She can be sly like that.
– We'll leave the pack where it is, then. Pick up in the morning.
– It is morning.

When they got into bed, Joseph said he could hear the first train running. Alice listened for a while, lazy and drunk, with the warmth of his legs stretched out against hers. Drifting, her limbs wine-heavy, she closed her eyes and remembered her grandfather, quiet and removed, out in the garden. *Did we have a reason for you coming?*

Alice called her mum the next day, partly to tell her about her grandfather's mistake, partly just because she missed her. Her mother lived three hours away by train. She'd come to London more often while Gran was ill, and in the weeks after, so seeing less of her again was another thing for Alice to adjust to. They'd had fierce rows while she was in her teens, and when Alice went to her gran for comfort, she used to say they were too close in age, and lived too close together. But their tempers were short-lived, and they stayed in that one-bedroom flat until Alice went to college. Her mum moved in with Alan a few months later, and a year or two after that he got a job back at his old school in York, so they moved out of London. Alan was head-master there now, and Alice's mum ran the biology department in another school, a little nearer their home. She used to joke about giving the sex education classes: ex-teenage single mother, not the best role model. Said she felt a fraud, warning them of the perils, because she'd never regretted having a daughter, even though Alice had come along a bit early.

Alice's mum wasn't worried about Grandad: told Alice she'd been waiting for something like this, ever since Gran died.

– He won't show it like we would, but it's bound to come out.

– I half feel like going out to see him today.

– I'd leave him be, love. I expect he does want to get some gardening done, he wouldn't have said it to be polite.

– No, I suppose not.

Alice liked the way her mum was about Grandad: clear, pragmatic. She didn't seem to get upset by his bluntness the way Alice did, so it was reassuring to talk to her. Alice often called her, in the evenings after she'd visited her grandfather, to get a bit of perspective down the phone. And she knew her mum liked to have a second opinion on how he was getting on.

– How's he been the last couple of times? Apart from forgetful.

– Fine. A bit weary. But he's keeping up with everything. The house, shopping.

– He can cope with more than you think.

They spent the rest of the call planning a week together for later in the year: Alice and her mum wanted to go up to the Dales, with Alan for a couple of days too, if his work allowed. His grandparents had farmed up on Swaledale and their house was still there, three miles from the nearest village. Alan and his brothers shared the upkeep, used it as a base for walking and holidays with their families. They'd got it hooked up to the grid for power a few years ago, but the water was still off the hill, so the supply was unreliable and had to be boiled for drinking, and the only good source of heat was from the kitchen stove. Alice remembered sleeping next to it her first time in the house: Easter was early that year and came with snow. The bedrooms were perishing, so they'd moved the mattresses downstairs. She was sixteen then and the three of them had spent the school holidays up at the farm. Her mum had been seeing Alan for a while and Alice knew the holiday was meant for her to get to know him properly. She hadn't done it consciously, but spent most of the fortnight avoiding him. They got on fine in London, and she couldn't explain it, but suddenly couldn't bear to be at the table with him eating, hated seeing his piss in the toilet in the mornings. Flushed it away before sitting down, although she knew she wasn't meant to because the water was low. She was amazed that Alan never lost his temper, despite her behaviour. Even after she had a bath without asking and the tank ran dry, and he had to get gallon cans from the outhouse and drive miles to the nearest standpipe.

Alan was always generous with the house: let Alice use it, would never take money for bills or maintenance. He'd long ago shown her all the best walks, how to keep the stove lit if you were out all day, and where the water tank was on the hillside, so she could keep an eye on the level. Alice usually went there with her mum now, but she'd taken friends up before, and boyfriends. The old farm was an acquired taste: the country was bare, the slopes around grey with scree, and the house was a steep walk from the only road out. Not always inviting, especially in winter, when you had to leave a warm car and scramble up the track with rucksacks and supplies. Alice tried to remind herself how awkward she'd been that first Easter visit, but it was hard not to be disappointed if friends ignored the sky and heather and complained about the draughts instead, the lack of mobile reception. She'd cut short a stay once, driven back south three days early, because she couldn't take any more of her then-boyfriend's moaning. Late summer and the house had been full of daddy-long-legs, dancing along the walls. For Alice, these were a familiar part of August at the farm, but they just drove her boyfriend mad. He couldn't sleep with the rustle of their spindly limbs in the room, spent the evenings battering them with newspapers until Alice decided she'd had enough. She told Alan about it a year or so later, after they'd split up, and he laughed when she apologised, belatedly, on behalf of her sixteen-year-old self.

Alice didn't have many friends who still went on holiday with their parents. It used to embarrass her a little when she was younger, after she'd left school, and while she was at college: summer weeks spent walking the Pennine Way with her mother while everyone she knew seemed to be hitching around Italy or clubbing in Barcelona. Took Alice years before she admitted, even to herself, that she enjoyed walking more than dancing all weekend and the come-down after.

Alice was six the first time they went away, just the two of them. Her mother had just qualified, had her first teaching job lined up for the autumn, and they spent three July weeks in Dorset: a graduation present from Gran and Grandad. The money had been intended for a week in a cottage, but Alice's mum decided on staying away longer, cancelled the reservation her parents had made and booked a caravan instead. Alice loved the instant mash and tinned spaghetti meals her mother cooked those weeks, the biscuits eaten straight from the packet. They stayed up late together playing memory instead of washing up, and kept their pyjamas on until lunchtime, both knowing Gran and Grandad would have dressed hours before them. The nearest beach was shingle, and rough on cold toes after swimming, but Alice asked to go there nearly every day because she liked the pebbles. Local legend had it that they were larger at one end of the beach than the other, something to do with waves and current, and fishermen sent adrift could always tell where on the wide bay they had landed by the size. Alice and her mum tested the theory, working their way along the beach, filling their pockets. She couldn't remember if they'd drawn any conclusions, just that she'd spent hours laying the stones out in size and colour sequences on the windowsills of their caravan. Milky blue-grey, deep red-brown, some green and some almost orange: all of them were prettier when they were wet, and she dribbled water onto them from the teapot, until her mother started frowning about the puddles on the lino. So Alice waited until she wasn't looking and spat on the stones instead, rubbing them against her palms.

The caravan site was small, but had space for tents, and in their last week three students pitched next to them. Postgraduate, geology, two men and a woman, on a summer field trip. They admired Alice's pebble collection, and told her the names of the stones: quartz, flint and chert, and one she could never remember, but they said it was harder than steel. The students seemed ancient to Alice at the time, but they would have been early twenties, like her mum. Her mother never spoke much to the parents in the other caravans, but she took to drinking her morning cup of tea out on the steps around the same time the students were eating breakfast outside their tents.

The caravan didn't have a bedroom, but the dining table folded down and there were spare foam cushions under the benches, so in the evenings, after dinner and card games were over, Alice and her mother would rebuild the narrow double bed, which they shared. They hung a blanket across the caravan so her mum could read at the far end by the door after Alice had gone to bed. Once the students arrived, her mum started spending her evenings with them, sitting and talking outside their tents. Not far away, not much more than thirty feet, and if she wasn't asleep yet, Alice would listen to the murmur through the metal walls.

One night, towards the end of their stay, Alice woke up and panicked. No light leaking around the edges of the suspended blanket. Miles from a street lamp and she couldn't hear anything. She needed the loo, and she'd been in the night before, knew the layout of the caravan, but this time her mum wasn't there.

Alice fell asleep again, despite the worry and the seeping wet, before her mother came in and moved her over gently to get into bed. And she cried when her mum peeled off her sleeping bag, sodden pyjamas. *Doesn't matter love, doesn't matter.* Her mum's voice was quiet, not angry, but Alice could see her neck, flushing red above her T-shirt.

The foam cushions and the sleeping bag were laid out on the sunny grass beside the caravan in the morning, and Alice stayed inside, thinking everyone on the site would surely guess what had happened. But she never heard her mum say anything to the students, not even the tall one who got a bucket from the site manager and helped her wash everything.

– Oh God, yes. Rory.

Her mum laughed when Alice asked about him, years later.

– You still remember his name?
– I was in his tent when you wet yourself, I think. Guilty conscience.

Her mum shrugged, smiling. They were on holiday again, one spring when Alice was studying. At the old farm: now part of their annual routine. Gran was with them that year, and Alan too, but Grandad had stayed at home. He'd rarely left London since retiring, and Gran going away for a few days without him was normal enough to them all by then. Alice, her mum and Gran spent the days wrapped in conversation, and Alan had come prepared: a car boot full of contracts and time-tables to keep him occupied at the desk in the upstairs bedroom, while they filled the kitchen with talking.

– Did you like him, though, Mum? Rory.

Alice poured more tea, reaching the cup across the table to her mum, who was smiling again, perhaps a little embarrassed because her own mother was there and listening.

– Enough to take up the offer of his tent, anyway.
– But did you see him again after?
– No, no. Nothing like that.
– Why not?

Her mum shrugged again. Alice didn't really need an answer: there had been nothing like that in her mother's life until Alice was a teenager. She'd had evenings out, of course, but Alice remembered them being very occasional, and usually with female friends. Her mum would cook dinner for people at the flat sometimes too, and Alice was allowed to stay up for a while then with the grown-ups, but the first regular male face she could recall from those evenings was Alan's. Alice used to press her mother about her love life. Started when she was seventeen, eighteen: the same age her mum was when she'd had her. Got more insistent as she got older. That spring break in Yorkshire became dominated by such conversations.

– But you must have been asked out.
– Sometimes. I did the asking sometimes too. Easier that way, because I'd pick evenings I knew you'd be free to babysit.

Her mum nodded across the table at Gran and they both laughed. Alice smiled with them, but persisted:

– Didn't it ever bother you?
– Of course. Of course it did.

It exasperated her mum on occasion, this line of questioning, especially during that holiday because it came up so often, but she never got annoyed enough for Alice. The subtext was clear to all of them: Alice's father. But Alice's mum refused to let slip any resentment of him, even though Alice did her best to provoke. Teasing, needling:

– He never interrupted his sex life to change my sheets, did he?
– I think Rory and I had finished whatever it was we got up to before I discovered your predicament.
– You know what I mean.
– Might have been better if you had stopped us. The

fact that you'd gone to sleep again used to bother me the most. I must have been away hours. Thoughtless.

Her mother shook her head, smiling, but still shuddering at the memory. She hadn't known Alice's father long before she got pregnant, just a few weeks in her first term at university, and they split up a good while before she took the test. Alice knew all that already, and it was a perfect walking day outside, blue and mild, but she kept her mum at the table with questions. Couldn't understand it, why she wouldn't get angry.

– It was just as much my fault for going to bed with your Dad. We were both naïve, love. Just didn't think it would happen to us.

Alice didn't remember her gran saying much while she and her mum were talking, but she stayed with them there in the kitchen, clearing away the breakfast plates, or just sitting. Watching Alice's mum, checking. Ready, it seemed to Alice, to step in if she got the signal that help was wanted. It annoyed Alice at the time: she didn't think her mum was the one who needed support. She always seemed so certain. Said it was her choice to have Alice. Not to get pregnant, but to keep her, and she never talked to Alice's father about it, just told him it was happening: part-way through the spring term, almost three months since the last time they'd spoken. Alice's mum said he turned up at the house she'd been staying in a few days later, with his parents, but she'd already packed her things and gone home.

– It wasn't as though I wanted him to marry me or anything. And I know he didn't want that either.
– He's never thought about us. Me or you.

Alice remembered being surprised at herself, her tone of voice, the anger that shot across the table at her mother. Her mum held up her hands, briefly, and then put them down next to her cup again, as though surprised too, but trying not to show it.

– You don't know that, Alice.

Her gran took the final word: soft, but spoken clearly enough to end the conversation, and Alice was glad of it later. She was twenty then, and frightening: could sound so sure of her own opinions. Gran had been good at timing her interventions.

They'd had plenty of those conversations before, Alice and her mother, but never with her gran there. It wasn't until that week away together that Alice saw how hard it was for her mother, to hear how angry Alice was about her dad. *Just as much my fault*. It must have been tempting: her mum could have joined in with the character assassination, agreed with Alice about her father, shifted the blame for Alice's hurt away from herself at least a little, but she'd held back. Not just because Gran was there, this was the way her mum always dealt with Alice's questions: shrugs and smiles, and calm acceptance of the way things turn out. Alice had been fooled by that. Too easily, she thought: too self-absorbed. It took her gran's concerned glances across the kitchen table to show Alice the effect her probing had.

She knew her gran was right about her father too: how can you be sure what he thinks or feels or doesn't? Unfair to make such a presumption. Her gran never said as much, and neither did her mum, but the implication was plain: Alice could be the one to make contact, if she wanted to find out.

They'd all been quiet after that, but they'd stayed at the table together. Long enough for Alan to think it was safe to come downstairs and put on the kettle. He'd started when he opened the door and found the three of them still in the kitchen.

– Oh! I thought you'd all gone out.

Four

Joseph didn't see Alice for well over a week. Didn't plan it that way, just days went by and he was working late or tired. She left a message and he called her back but made an excuse when she suggested meeting up. Bit of flu coming on or something. He didn't think about it before he said it, it just came out, and he felt bad after: lying to her like that for no good reason, just because he wanted to sleep in his own bed. Monday night knackered, he'd been working over the weekend, and he said he'd see her Wednesday maybe, she could come round then. Only he must have made it sound vague enough for Alice to say she'd call him first, make sure he was better: still friendly enough, but she knew he wasn't ill. It was a relief, though, waking up alone in his empty flat, and he didn't start work until nearly lunchtime on Wednesday. Still sleepy, he keyed in the wrong code when he got there, set the alarm off in the house he was plastering. He was working with Tony, who didn't want to wait for the police: his parents were West Indian, and the last time this happened they didn't believe he was a carpenter and took him in to get his fingerprints. Tony jogged down to the pub on the corner and Joseph went to find him after the police had been and the alarm was reset. Stan arrived a bit later and Joseph ended up staying in the pub with them until after closing. Didn't have his mobile on him, but from where he was sitting, Joseph could see the payphone at the end of the bar. Thought about calling Alice to let her know where he was, but he never made it up there. He went to see Eve and Arthur on the Thursday, and was glad when his sister didn't ask about her: she was good like that.

Joseph went home early that evening. Passed the end of Alice's road and thought how he didn't really understand what was going on, because he'd been into it, right from the beginning. Hadn't felt like that in ages, but he liked her. The sandy red hair growing back in under her arms, that she apologised for, laughing, but that sent him searching, unbuttoning, with her lifting and shifting and helping him find the same shade curling over the top of her knickers. He remembered her wandering half-naked around his flat one morning before work, looking for her socks. Not thinking he might be watching, still half asleep maybe, her face all squashed from the pillows, she looked great. But it took getting used to, being with someone again. All the time spent and all that talking. Tired him out, made him want to shut his mouth and keep it shut for a while.

– I've never told anyone that before.

That's what she'd said. The second time they talked about her dad. After she told him it had been hard sometimes, not knowing him, or what he was like.

– Not when I was little. I never missed having a dad then, not really. I knew my family set-up was a bit odd and everything, when I was at school. But I remember another girl in my class whose parents had split up and one boy who lived at his gran's too. Mum says kids have such complicated families now. She has to draw little trees to keep track of them for parents' evenings.

It was a few days after that dinner with her flatmates. Alice had got a puncture on the way over to his place after work. They cooked together, and while it was in the oven, she carried her bike up the stairs and turned it upside down to mend it in the hallway, so she wouldn't have to get up early for the bus in the morning. Alice was kneeling on the floorboards, working the bolts loose when she started talking, and it took Joseph a few seconds to catch up somehow: thinking backwards through what they'd been saying since she arrived that evening. He'd asked Alice before, about her dad, but not today, and it hadn't seemed like she'd wanted to say much about him, either. Joseph filled the washing-up bowl for her and found an adjustable spanner, and then he waited.

– I started to lie sometimes, when I was at college. If friends asked about my parents, I'd say they were divorced and I didn't see my Dad. Seemed like an easier explanation. Plenty of other people in the same situation.

Alice looked up at Joseph, standing in the kitchen doorway, and then down again. She stopped after that, talking and working, and so Joseph crouched down. Thought that might make it easier for her: make her feel more listened to than watched, because he did want to hear about it.

Alice stayed quiet for a while, working the tyre irons around her front wheel, her palms turning grey with dirt. Joseph liked the way she always had oil smears on her legs, from her bicycle chain, and that she mended things herself: punctures and brake cables, and the dodgy light switch that gave Martha shocks. She never made a fuss or waited for someone else to sort it, just turned off the mains and got a screwdriver out. Started on things she didn't know how to finish sometimes, but Joseph liked that too. The way she'd stood looking at the wires coming out of the wall that time, with the switch in her hand. She'd been stuck, but she found her own way out: unscrewed the switch in the living room too, and worked out the wiring from there.

– Mum met him through a girl she knew from school, went to uni the year before her.

The tyre came away, and Alice said they lived in the same squat, this girl and Alice's dad, and Alice's mum was living with a family then, friends of her parents, in a different part of town.

– She was only seventeen, young to be studying. The idea was that my grandparents' friends would look out for her. Didn't do a very good job.

Alice laughed and stood up to get her bike pump out of her bag.

– I think the squat was just that bit more exciting, and the area. They'd done the house up really well, she said. It was a big place, and it wasn't only students who lived there, but older people too, locals. One was a stone-mason, I remember Mum telling me he did these Celtic knots all around the front door. Everything was put together out of bits they'd found or been given, but everything worked. I think my Dad spent more time on the house than in lectures. They turned the back room into a big kitchen, for everyone to sit in, and he helped the stonemason lay all the floorboards in there.

She smiled about that and then she said they weren't together long, her mum and dad. Stopped seeing each other even before her mum found out about Alice, and her dad panicked when she told him. Her mum never thought about staying with him, just wanted to go home.

– She says he didn't want to be with her either. She's probably right. After I was born she sent him a letter. To say I was a girl and what I was called, and he never wrote back.

Alice shrugged and Joseph waited for her to go on, watching her while she held the inner tube under the water, looking for the leak. Her fingers were dripping when she pulled the tube out, so he grabbed a tea towel from the back of the kitchen door for her.

– It'll get filthy.
– Doesn't matter.

He didn't want to go off looking for a rag and hold up the conversation. Looked like it was hard enough for her to say all this without interruptions. Alice dried her hands and then the tube and chose a patch from the kit. Still nothing.

– He never got in touch? Your Dad.

She shook her head. She didn't look at him, just at what she was doing.

– He never got curious enough. That's how it seemed to me anyway. I spent years going on about it with my Mum. She wanted to keep me, and she said it was her decision, pretty much. Took it out of his hands. But then, he let that happen, didn't he? Never made contact. So I thought he didn't want anything to do with me.

Alice spread glue onto the patch, frowning concentration, then she put it to one side and looked up at him.

– It was probably just a relief. For my Dad, I mean. He was nineteen and he wasn't in love. No one was pushing him or asking him to take responsibility. I don't know.
– You can't blame him for turning his back?

Alice looked up at him, like that was a harsh way to put it, but then she smiled. Self-conscious.

– Yeah well, maybe. If it wasn't me he was turning his back on.

She picked up the tyre again and Joseph thought about his own mum and dad, both of them teenage parents. But they'd wanted to be: got engaged, saved up, so it didn't compare. Still, listening to Alice, it was hard not to think of his dad and what he did for them. Years of night shifts, and he'd wanted to be a cabinet maker, like his grandad was, only the apprenticeship was a long one and you couldn't keep kids on apprenticeship money. That's what he'd said when Joseph asked him about it. Like it was something you didn't have to think about, just obvious: no point moaning, just get on with it. Alice was still watching him, as if she was thinking, and then she said:

– I had a hard time understanding my Mum. Always so bloody fair when she talked about him. My Dad never helped her look after me, or supported us financially. But Mum said she had all the help she needed, from

Gran and Grandad. I suppose she did. I think Mum always wanted me to get in touch with him, basically. She didn't want me to be angry with him on her account. Didn't want that to stop me.

Joseph had thought maybe Alice wrote her dad a letter: the first time they'd talked about this, he'd thought that was what she was going to tell him, but then she'd stopped. She was quiet again now, looking for the mark she'd made on the tube, so he said:

– He doesn't still live in that squat, does he?

Alice looked over at him and laughed.

– No. He doesn't.

Then she held out the patched tube for him to hold while she wiped the splashes off the floor and poured away the water. Joseph pressed his thumb down onto the sticky rubber and listened to Alice describing her dad while she worked, things he'd told her in his letters. He was a doctor, a GP. Had a surgery in Bristol, same place he went to university. He was an astronomer too, amateur, had a telescope in his garden.

– I don't know. I just really liked the sound of him.

She didn't always like reading his letters. He never said sorry or why he hadn't got in touch, but he'd wanted to know about her: his first letter came three days after she'd sent hers, and it was a long one, nearly four pages. He asked lots of questions, and when she did the same, he wrote a lot about himself in return.

– I thought that was more important, you know? Finding out about each other. I didn't want anything to get in the way of that, not so soon in any case.

Alice sat down by her bike again, opposite Joseph. Said they wrote to each other about work, because they had that in common: debating the NHS cuts and squeezes, the good and the bad in policy changes. She was retraining at the time, for post-operative, and enjoying it.

– Much more interesting than where I was before, in antenatal. You see people more often and for longer too, over weeks. Get to talk to them about more than just what hurts and what doesn't.

Her gran had been the one she usually talked to about work, but her dad was better, his knowledge was that much more up-to-date, so Alice wrote to him about hip replacements and her spinal patients.

– I told him I like walking, so he wrote to me about good places he knew. I drove out to the Mendips after I got that letter. Borrowed Martha's car. Middle of the week, so he wasn't likely to be out there. I wasn't even sure he was a walker, but any middle-aged man I came across in hiking boots had me thinking about turning and running. We hadn't talked about meeting up yet. I mean, I wanted to bump into him but I didn't want to look like a stalker, did I?

Alice smiled a bit, and then she said the address he gave her was his surgery. They'd been writing for months by then, letters going back and forth every few weeks, but she still didn't know where he lived. She found out she'd been writing to his work because he never gave a phone number, and she'd called directory inquiries.

– Makes me sound so desperate.

She shook her head.

– Maybe I was. I had to wait weeks between letters sometimes. I know it took me a while to reply too. Wasn't always easy to write, but waiting was worse. I never knew for certain I'd get more.

It wasn't residential anyway, the address, so Alice told the woman to check under business instead.

– I couldn't not ask him, could I? Why he didn't want me writing to him at home.

Alice picked bits of glue off the ends of her fingers. Joseph watched her pulling the words together.

– So that was all I wrote in the end. Just that question. He's married. They don't have kids. Maybe they couldn't, I think that's what he meant. His wife doesn't know about me, anyway. He wrote back and said he wasn't sure how to tell her yet. I thought that meant he was going to, but I don't know now.

Joseph held the wheel steady while Alice fitted the tyre again. When that was done she said:

– I brought you a picture anyway.
– Of your Dad?
– Yeah, well. You were asking, so I thought you might like to see him.

She went over to her bag and dug it out for him. Joseph thought he was getting a doctor in a shirt and tie, but it was an old picture, in a little plastic pocket. There were a few of them on the photo, her mum's friends at university. All of them with the same hair, long and in need of washing, the blokes too. Sat with their backs up against a wall, the steps of someone's back door, Joseph thought it was the squat maybe. Bare feet in the long grass in front of them, a couple of wine bottles open, leant up against their knees. Alice pointed to him, one along from her mum.

– I've always wondered if I look like him. People say I'm like my Gran, but I'm not really. Same hair, same colour eyes, but that's as far as it goes. And I don't look a bit like my Mum.

Joseph looked at her mother's face in the picture and thought Alice was right: her mum was all dark and round. He looked at her dad, and Alice laughed.

– No, you can't tell from that.

He was a student, all scraggy beard and glasses, so much on his face you couldn't get past it. He did look young, but Joseph didn't want to say that, in case it sounded like he was making excuses for him. The same age his parents were when they had him. It wasn't getting her mum pregnant that Alice was upset about anyway, as far as he could tell. The guy wasn't too young to be her dad now: that was the problem.

– I sent him a photo of me. Should have waited before I did that, probably, but I wanted to push him, you know?

I thought he might send me one back, but he never wrote again after that.

Alice put the picture away in her bag again.

– When did you send it?
– A year ago, a bit more than. It was after Gran got ill.

She was trying not to sound too sad, and Joseph couldn't understand that. He thought she should have been angry, like she was before she started writing, and he kept waiting, couldn't believe she wasn't going to say any more about it. Wasn't expecting her to shout or cry exactly, but something. Thought if she asked him, he would have to say her dad was a coward. The way Alice talked, made it sound like it was her fault the letters stopped coming, and it didn't make sense to him. He didn't want to upset his wife, Joseph could see that part: first you have to say you've got a daughter, then you have to explain why you've never told her. But her dad never even sent Alice a picture, he couldn't even get it together to do that much for her.

Alice didn't ask Joseph what he thought, she just said:

– I've never told anyone that before.

He could remember standing next to her in the hallway and how she spun the wheel of her bike a few times, like she was checking if it was on straight, even though she'd done that already. He'd been angry about her dad, but she just looked relieved. Glad to have said all that to someone, maybe. And Joseph thought it was better not to have said anything about her father, not then anyway, because that would have spoilt it for her.

Friday night, he went to his parents', didn't tell them he was coming. Drove there straight from work, bought a bottle of wine on the way, some cans for his father, and some flowers for his mum. From a garage, so they weren't up to much, but it was the only place he found open. Eve had got their mum used to much better over the years, but she laughed when he apologised for them.

– I'm always happy to get flowers, Joey. Especially when my son comes with them.

His dad was in the kitchen, peeling potatoes, and he grumbled about having to do a couple extra for Joseph, but he was smiling. Joseph took them out for a drink after dinner. There was a quiz night on in the bar at the snooker club, and they were talked into staying. Phil, one of his dad's old workmates, was doing the questions, and half of them were about the cars they used to assemble and the union they belonged to. Most of the regulars at the snooker club worked at the plant or used to, but there was a younger crowd in too, and after a while they started whistling and heckling. Phil threw in a couple of telly questions to keep them happy, but then his mates started in on him, and there was more banter than quiz until he threatened to hold over the prize pot until next weekend. It made Joseph laugh, seeing how much his dad enjoyed it, all the kidding, and how much about his old job he still remembered. They came second, won a set of glasses, it got late and Joseph had had too many to be driving, so his mum made up the bed in his old room upstairs.

The mattress was narrow, and Joseph knew that Ben

slept there now, if Eve and Arthur stayed over. He couldn't get to sleep for a long time: had to be up early, but he'd had too much to drink, and so he spent too much time thinking about what it was like when he and Eve still lived here. The estate was out in one of those dog-end bits of London, always felt nearer the coast than the centre. Not great, but not so bad either. Rows of brick-and-tile semis built after the war, roads laid out in crescents with endless pavements, their kerb stones dipping for the countless driveways. Shops on one side, primary school on the other, and beyond that came the industrial units and the railway siding. Their house was in the middle, where the gardens backed onto each other. They were mostly kept neat these days, but Joseph remembered long grass and low fences when he was younger, all sagging and ignored by the kids, their games played across and through them.

Hadn't thought about any of this in years. He'd maybe caught it off being with Alice so much, listening to her, and telling her about himself. Joseph wasn't used to it. Lying in his old bed, he couldn't stop it all coming, and there were plenty of good things to remember too. Kids' things mostly, wouldn't mean much to anyone else, probably, but he enjoyed thinking about it all again. Walking to school the long way by the canal, after his paper round, football and cigarettes at the rec, Sunday dinners with everyone at his nana's house. Auntie Jean, who wasn't really his auntie but lived next door, her kids grown up and gone. She looked out for him and Eve after school when his mum was working, took the fence down between their bits of back lawn. His mum and Jean used to sit together on the back step, smoking in the evenings after his dad left for work, and Joseph liked to listen, not to what they were saying so much as the sound of their talking. Lying on the rug in the front room with the gas fire on; cool air and warm cigarette smell from the open kitchen door; half-listening to his mum laughing, half-watching the telly.

None of that was what Joseph expected to be remembering. He knew something was on its way back to him: it was like he'd been waiting all week, getting ready, but then all this stuff from when he was a kid surprised him. He lay in his old bed and thought this wasn't such a bad way to be feeling, they were happy enough memories and he should be glad of them. Usually it was different. Days ahead he could predict it, and he'd felt it happening this week too: going home, not answering the phone, avoiding Alice. He'd been crawling into himself, and that meant he had to be careful.

Saturday and early, but there were kids out already on the estate, playing, standing at the street corners when Joseph was driving away from his mum and dad's place. It was quick, the memory, when it came, and he was ready for it.

Up in Portrush, two days on R and R, halfway through his tour, end of the summer. Four of them in a taxi, going back to the hotel: civilian vehicle, civilian clothes. Three small boys at the side of the road, couldn't have been more than six years old: hard little faces, spitting, giving them the finger as they were passing.

Joseph drove off the estate. Been a while since he'd remembered anything like that too, but it was more the kind of memory he was used to. Stones thrown, people staring, mums shielding their babies from you, like you were infected or dirty. Didn't matter if you weren't in

uniform, there was no getting away: even on leave,
everyone knew who you were, even the kids. Was a time
he'd have had to stop the van, hands useless, feet shaking
on the pedals. Not today, though. It was just that feeling
that stayed with him: years gone by and still no escaping.

Alice called Joseph again at the end of the week. Still just the machine doing the answering, so she hung up. Called her mum a few hours later, not intending to talk about Joseph, but she ended up doing so anyway.

– It's too bloody stupid, this. I feel like an idiot. Adolescent. Waiting for some spotty boy to phone me.

It was a relief to laugh at herself with someone. Her mum said:

– Maybe he's in bed. I don't answer the phone when I'm ill.
– No, he's fobbing me off. He doesn't pick up if he doesn't want to, I've seen him do it. Just lets it ring and gets on with whatever he's doing.
– Are you a bit in love with this one, maybe?
– Not today I'm not.
– Sounds to me like you are, sweetheart.
– I think he's a wanker.
– Well, in that case, so do I.

Alice had to laugh again, properly this time, and it helped that Martha agreed with her later too:

– If he's being a berk, you just have to ignore him until he stops.

Alice thought of the days, weeks even, that Keith and Martha could be angry with each other and still stay together, and it was comforting. She took her mother's advice and went out with Martha, to the pub first and then a late show. They queued too long for coffee and chocolate and sat down a few scenes in. Alice couldn't get interested in the film and irritated herself again thinking about Joseph instead, how much she'd liked being with him. She wouldn't be the first to confuse sex with something else, but it still made her flinch: to think that's what it might amount to, just the familiarity that comes from knowing someone's body. Should know better than to trust that. Patients would sometimes tell her the most intimate things, all about their childhoods, their divorces and bereavements. Because we touch them, that's what Clare said: they put themselves in our hands. Alice thought of the past weeks with Joseph and all that she'd told him. Too much, probably. *You can go too far with people.*

Alice had told her mum that she was writing to her father, but they'd never really discussed the letters.

– I'm sorry, Mum.
– Don't be, love. None of my business really.

She was patient like that, her mother: Alice thought maybe it had been enough for her to know they'd made contact, and that the letters were ongoing. Martha got to recognise the envelopes after a while, and she used to slip them under Alice's door instead of leaving them on the kitchen table if she picked up the post downstairs. Alice had thought she would talk about it with all of them later: her mum and Gran, Martha and Clare too, once there was something to talk about properly.

But then it was all over, when it had just got going, and telling anyone had seemed too difficult. Joseph had sat quietly for the most part and let her get on with it, but he'd wanted to hear, and there was no pretending with him either: *you can't blame him for turning his back?* He was right: it had been daft to make out she wasn't hurt by her father's absence, or that she understood it. In theory, yes, but Joseph could see that's all it was. He had been teasing her, but he'd been gentle about it, and she felt sad, remembering how it felt to speak to him: he'd been interested and she'd wanted him to know.

She didn't have a lot to base that trust on, Alice was aware of that. Never met his family, and it had been weeks before she'd even stayed at his flat. He'd somehow never invited her back, and she'd thought he had some dodgy flatmates, perhaps, even started wondering if he lived at home with his parents. Alice had been absurdly nervous the first time she went round there, but it turned out to be fine. He lived on his own, in an ex-council place in Streatham. It was a small estate, three blocks, and he told her most of the flats were owner-occupied now. Alice thought it was a bit grim at first: the stair-wells and walkways seemed unfriendly after dark. But in the morning she saw the window boxes and net curtains and changed her mind. The three blocks faced inward, and every front door was a different colour. Joseph's neighbours nodded hello to him across the courtyard and she felt stupid and prissy for having been worried the night before.

– It was a state when I bought it. Pulled everything out.

Joseph told her about doing it up, with his brother-in-law, how they'd thrown the old carpets and cabinets over the side of the walkway, had two skip-loads of junk piled up in the courtyard. It was very plain inside now, new floorboards and plaster walls, and Joseph said it wasn't finished, but Alice thought they'd done a nice job. She liked the sun in the bathroom in the mornings, the big kitchen table his dad had made for him, and the view from the bedroom too, over the allotments. The flat was on the fourth floor and the whole place was on a hill: from the living room window, Alice could see trains, gas towers, the trees on the common.

But that was his flat, not Joseph. What did she know about him? He drank Guinness, mostly. He grew up in London, like her, but a bit further south. His music collection was eclectic: Marvin Gaye, The Jam and Johnny Cash were the tapes he kept in the van. He had no vanity about him, which Alice found appealing. When he cut his hair it was short, a number three all over, and he did it himself, but not that often, and he didn't shave every day, either. Only when his beard got long enough to be uncomfortable, and then only in the evenings, because he didn't like getting up any earlier than he had to. He voted Labour but said his family had done well out of the Tories: he wasn't mad about council sell-offs, but he knew how proud his dad was that they all owned their own houses. Socialism was one thing, security another. Joseph played snooker, wasn't really interested in football. He'd been in the army for a while, after he left school. Spent a year or two in Spain and Portugal after that, plastering retirement villas for expats, and it was someone he'd worked for out there who introduced him to Stan after he came back.

It didn't add up to much, but then she really hadn't known him that long. Alice still felt surprised by Joseph, and how much she liked him. When she'd told him about the old farm and suggested going up there some-time, it hadn't been the wildlife and ancient plumbing he'd picked up on, she didn't think they'd bother him. He said he liked the sound of the house and the hills around it, but he'd never tried going to the same place over and again: *I've never wanted to do that before.* Familiar routes and views, knowing which tracks were best at what times of year: that was all part of being at the farm for Alice, but she hadn't been disappointed by Joseph's comments. He hadn't been turning her down, and there was no criticism in them. He was his own person, that's what Clare said, and Alice agreed. Self-contained, but not unfriendly with it, not until now at least. She liked that about him: self-possessed, something she'd always wanted to be herself.

Joseph rang early on Saturday morning and said he was sorry. Just after she'd picked up the phone:

– It's me. It's Joseph. I'm sorry.

No lead up, and then quiet afterwards. Alice couldn't even hear his breath. Thrown, she said nothing, and then he asked if he could see her, and Alice said yes. Much too quickly she thought, and cursed him for it when he came round. Standing in the kitchen, relieved to see him, despite herself. Pouring him tea and calling him an arsehole at the same time, which made them both smile.

They spent the afternoon in bed, and then when it got dark, they wandered out together for a late drink. Stan was at the pub, with Clare and a few others, so they pushed the tables together and played cards. Stan persuaded the publican into a lock-in, but Alice and Joseph didn't stay long. Just until Alice won, then Joseph took her home, and made her laugh again by waiting to be invited upstairs. He stayed over and it was lovely, but Alice kept expecting him to say something about what had happened the week before. She was very glad to have him back, but angry too, because he never explained. Wasn't sure she wanted just to start up again like that, without reasons given or any discussion. Clare smiled when Alice talked to her about it.

– Looks to me like it has anyway, whether you like it or not. Or it did last night. I'd never have guessed you'd fallen out.
– We haven't. Not really.

Late Sunday morning and Alice had taken a detour on her way to her grandad's. Stan had taken the boys swimming, so she and Clare were alone, and they sat in the kitchen, talking.

– He's apologised, Alice. Be happy.
– I am. Except I don't know what he's sorry for, do I? He might have been sleeping with someone else for all I know.
– Have you made any promises to each other?
– No.
– Do you want to stop seeing him?
– No, I don't.

Alice had been through her options already. Either she talked to him about it or she left it. The former was too possessive, and the latter wouldn't work for long: she was bound to start thinking about it again. But Alice didn't want it to be over. She liked being with Joseph too much. He'd said sorry. Last week had thrown her: she hadn't seen that coming. But then there was yesterday, last night, this morning. Clare walked her down as far as the corner, and smiled when Alice said she wanted to give him the benefit.

– Good. I don't think a relationship's got going till you've had a bit of bother. Not properly. Don't make too much of it, will you?

Five

Another Sunday at her grandfather's, another month or so later, and the first rainy day in weeks. Alice arrived soaking and her grandad hung her jacket over the boiler, fetched a towel from the airing cupboard for her hair. She had a dry T-shirt with her, changed in the downstairs toilet, and her grandad pointed at her rucksack when she came out.

– Are you going away?
– I've just been. Camping with Joseph.
– I thought you'd caught the sun.
– Freckles, like Gran.

Alice held out her forearms and her grandfather smiled, said they suited her well. Joseph had been talking about going for ages, ever since that weekend he was down in Brighton. He'd picked Alice up from work on Friday to surprise her: she saw him when she came down the steps, standing by the railings where she locked her bike. He called to her across the car park, said he'd read the weather forecast and it was too good to stay in London, so he was driving her home to pack. Two nights on the South Downs, and a hot day between, spent following the course of a river. It was Joseph's idea, and a good one, a tributary of the Arun. He'd shown her on the map after they'd pitched the tent: tracing the path he'd planned for them, his fingers excited, touching the blue curve of the water as it wrapped around the foot of a slope, marking out the highest point for miles around.

Joseph said he'd driven past the hill before but never climbed it, had kept it in mind for them to do together.

They waded under the trees to escape the sun, boots off, silt between their toes. Calf-deep water and slow, cool progress. The banks got steeper: twisted walls of root that they scaled, scrambling on elbows and knees, emerging smiling, blinking from the trees at the foot of the chalky rise. Joseph said it was still possible to find empty places, pointed east as they were climbing, told her about the country beyond the ridges and woodland, where the marshes started: wilder parts. He'd spent a lot of time down there a few years back, before he went to Portugal: every chance he got. Alice walked behind him up the slope, watching his arms and shoulders moving as he spoke. Enjoying his talk, this time with him, the invitation in what he was saying. The prospect of more time to come, over where he was pointing maybe, winter days together, like the ones he was describing, out on the empty coast.

– Smuggler territory, used to be. Best when the geese are flying and the low fields are flooded.

It was perfectly still at the top, only her own and Joseph's breathing, standing, shoulders touching, squinting down at the quiet, yellow country. The sun had burnt off the haze by then and they could see out across the escarpment, as far as the dark band of the Channel. In the morning they went down to the sea, although it was already clouding over. They had the far end of the beach to themselves and made the best of it. Swam out beyond the breakers, then ate biscuits and apples for breakfast on the sand, because that's all they had left. They were late packing their things up, even later back into London, and then the traffic slowed when the weather turned, rain driving everyone into their cars. Joseph had to drop Alice at a station so she could get to her grandad's in time. She almost invited him to come along, but then apologised.

– I'd feel a bit bad, springing it on him, you know?
– Don't worry about it. I'll just see you tomorrow, will I?

The rain continued into the afternoon. Fell hard and steady, spattering off the patio and against the French windows, so Alice and her grandfather sat at the dining table with their cups of tea. She'd mentioned Joseph before, perhaps once or twice, and her grandad had shown polite interest. No more or less than with any of her boyfriends, but today he said he'd appreciate Joseph's advice.

– I want to have the house decorated. Some of the rooms. I'd like to be sure I'm paying a good price.
– Which rooms?
– In here. The hallway. Our bedroom upstairs.

Alice knew those had been her grandmother's plans: she'd wanted to have them done last summer, but then she got too unwell. Alice's grandfather got up from the table, motioned to her to stay in her seat. He got a folder out of the drawers by the window, and held it up to show her as he came back across the room. He spread the contents out on the table, pushing the tray and the biscuits away. Alice cleared the cups and plates for him as he laid out the colour charts, and then she sat down while he arranged the wallpaper swatches, hand-drawn sketches of the rooms, her grandmother's notes and arrows of explanation on the pencil walls. Alice picked up the picture of the hallway, eyes moving across the page, taking in her gran's lines and words. Her grandfather was still standing, so she got up again and moved to the top end of the table next to him, watching while he pointed to each item and explained it in turn.

– This was the paper she chose for the hallway, and this for in here. That's to be painted, of course. White with a hint of something. Here: cream, I'd call it. Same for the bedroom.
– And a new runner for the hall.
– Yes. We thought about carpet out there, but it's the original tiling, so we decided to keep it that way.
– Yes. I would too.
– Yes?

He nodded at her briefly, approving. Most of the other houses on the street had new porches and double-glazing, but her grandfather had stubbornly resisted, preferring to maintain his woodwork and keep the stained-glass inserts at the top of the front door and bay windows. They were unique, Alice knew, because he'd often told her: no two the same on the street when the houses were built. He was still looking at the papers laid out before them, fingertips resting on the tabletop, blinking. Alice asked:

– Have you got any quotations yet?
– Only old ones, from last year. I'll have to call them again.
– Maybe I could show them to Joseph anyway? He might know the companies, or at least he can tell you if their prices are reasonable.

Her grandfather pulled the relevant pieces of paper together for her, and started to clear the table again, but then stopped.

– I went to the DIY place last week but they don't stock this wallpaper any more.

He pointed to the hallway pattern. Pale blue stripes on a cream background, and yellow in the border. Alice picked it up.

– We'll be able to get something similar, I'm sure. I'll ask Joseph for you. He'll probably know of other places we can look.

She made her way home once the rain eased off, walked to the station under one of her gran's umbrellas, though the weather wasn't really bad enough to warrant it any more. Her grandad had opened it ready for her in the porch, and then she hadn't liked to refuse. It had been an awkward goodbye altogether, prolonged by bag and brolly and jacket, her grandfather standing, silent, waiting to wave to her at the gate and then close the door.

They'd never spent time on their own together as adults: not used to it, and they were not much good at it. He'd had the table set and the kettle filled when she arrived, as he often did on Sundays now. Her mum said he was just looking forward to her visits, but Alice suspected he was impatient to get them over with. She'd been relieved to have something to talk about this time. When her grandad first mentioned the redecorating, she'd wondered if he was just making conversation, but he'd obviously been looking for wallpaper this week, so that was probably unfair.

She walked the rainy pavement and platform, tried to remember a time when it was better, a clue to how to change it, but all she could recall were Saturday morning trips to the library while her mum and gran went shopping together. She was still in primary school then and her grandad would take her hand while they crossed the main road. He kept her library tickets in his wallet and gave them to her at the desk after she'd made her selections. He never chose books for her or with her, would walk the shelves with his hands folded at the small of his back while she went to Junior Fiction.

They didn't talk to each other then either, but what should they have talked about, an eight-year-old girl, and a man already past his middle age? It wasn't as though there was no love between them. He was never like the fathers she knew, the various dads of her friends at school. Older for one thing, more reserved, more formal, always wore suit trousers, leather shoes, never carried her on his shoulders or called her pet names, but then he wasn't her father, so none of that mattered. Part of her always enjoyed it too: that he was unusual. Embarrassed and proud of him at the same time. She liked his arm swinging as he walked, the clipped, white hair at his neck, his smooth-soft ties hung on small wooden pegs in the wardrobe: so many patterns and they smelled of him too, the soap he used for shaving. On their library trips, he always dropped her hand again as soon as they got to the far kerb, it was true, but she liked the quick squeeze he gave her fingers before he let go. *Blink and you'll miss them*: that's what her mum said about Grandad's fleeting displays of affection.

Her grandfather worked until she was in her teens: her last years at school, his last years tying his tie in the hallway mirror weekday mornings. He saved enough to retire a few years early, but until then, he commuted halfway across the city. Always caught an early train, and rarely came home before evening. While they lived at her grand-parents', Alice and her mum would eat most of their meals with Gran, just the three of them. Breakfasts after Grandad left for work and often their suppers too, before he came home. They would talk about school and friends, and they'd have the radio on in the background while they ate in the kitchen. Alice loved her grandfather, but she always liked this better than the meals when he was home and their places were laid at the dining room table.

Her train was late but the rain had stopped and Alice folded the umbrella, zipped it into a pocket of her rucksack. It was harsh, realising how little they knew of each other, how many years her gran had been compensating, providing ease and conversation. Alan said once that her grandfather just didn't care enough about him to bother with talking. It had stung Alice, because she'd thought it might be true, and it did again now, thinking it might apply to her too. After they'd finished their tea, her grandad had washed while she dried and put away, everything familiar and in its own place. Alice wondered then if he found their silences companionable, or if he was just as uncomfortable. Looking at him, absorbed in his washing and rinsing, it had been impossible to tell. She was almost glad when the rain had let up, because it had given her a cue to go. Alice watched her train arriving, reminded herself he'd lost his wife and felt ashamed.

Alan didn't get on with Grandad. They never argued, but they never really spoke either. Alice's mum didn't agree, but Alan insisted David didn't like him:

– He acts like I'm not there. He does it with everyone who makes him uncomfortable.
– Don't exaggerate.
– Even you sometimes.

Grandad was the only thing her mum and Alan ever rowed about, as far as Alice could tell. It was usually good-humoured, while she was around in any case, but serious enough, despite the smiles. Listening to them, Alice would often feel defensive like her mother, but usually thought Alan was right. He'd come to London for a conference once, a few years ago, and stayed at her grandparents' on his last night, instead of the hotel. Alice cycled over early the next morning to see him, and found her grandfather and Alan at the breakfast table, absorbed in separate sections of the paper.

– He was already reading when I came down and I felt stupid just sitting there after your Gran went out to the shops.

Alice had walked with Alan to the station when it was time for him to leave, and she'd tried not to apologise for her grandfather, or find excuses: she'd been in on enough of Alan's discussions with her mother to know that would only annoy him. Better just to let him laugh about it:

– It's probably the best arrangement. We both keep schtum, we can't piss each other off too much, can we?

That was how Alan dealt with it mostly, and Alice thought he didn't have much option. Her mum agreed that Grandad could be standoffish, but she refused to see it as deliberate, or directed at Alan.

– It's just his manner, love. I wouldn't take it personally.

She was impassive, and while Alice found that re-assuring in her mother, she knew it was just frustrating for Alan. He teased his wife about her parents' colonial past, because he knew that was the one way to get a rise out of her. Alice's gran was from Fife, her grandad from London, but they were both in Nairobi when they met. She was a nurse, and had been recruited to Kenya after the war. He was an RAF pilot: had joined up in 1950 for his national service, and stayed on. He got posted to Africa twice in two years: first Rhodesia, as it was then, for training, and a few months later Kenya.

– Keeenya.

Alan would elongate the vowel and smile when his wife didn't respond: David's colonial intonation didn't bother Alan, but he knew very well the effect it had on her. He said once he couldn't understand her: so impervious to her father's lack of grace, and yet so painfully aware of his occasional slip in pronunciation.

– That's just the way your Dad learnt it. It doesn't mean anything.
– I'm not dense, I know the way he comes across. Anyway, I'm not sure many Kenyans would agree with you about that.
– I'm sure most Kenyans have got more important things to worry about, no?

Alan usually knew when to stop: Alice's mother would throw something at him, a sofa cushion, a newspaper, anything soft but big or noisy enough to make them both laugh. But Alice had been present a few times when teasing wasn't enough. She'd spent a weekend up at the farm with them not long after Alan's conference, and the silent breakfast with his father-in-law obviously still irked. Alice remembered her mum and Alan debating Grandad while they were packing up the car to drive back to York:

— I never know what he's thinking. Not just about me, about anything. I can't be around someone like that for too long. It makes me nervous.
— Maybe that's your problem then, not his?
— He's such a stuffed shirt.
— Do you have to be so rude about my Dad?

Alan blinked at her. Then went on.

— I'm sorry, Sarah, but I think he's rude. It's arrogant to think you're above conversation.
— You've got him all wrong.
— Well, he doesn't give me much to go on. Maybe he should risk an argument with me. At least we'd get to know each other that way.

Her mum didn't respond, just shifted an awkward box from the boot to the back seat, and Alice wondered if she was swallowing something: the risk of this argument turning serious too great for her to take. Alan was quiet too, shoving their rucksacks over to make more room, and it seemed as though he might be regretting what he'd said, or at least how he'd said it. Her mum got into the driver's seat, and Alice picked up the last of the bags from the path, finished packing the boot with Alan, in silent solidarity. *Hard to love someone if you don't know much about them.* Her grandfather didn't dislike Alan, she was sure of that: he could be just as offhand with her and her mother, but at least they knew he was fond of them too.

Joseph had been on that part of the coast a few times. His dad used to take him camping, just the two of them: places a train ride away at first, then further afield after they got the car. They never went away long, just a night or two, a weekend here or there. They didn't have a stove or build a fire, just took sandwiches, ate pies and things from packets. Flew kites they made themselves and crashed them, got better at them over the years. His dad always had a can and a cigarette last thing, outside the tent when Joseph was meant to be asleep, and Joseph could remember listening to him, sitting quietly out in the dark, and the smell of it all too: night air, fag smoke, the earth underneath. They drove to the Kent beaches mainly, Herne Bay, Whitstable and Deal, because his dad liked the sea, but he took them to the Downs sometimes too, the High Weald. Joseph wasn't sure he liked it there at first, missed the seaside towns, piers and arcades. But there were cliffs and woods as well as beaches, and chalk in the ground that came up with the tent pegs. The longest they were away was a week, when Joseph was about thirteen: the last proper trip they did together, too long probably, and Joseph was too old by then. Navigating while his dad drove them further every day, when all he wanted was to turn back and head for London again. He remembered making a box kite with his dad on the dunes at Rye. For auld lang syne, his dad said, and Joseph said nothing because he didn't want a sentimental morning. But the kite was one of their better efforts, and Joseph remembered the beach too, curving for what seemed like a day in either direction. It stuck with him anyway, the area, because he carried on going there after he left school. With his mates usually, car boot stacked with cans and plenty to smoke, but also on his own. Never the same place twice, and the further east the better: the wide flats of the Romney Marsh, all horizon and pylons, and the coast beyond Hastings, where it wasn't crowded with towns any more. The cliffs gave way, the country behind was rough and the sands out there got longer and emptier. That was where he went after he left the army: a year or two later, when he couldn't get it together, it seemed like the best place to go.

Days at a time out there, mostly. Turned into weeks when he was at his worst. No warning, no reason, but it was always the same routine: like everything was getting away from him and there was no way he could stop it. Could be anything that set him off, no way of knowing. Too much noise, too much talking, a car driven too fast past him, wrong words said on a bad day and that would be it. Job chucked, or he'd get the sack, or he'd be shouting at someone he'd never met before over nothing. Pints all over the bar, wet sleeves and faces. A supermarket full of people, shocked quiet and staring. Fighting too: when shouting didn't do it, he'd start shoving and kicking. Had to have the rush of it sometimes, and the damage. Last one was a bloke he'd been working for and Joseph couldn't remember what started it, just how vicious it got, and how glad he was when it was over. Winded, on the floor and frightened. Hauled up and pushed out onto the pavement. Hard to walk, but the pain got much worse later, after the adrenaline was gone again, sitting in the kitchen at Eve's, with the bones in his face aching.

Mostly it was no drama, nothing that obvious. It was just like he couldn't be staying so he'd be gone again. Not turning up for work or answering the phone. Trying to go as many days as he could without talking, no contact with anyone. Hard, because he didn't have his own place then, and most of the time no money, so the only way to sort himself out was to go missing.

It took over everything sometimes and there wasn't anywhere he could settle. Only a few days in any one place, if that. Friends' houses, then friends of friends, sometimes hostels. He was in a place for veterans for over a week once and that was easy at first, familiar: the sharing and the three meals a day, all the army jargon and the black and blue humour. But the man in the next bed had screaming nightmares, and the dayroom was full of bitter talk about compensation and pensions. A lot of Gulf War blokes there, all of them angry, and it scared Joseph thinking he'd get to be like them.

People he knew from before the army, most of them were married by then, and some had kids already, couldn't be doing with him. For a while he still had Malky's to go to. Grew up down the road from him, and he was still in the same life as before: drinking, smoking, living off dole scams and killing boredom. Being with him was easy in that way. Days went by and Joseph lost count of them, slept on the couch and Malky never asked questions. Always a bit of something floating about to be taking. Ate up the time well enough but there were always new people: ones Joseph didn't know, and he didn't think Malky knew them either, but Malky didn't seem to give a toss who was in his flat, long as they brought something with them.

After he'd used up his money and his possibilities, Joseph split his time between Eve's house and his mum and dad's place. South London streets he didn't know or the old estate that was too familiar. He started leaving a couple of days in between, and then that turned into weeks where he'd go wandering. Sleeping rough, he used to try and get out of London. Hitch down to the coast, Brighton was usually easy enough, and then over the Downs and on, until he got to the long beaches. He knew how to live out: that was part of what they'd taught him. Cold, salt and wet in a bin-liner bivouac. Broke into a beach hut one night, and ended up staying. It was a quiet place, holiday season over, the sands were mostly deserted, just the odd dog and walker, nothing else to disturb him. Late summer, cool evenings, windy days passing, sleeping, smoking. Wooden walls and shingle, the paraffin smell of the stove when he'd got it up and running. Walking back along the low cliffs from the village with food and tobacco. Hitching up to London every two weeks, signing on, but he lost track of the days and then they stopped his money. Went home and took a bag of food from his parents' house while they were out, got more on tick from the shop in the village nearest the beach, but after three weeks the owner put the closed sign up when she saw him coming.

Stove ran out, weather turning colder, and after that everything started hurting. Skin cracked, round his mouth, under his nails. Great sore patches, red raw under his clothes. Woke with the taste of sea but the summer was gone. Still dark, pitch, and freezing. Tried but couldn't stand, crawling. Scared then, and crying. Reversing the charges from a phone box when the light came. Eve shouting and then Arthur saying what was

the place called, what was the number, the bloody
dialling code, just stay put, stay fucking put and he'd
come out and get him.

Joseph owed everyone then. Money, explanations. It felt
like a long time ago. He'd been glad of that, while he
was down there with Alice. Not the same place, he'd
never been back to the hut, but it was near enough.
Joseph had worried about it, but he'd wanted to take
her: to show her, and maybe just to see, and it had turned
out fine. Better than that. Some of the best days they'd
had together. Nothing complicated about them. Her
arms and legs all rough and cold from the sea and
wrapped around him. Sitting stomach to spine on the
sand, her warm mouth against his shoulder blades,
talking and shivering, smiling and sweet-talking him
back into the freezing water with her. He liked to
remember that feeling, of having her pressed up against
him and laughing.

Keith had given Alice a bit to smoke when they left, so
they'd had that the first night and Joseph was glad of it.
They'd had nothing on the second, though, not even a
drink, and he'd still been alright. A bit edgy at first,
maybe, after they missed the off-licence and then the
shop on the campsite was closed, but they drove back
to the beach, built a fire and stayed down there until
after it got dark. Joseph woke up early, but only because
the sun was out and shining on the tent. He unzipped
his sleeping bag and enjoyed that clear head feeling,
being awake and staying in bed, waiting for Alice to turn
over and open her eyes. Crawl out of her sleeping bag
and join him in his. She was lying on her belly next to
him, covers pulled high, her tangle of hair the only thing
showing, and the tops of three fingers, still black under

the nails from last night's fire. He rolled gently onto his side, curling himself around her sleeping form, its smell of woodsmoke and skin. Packing up the tent with her later, Joseph thought if something was far enough passed, maybe he wouldn't have to tell her.

When Alice showed him the quotations, Joseph said her grandad was being ripped off. Didn't know the companies, but he saw what they were doing.

– They'll chance a bit extra because they know he won't be able to do it himself. Old guy on his own with a decent-sized house. He's bound to have enough money and his kids will be too busy to help.

It was a Wednesday morning and they were having breakfast at the café round the corner from his flat. Alice had a training day at work, so she didn't have to be in until later, and Joseph had the rest of the week off. He was angry for her grandad, and he wrote down a couple of numbers on a paper napkin for Alice. Said they were nice enough blokes, and her grandad could use his name if he wanted, but then he screwed the napkin up.

– I could do it.

Alice blinked.

– You've got enough on, Joe.
– Not back to back, look at this week. I can do it between jobs, if your Grandad's not in a hurry.

Alice felt the conversation getting ahead of her. She said:

– I don't think he is. I can ask him.
– I wouldn't want paying, just the materials, and I can get them trade.

Alice wasn't sure about this: she should have thought before asking, should have known Joseph would feel obliged to offer.

– I wasn't angling for that.
– I know you weren't.
– He might want to pay you. He's like that.

Joseph smiled at her, shrugged. Alice didn't know what her grandfather would say.

She took a half-day at the end of the week and they went over to her grandad's on the train together. He'd sounded a little dubious about it on the phone, but was welcoming when they came round. Alice made tea while her grandfather showed Joseph the rooms to be done. She heard them discussing different types of paint up on the landing, and watched through the kitchen window while they checked the old pots and kit in the shed. Joseph sorted everything into two piles on the patio, one good, the other to be taken to the dump. The paint was all useless, a thick plastic skin had formed on the top of each pot, which Joseph poked a stick through, but the rollers and brushes had all been carefully cleaned and stored.

– The wallpaper table is in good nick too, and you've a decent set of steps in the shed.

Alice watched her grandfather nodding as Joseph spoke. He looked happy to have someone there who knew what he was talking about. They hadn't discussed money yet, but Alice thought if they could resolve that one, then her grandad would be glad to hand over to Joseph in any case. She could remember from her childhood that he always preferred the garden: weekends spent doing jobs around the house tended to spoil his mood. Alice only knew of one exception, and that was a long time ago now, shortly before she was born. He and her mother had decorated the box room together, made it into a nursery for her, and he'd also given her cot a new coat of paint. Gran had told her this, on one of their after-school afternoons, and it became a favourite piece of family lore. As she got older, it occurred to Alice that it couldn't have been easy for her grandad: his young daughter pregnant and unmarried. But Gran said he'd been the one who suggested repainting together, and Alice liked that part of the story: her grandfather's happy anticipation of her arrival in the world.

— How did you sort out the money, then?

Joseph laughed because Alice couldn't believe it had gone off without a fuss. He wasn't used to seeing her all nervy like this. They were on the train again, on their way home together, the carriage filling up in the Friday evening rush. He found seats for them, across the aisle from one another, and they sat smiling, both glad the afternoon had gone well, and relieved that her grandad had agreed to Joseph working for free.

— He wasn't happy about it, but he couldn't embarrass me by insisting, could he?
— I suppose not.

Joseph had always thought Alice was close to her grandad, she spent so much time with him. She'd made a show of leaving them to get on with it, but he could tell she was listening, the whole time they were talking. Like she was ready to step in if things got difficult, or something. The old man had been fine, a bit stiff with him at first, asking him all sorts of questions about the jobs he did normally and where he was trained. Joseph couldn't decide if he was checking his credentials as a decorator, or as the right kind of boyfriend for his granddaughter. He asked David at one point:

– Do I pass muster, then?

And he was glad when the old man took it well.

– You'll do, I'm sure.

A quick smile and nod. Joseph thought he was alright, a bit dry maybe, but at least he had a sense of humour. Alice looked better now than she had in the house: still a bit nervy, but happy with it, and Joseph wanted to make her laugh.

– You told him I was trained by the council.
– You were, weren't you? After you left school.
– Not exactly.

Alice swayed a little with the movement of the train, smiling at him, eyes narrowed, ready to be teased.

– What exactly, then?
– It was my community service. A hundred and twenty hours for harbouring stolen goods. We had to paint over graffiti in subways, that kind of thing. The man in charge

of us, Clive, he knew my Dad. I got on with him, and
he took me on when he set up by himself.
– Okay.
– We did do a lot of jobs for the council, I suppose, but
it was Clive who trained me up.
– You didn't tell him all of that, did you?
– Your Grandad?
– Yes.
– No.

Joseph heard Alice let out her breath, and then she leaned
across the aisle and thumped his knees. But she wasn't
angry, just laughing, eyes bright with relief.

– A hundred and twenty hours for harbouring stolen
goods.

Alice was making fun of him and he had to smile.
Recognised the tone of voice he'd used, the slight touch
of pride: coming up for thirty and still parading his
teenage rebellion. She said:

– Bet you were the one sprayed the graffiti in the first
place.

Alice leaned back and looked out of the train window,
still smiling. The sky outside was torn clouds and
sunshine, and she blinked at the houses going by, he
couldn't tell what she was thinking. The skin on her
cheeks still looked hot somehow, but Joseph thought she
looked good: relaxing properly now, laughing again,
about both of them, wiping her eyes on her jacket
sleeves.

– Oh dear. Oh dear, oh dear.

Six

Joseph made a start on the upstairs bedroom the following week, and Alice looked in there on her Sunday visit. The old wallpaper had gone already and she knew Joseph would be coming tomorrow to skim the plasterwork around the windows. He'd told her he'd finish this room by the end of the month, and that he had a run of days coming in September, so he could get on to the hallway then. It had made her nervous at first, but Alice found she liked the idea of Joseph being here when she wasn't. Had to smile when she saw the neatly laid dustsheets, the stepladder folded and lying down against the skirting board: her grandfather had said on the phone that Joseph was a careful worker. He had to park his car in the driveway these days, because the garage was full of painting things, took Alice out there to show her the wallpaper Joseph had found for the living room, pleased it was such a good match.

– He went out to Kent to get it.

Her grandad tapped the shop label on the side of the roll, appreciative. Joseph had left some overalls there, a pair of his work boots and a radio, caked with paint and plaster gobs. Her grandad pointed at the radio.

– You wouldn't think that could make much noise, would you? I can even hear it from the garden.

But he was only pretending to be annoyed, and while they were walking back to the house, he said he was very impressed with Joseph, so far. Something in her grandad's voice made Alice look over at him: the tone was dry, deliberate, as though he were teasing her, or mocking himself. He didn't catch her eye, but again Alice had to smile.

In the living room, sitting in one of the armchairs with the newspaper folded open on her knees, Alice saw that her grandfather had been moving the pictures again. They had just started the crossword, and he was waiting for her to read the next clue, but Alice was distracted. The wedding portrait was still on the sideboard, but her gran's engagement picture was now on the small table next to her grandad's chair. Alice thought he must have been looking at it, last night maybe, and forgot to put it back before he went to bed.

– When did Gran have that taken?

She knew the answer already, but just wanted him to know she'd noticed, appreciated the fact he'd had the pictures framed. Her grandfather looked at the portrait next to him, a little surprised, waited a moment and then said:

– It was not far from the library, a studio in the centre of Nairobi. I'd just proposed, and I think she went there that afternoon. I did the same, a few days later. Same place too. It was a bit silly really, but we wanted to surprise each other.

Alice had always found her grandparents' story romantic. When she was a child, she'd often asked her gran to tell it to her, because it was so different to their suburban reality, and she was fascinated by the idea of their other life elsewhere. It was only later, when she got into her teens, that she began to put their story into context, prompted largely by the realisation that her grand-parents' time in Africa made her mother so uncomfort-able. It was her mum who told her that Gran had worked in the European hospital in Nairobi.

– White, that meant. Africans and Asians were treated elsewhere.

Alice remembered this information came unbidden. She'd wanted to hear some detail about how her grand-parents got to know each other, and her mum had been quite impatient, as though she realised Alice wouldn't put the backgound together without a bit of prodding. She remembered how it had smarted too, her mother's tone. Later, they talked more about it, all three of them together. Gran said she'd got to know a few older nurses while she was training in Dundee. They'd worked abroad, in Italy and North Africa:

– The war had taken them there, of course, but they opened my eyes to the idea.

Alice could remember asking what her grandmother had thought about the segregation in Kenya:

– I suppose I didn't think about it enough.

Her answer had been brief, matter of fact, but it came after a pause, and Alice knew she'd put her grandmother on the spot. She could remember her gran telling them about the general strike, called by African workers on the day King George deemed Nairobi a city, and they spoke about the White Highlands too, on a number of occasions: the Kikuyu farmers who worked for the settlers out there, north of the capital. Gran said the farmers' homelands were taken over by European migrants and they'd had little choice but to become squatters. *They resented that. Of course they did. That's understandable.* Alice remembered her grandmother's hesitant explanation and that it had surprised her when her gran embarked upon the topic: cautious, but it had been of her own accord, because Alice hadn't known enough then to put such questions together. She'd wanted her granddaughter to know about the Kenya she'd lived in, that much was clear, because she initiated discussions like this one more often as Alice grew older. It was Gran who told her about the detention camps, set up during the Emergency. *The Pipeline, a whole system.* And that their reputation for brutality preceded them. She said fear of imprisonment turned people against one another, destroyed communities, as did the torture meted out by the security forces. Alice's mother told her about how confessions were forced: ropes and rifle butts, wet sheets and electric currents, long-necked bottles filled with scalding water. Gran never went into detail, but she said the methods were crude, and that many of those arrested were innocent of involvement with the Mau Mau. The police would promise anonymity to informers, and people learned to dread being lined up in front of a hooded figure: a neighbour or friend or cousin who might try to save themselves further pain and point their finger.

At some stage during these conversations, Gran would always stop and remind Alice that she hadn't learnt about much of this until after it was over. She remembered the strike, of course: transport was at a standstill in some parts of the city, and she'd read about battles between strikers and police in the next day's papers. But Gran said she didn't realise until later that so many of the strikers lost their jobs, even though the numbers ran into the thousands. Alice could see it embarrassed her, this admission. *How could you have lived somewhere like that, at such a time, and not have been aware what was happening?* For all that she was fascinated, Alice was always relieved for her grandmother when their conversation returned to the safer ground of first meeting, courtship, proposal. It sometimes felt there was enough complication there to be getting on with.

As a child, Alice had been intrigued by the idea that her grandmother was a few years older and already married when she met her grandfather.

– In the process of getting divorced.

Gran always stressed this, and it made Alice smile, the insistence on propriety. Her grandmother caught her smiling once, and was unusually stern:

– It was the fifties. Such things mattered.

Besides, there were only five years between them, which was hardly an age gap. While they still lived together, these stories were told over their kitchen table meals; later they were saved for birthdays and anniversaries, family occasions. Christmases usually involved long walks together, through winter-quiet streets and parks. The three of them, Alice, her mum and Gran, talking talking, among the sodden suburban trees and grass. Catching up with the current events of their various lives, rehearsing memories, wrapped in their coats, breath coming in clouds. Alice liked hearing about her grand-mother's childhood in Fife, and what she called the beginning of her Real Life, when she moved to Dundee to train as a nurse. Everything got repeated over the years, but it didn't matter to Alice that she already knew her grandparents got engaged only a few weeks after meeting. Her gran enjoyed the telling, and that was part of the appeal, hearing again how reckless it felt, and how her grandmother had never been so certain of anyone. Gran liked to make fun of them both, the portrait she'd had taken, Grandad too.

– Scrubbed up and posing like matinee idols.

She laughed about his deliberately thoughtful expression, and the way his ears curled over at the tops. And she said her cheeks had always been too soft, her chin as well: more suited to a grandmother's face than a starlet's.

Alice sat opposite her grandfather in the living room now, and watched him holding the picture of his wife. He used to come on their Christmas walks, but rarely joined in with their conversations. He never seemed offended or excluded, but Alice couldn't believe he had nothing to tell: he'd fallen in love with a married woman at a time when divorce was still considered scandalous. His superiors admonished him, his friends in the air force advised him to end the affair. His parents refused to come to the wedding, and didn't speak to him for years because he went ahead regardless. Gran said her in-laws never warmed to her, and even after contact was finally resumed, it was clear to everyone that this was primarily to see Sarah, Alice's mum: she was their only grandchild. Alice had no idea how her grandad had felt then, if he'd been as certain as Gran, and wondered if he'd tell her. He was still looking at her grandmother, so Alice thought she would try.

– Weren't you ill when you met Gran?
– Yes. Jaundice. After a bout of dysentery.
– And you were staying in the same house?
– Yes. They were friends of your grandmother's. She'd got to know them early on during her time in Nairobi. She taught their oldest daughter while she was still living at home. Piano lessons, twice a week. Gran was just married then, and they were very good to her after that broke down.

Gran had told Alice about her first husband. He was from Dundee, but they met in Nairobi, he'd been stationed there during the war and went back after he was demobbed. He was an engineer and liked it out in Kenya because there were plenty of opportunities for ex-servicemen there: more interesting work, and better paid than at home. When they married, Gran had presumed that, like her, he'd want to go back to Scotland in a year or two. *Only the first of many mistakes.* Gran kept in touch with one or two Kenyan friends after she left, and gleaned a few things from their letters over the years. He remarried twice, but never had children, and he went on to work for the new administration, after independence. *He always was pragmatic*: that was her grandmother's verdict, and Alice thought it wasn't entirely disapproving. She wondered if her grandfather might have met him, while they were in Nairobi, but she wasn't sure she wanted to ask. She didn't want to get into difficult territory, not so soon in any case. Her grandad had been gazing down at his hands for a minute or so, and then he smiled:

– I was still yellow all over. I remember it on my palms especially, my fingernails, even my eyes. A bilious sight in the shaving mirror every morning.

He laughed a little. Alice knew he was on leave when he met her grandmother, convalescing, and that it was not unusual for better-off Nairobi families to open their houses to officers that way.

– I'd been in hospital for two weeks and needed another six to recover. The facilities up at Eastleigh, at the airfield, they weren't up to it, and many expats were keen to help. To show their gratitude, I suppose. The family was very welcoming, I can't remember their name. It'll come to me.

Her grandfather said their hosts were a little older, their children grown up with families of their own. Their house was large but somehow always full of people. They all played instruments, used to hold informal recitals, out on their veranda. Mostly it was jazz standards, but they'd sometimes put together a string quartet. Guests would come for cocktails at sundown, violin cases tucked under their arms, and after the playing was over, they were usually persuaded to stay on for dinner. Mostly it was friends and colleagues or neighbours, and he and Gran were often the youngest at the table.

– They'd sit us together. I don't know that they were match-making exactly, but I remember being very aware of it. I wasn't used to eating in female company. Or to good food, for that matter. I had my first curries there. It was corned beef in everything up at the airfield, condensed milk puddings in the mess hall. Isobel had been staying at the house a while, of course. But we were both fish out of water. I think we recognised that in one another.

It was strange to hear him say her grandmother's name. There was something intimate about it, a small shock to see her as the woman before she became her gran. Her grandfather was quiet for a while after that, but it wasn't an expectant silence, as though he wanted Alice to respond. His eyes had turned inward. She waited for him to continue.

– I'm sorry. We were halfway through the crossword, weren't we?

He put the picture down on the table next to him, smiled across at Alice. She still had the newspaper ready on her lap, but it took her a moment to catch up, find the clue they'd been working on: hadn't thought he'd stop talking when he did. He didn't offer any more that afternoon, but Alice was more pleased than disappointed. Such a brief conversation, but it felt like a start. She called Joseph to tell him about it when she got home. Said it had been the best visit since her gran died, and she almost felt like celebrating.

– That sounds daft, doesn't it? But it was so nice to hear him talking about her.
– I'll get a bottle of wine in for tomorrow, then. We can drink to David together when you come round.
– Don't make fun.
– I'm not. I like your Grandad.
– Do you?
– Yeah.

Alice called her mother after that, and she agreed that

Grandad had seemed very well over the past week or two.

– I thought he was very chipper on the phone. He must like having your Joseph around.

– Did he say that?
– Not in so many words.
– I hope he didn't think I was being nosy this afternoon.
– Doesn't sound like it to me.
– I've never thought to ask him before, don't know why. We never gave him the chance, did we? The three of us. Too busy talking to each other.
– Alan says Grandad listens to us. He's watched him, out on our Christmas walks.
– I was wondering about that today. Made me want to ask him. Seemed alright at first but then he just stopped.
– Don't worry about him. He loves you.
– Do you think he'd ever really talk to me about Kenya? I mean how he felt about what he was doing there.
– I don't know, love. Hard to say.
– You think I shouldn't try?
– No. Just be careful about it, won't you?

After Alice left home, her family started spending Sundays together, once a month or thereabouts, and usually at her grandparents' house. Alice couldn't say now who had initiated this, but supposed it must have been her gran: recalled her saying she'd miss them when Alice started college and her mum moved in with Alan. No longer three streets away, but scattered across the city. Those Sundays weren't as frequent as her current visits, but somehow they seemed more of an effort. There were just so many other, better things she would rather have been doing at the time, and Alice sometimes wormed her way out of going, pleading too much study or a bar shift that clashed, but mostly she went: dutiful, reluctant to give her mum cause for a row. She could remember Alan felt the same way, especially after they'd moved up north, and the journey ate up most of his weekend. They often ended up doing the dishes together, in irritated sympathy, sneaking nips of sherry out of the bottle her grandmother kept in the kitchen. Alice said those Sundays were boring, he said they weren't so bad, just a bit stilted, but they both agreed it was the having to be there they resented.

It was usually all over within a couple of hours, a meal and then coffee, and coats and goodbyes. There was only one visit that ended more quickly, abruptly, the day gone badly wrong. It was before her mum and Alan got married, but just after they'd bought the house in York together, which Alice's grandparents took to be the next best thing. Alan was due to take over from his retiring headmaster when the new term started, and Alice remembered her grandad greeting him at the door, saying how pleased he'd been to hear about his promotion. Everything was friendly until Alan asked David about his time in Kenya.

– I just wanted a real conversation for a change.
– Excellent choice of topic.

That was in the car, on the way home, their visit cut short by the row. Her mother was furious and so was Alan, but he was shocked too: sitting quiet in the front seat while his partner drove and tried, unsuccessfully, to stop herself shouting. Alice sat in the back and kept out of it. She thought her mum was being unfair: the row had been just as much her grandad's fault. He'd seemed amiable enough, answering questions about the RAF and his training, pleased maybe that Alan was interested. But then he reacted badly, rudely to Alan's mention of Kenya.

– Where is all of this leading?

Alice had left the dining room by that stage, clearing the plates ready for the next course, but she could remember listening to them from the kitchen, hearing Alan faltering and then persisting:

– I'm just interested. Because the way I've always understood it. The insurgency was about Kenyan independence, wasn't it?

Her mum sighed down the phone when Alice reminded her.

– Oh dear.
– It didn't seem such an unreasonable question to me.
– No, I know. I don't think Dad was disputing that, actually. The point he was trying to make was more about hindsight. Independence was still over a decade away when the Emergency started. Oh God, he just kept on saying that, didn't he? The Mau Mau were killing white settlers and Africans loyal to the state, the country was being terrorised by a minority, blah blah, and so British forces were called in.
– I remember him saying terrorised. And Alan picking him up on it.
– Me too, he shouldn't have gone on the attack like that. But it was all degenerating by then, wasn't it? Alan waiting and Dad refusing to look at him. I was sitting next to him

at the table, and I couldn't work out if he was going to say something important, or just hoping we'd disappear.

Her mum was almost laughing, exasperated by the memory.

– Dad was right in a way, though. I mean, most Africans probably wanted independence by then, but not through violence. African Christians were being killed, people were being coerced into taking Mau Mau oaths. I talked to Alan about it afterwards. I didn't think terrorised was Dad's word, maybe he was just explaining what they'd been told. It was a civil disturbance: that's what they called it, the authorities. Didn't wash with Alan, he was still too wound up about it. Said he'd wanted to hear what Dad thought, and he didn't give a shit about the official version. I'm not sure I blame him.
– But you got so angry with him. I was glad to get out of the car.
– I know. I'm sorry. They just pissed me off, the pair of them. Dad was being so pig-headed, and Alan kept backing him into a corner. Wasn't going to get anywhere. If Dad agreed with him, it would mean he fought against people who had a legitimate cause. I wouldn't want to give someone the satisfaction of pointing that out, would you?
– How do you think Grandad felt at the time?

Alice thought she heard her mum sigh again.

– You'll have to ask him that one.

Joseph finished the bedroom and David invited him for dinner to say thank you. Alice laughed when he invited her too, said it was probably so she'd help him with the cooking, but Joseph could see she was pleased. Her bike was locked in front of the garage when he got there Thursday evening, and she opened the door for him. Her grandad was busy in the dining room, laying the table and opening the wine. When he saw Joseph through the hatch, he came into the kitchen, smiling, to shake his hand and apologise for not letting him in personally.

– I didn't realise you'd arrived.

The talk over dinner was mainly about the redecorating: how pleased David was with it, and what Joseph would start on next. He was busy until the middle of September, but they'd agreed he would do the front room after that: it was only a few weeks away now, they were well into August already. There had been another run of hot days that week, but they all said it felt like the last of the summer. It was nice enough chatter, no big silences to fill or anything, but Joseph knew Alice was hoping to hear more about her gran, and when David met her in Africa. He could see she was waiting for the right moment, so he was happy for her when David started without her having to ask.

– We were talking about the family in Nairobi last
Sunday. I couldn't remember their name.
– The people you stayed with?
– Yes, the Sumners. Alexandra and Iain. It came to me
just after you'd gone, of course. They'd been in Kenya
for years, came out between the wars, he was in
construction as far as I remember. They were both from
Scotland in any case and Alexandra grew up in Fife, like
your grandmother. I think that's why she took to her.

It was still warm out when they finished eating, and still
just about light. Alice said they should make the most
of it, take their glasses into the garden, and she sent
Joseph ahead with her grandad, promising to bring out
coffee for all of them. The sun was just behind the roofs
when she brought the tray out onto the patio, the bottle
of wine they'd started over dinner wedged under her
arm. The sky was still bright at the horizon but the long
back gardens around them were just shapes of shed and
fence and tree. Joseph had smoked half a cigarette out
there while they were waiting for Alice to join them,
watching the planes go over and the light slip out of
the day. The old man had sat next to him, not saying
anything, and when Alice came out, Joseph thought
maybe he should have asked him something about
Africa: kept the conversation going for her sake. But
when she started pouring the coffee, David picked up
anyway.

– No long evenings like this so close to the equator.
More like a light being turned off. Took some getting
used to. Kenya was like that altogether, somehow.

Alice passed a cup to her grandad and he nodded his
thanks, told them Nairobi was quite high up, over five

thousand feet, and the air could be cool all day, but the sun still so strong that it burned.

– I learnt that to my cost, sitting out in the Sumners' garden, writing home. Only half an hour, and with a sweater on, but come evening the tops of my ears and the backs of my hands were pink and sore.

Alice sat down next to Joseph, opposite her grandad, who was looking out at the darkening garden. He said he remembered the gardener in Nairobi, and the pride he took in the Sumners' lawn. Alice was sitting forward in her chair, holding her coffee but not drinking it, watching her grandad. He said that at first glance the grass looked like the suburban patches he knew from home, but it was tough and springy to sit on, not soft.

– That's the kind of thing I mean: things out there were familiar and unfamiliar at the same time.
– Were they quite wealthy then? The Sumners. To have had a gardener.
– Comfortable. Nothing more. They weren't at all keen on Baring, the governor, I remember that. Iain Sumner thought he was far too heavy-handed, the way he dealt with the Emergency. Thought the British might be a steadying influence, the military, I mean. On the Kenyan police, on settler politics. The Sumners would probably have counted as liberal.

The old man shrugged, and said that if you were white, and had any money at all, you had servants. Told Alice he'd had a dhobi boy up at the airfield, did his washing and ironing, and when he came to the Sumners' house, they assigned a maid to him. He could remember her bringing vinegar solution, for his sunburn, and that she never wore shoes.

– None of their house servants did. Had them all barefoot. Alan would smile at that one, wouldn't he? It would confirm things for him, I'm sure.

Joseph watched Alice blinking, and was glad when she said nothing: he knew her step-dad and David didn't have much time for each other. The old man hadn't been up north to visit them for years, and it was a bit of a sore point with Alice's mum. Joseph didn't mind listening to David reminiscing, but he didn't want to get into their family politics, not this evening anyway. He had a job starting tomorrow, out in Kent, and a long drive in the morning. He'd switched to juice after dinner because he'd come over here in the van. Alice and her grandad hadn't drunk much more than a bottle between them, but Joseph could still feel the difference. Alice had to go to work in the morning as well, but she wasn't checking her watch, neither of them were, too wrapped up in talking. Joseph rolled himself another cigarette, thought it was someone else's family, people he didn't know, not really, and maybe that's why he couldn't concentrate. He'd seen the pictures in the living room, Alice's mum and gran, and Alan, and he knew what David looked like too, when he was young and in uniform. Should try putting those faces into the stories he was hearing, maybe. David was talking about the people he stayed with again. Saying how they invited him to everything, but he knew he wasn't obliged to attend.

– It was a good arrangement, because I was still quite weak. Being ill was a lonely business, away from the squadron, all the men who knew me. It sometimes helped to join the guests out on the veranda or in the drawing room. I wouldn't stay long, but I liked to listen to their conversations for an hour or so. Gave me the illusion of company at least.

– Gran said she didn't go to them much.

– No, your grandmother had started working again, at the hospital, and I suspect she used to take her time about coming home, to avoid them. It meant I didn't often see her. I certainly enjoyed the evenings most when she was there.

Alice smiled at her grandad, and Joseph felt a bit awkward, sitting between them, watching her listening, and the old man getting lost in the telling. David said he'd been introduced to Alice's gran the day he arrived, but he wasn't told much beyond her name. She usually sat opposite him at the breakfast table, a young woman he'd assumed was a recent migrant, staying in Nairobi while her husband set up a farm or a business, and a house for them in another part of the country.

– What did you talk about?

– We didn't actually. Not at first. I think we both enjoyed having someone to be quiet with while all the others were talking. I found out about her from other people. One of her husband's colleagues used to come to the sundowner evenings. He worked for the same construction firm, and they had dealings with Iain Sumner too, as far as I remember. They were all connected to each other somehow, British in Nairobi. Knew each other's business. I didn't have to press the man. I think it was only the second time I met him that he told me Isobel was divorcing her husband.

– Were you shocked? About Gran, I mean.

– Perhaps a little. But then I was quite pleased too.

They were both smiling now, Alice and her grandad,
and both of them were quiet. Joseph didn't want to
interrupt them, but it was gone ten, and he needed to
get moving. He'd arranged to drop Alice off at her flat,
but thought maybe she'd want to stay talking with her
grandad and make her own way home later. He wanted
to give her the option anyway, but he didn't know how
to put it without sounding rude. *Do you want to stay on?*
Because I should shoot off now. Didn't like the idea of Alice
going home alone either: too far to cycle all the way,
but getting too late to stand around on station platforms
on your own. He shifted forward a bit in his chair to
get her attention, but then David sat up and said it was
getting late.

– I shouldn't keep you any longer.

He looked at Joseph like he knew he wanted to be off,
but the old man wasn't offended. More like he was being
polite: ending the evening so Joseph didn't have to. Alice
was disappointed, he could see that. She stayed in her
chair for a minute while her grandad started picking up
their glasses. Joseph stood up to help him, but the old
man told him to stop, said he would do the washing up
after they'd gone, and then shook his head, smiling, when
Alice protested. As they were walking back into the
house, Joseph thought Alice was wrong about her
grandad on one count anyway: she'd told him David
wasn't good with people, but here he was, smoothing
their way to the door. Making up for the stopped
conversation, indulging Alice in a bit of friendly bick-
ering. She was still on about doing the washing up while
they put their jackets on, but the old man held his hands

up, said he wouldn't hear of it because Joseph was a guest and she'd done most of the cooking. He came to the gate with them, held out an envelope to Joseph as they were leaving:

– Thought you may as well have these.

House keys. Joseph could feel them through the brown paper, walking to the van with Alice, one hand on her waist, the other gripping the envelope.

He dropped Alice off at her flat, got her bike out of the back and watched her wheeling it up the path. She waved from the front door and then Joseph waited until he saw the hall light go on upstairs before driving away. He didn't go straight home like he'd planned, drove past the turning for Eve's and then doubled back on himself. She came to the door in her pyjamas.

– You alright, Joey?

Eve had stayed angry with him for about a year after he joined the army, the only serious falling out Joseph could remember. She came to his passing out parade, but refused the drink he bought her after in the bar. She'd dressed up, skirt and blouse, but couldn't bring herself to do more than that, standing with her face closed while everyone else in the room was laughing and chatting. Teasing Joseph's mum, because she'd cried when she saw him in uniform: Joseph's dad said she'd missed half the parade, dabbing at her eyes with his hankie. Eve was the only one who didn't join in, and Arthur told Joseph she gave their mum a row after, in the car on the way home. Went on at her on the motorway for a good twenty minutes, said she should be crying real tears about it, save the sentimental bubbling for weddings. Joseph's dad pulled over in the end, told her to leave off being such a stupid cow, spoiling the day for everyone, so she started in on him instead.

– He'll be sent off to God knows where for God knows why and get blown up for his pains. You'll see. Somewhere he's got no argument with in the first place, more than likely.

Joseph's dad laughed: he wasn't convinced.

– What's that supposed to be? Politics?
– Might be.
– Since when? Never heard a peep out of you before now.
– My brother wasn't in the army then, was he?

Eve was shouting by that stage, and she said it was her dad's fault Joseph had enlisted, because he hadn't tried hard enough to stop him.

– Not even nearly.

Three years later, Eve lent Joseph enough to buy himself out. It took him as long again to pay her back and she told him it didn't matter, would have written it off, only Joseph wouldn't let her. He knew she didn't want it back, but she never argued with him about the money, and as far as he knew, she'd never told their mum and dad about it either.

Eve made him a cup of tea and they sat in the front room. Joseph hadn't seen how late it had got, and thought he should make some excuse, but nothing came to mind.

– You had a row with Alice?
– No. Just wanted to come and see you.

He couldn't think how else to explain it. Eve was sleepy, said she was sorry for yawning, pulled her legs up under herself on the sofa.

– Do you want to stay over? I can get the spare duvet down.
– Yeah, alright.
– Art's due in from his shift about six, I'll leave a note for him so he doesn't wake you.
– No, tell him to give me a shout, I should get moving about then anyway.

Joseph hadn't done this in a long time. Stayed here in the spring, after Arthur's birthday, but that was different: they'd all had too many that night, and he just couldn't be bothered going home. Turning up like this was much more like he used to be, years ago, but if Eve was worried, she didn't let it show. She tucked the sheet around the sofa cushions with him and then kissed him goodnight. Said she'd most likely leave with him in the morning, because it was a market day tomorrow, and that was that. Both talking like this was normal made it feel that way too.

Seven

September came and Alice was allowed to take some time off again: she'd used up most of her last year's holiday looking after her gran and hadn't been away in ages. Joseph planned a week in Scotland with her for the end of the month, and Alice booked a train up to Yorkshire first, to see her mum, spend a bit of time with her out on the Dales, at her step-dad's place. Joseph was due to finish off a job for Stan, so he wouldn't be able to join them this time. He had some free days, but they were in the middle of the week, and he thought he'd spend them working at David's.

He took Alice to the station. The idea was to drop her off at King's Cross and drive on to work, but when they got there he decided to look for a meter, said he wanted to come in with her.

– Won't you be late, Joe?
– Doesn't matter. We might get a space by the arches if we're lucky.

They had to park a couple of streets away from the station in the end, and they were cutting it fine for her train by then, so Joseph took Alice's rucksack because it meant they could go a bit faster. He'd wanted to make it a proper goodbye, but the half-jog up the platform made it all a bit hectic. And then the train was packed, and it was hard to say anything to each other with all the people trying to shove onto the carriage past them, both out of breath and sweating. Alice smiled down at him from inside the door.

– I'll give you a ring later, yeah?
– Yeah. Take care of yourself.
– You too.

She pushed the window open further, so she could reach an arm out and touch his face.

– Don't spend all your days off at my Grandad's, will you?

Joseph walked along the platform, watching her through the windows, as she found her seat and lifted her bag onto the rack above. This time next week, he'd be getting on the same train and she would be meeting him off it at York: the plan was to have some lunch with her mum and step-dad before getting another train further north. He stayed on the platform, by her window, but Alice had a paper with her, and started leafing through it after she'd sat down, so Joseph thought she might not look out again. He felt a bit stupid then, waiting for someone who didn't know he was there. But when the train started moving, Alice raised her head. Saw him, and then lifted a hand to wave to him, surprised. Looked almost shy, pleased to see him still there, and then Joseph was glad he'd stayed.

There was no answer when he rang the bell, so Joseph went to the garage and got changed before he let himself into the house. It was cool and quiet in the front room and strange to be alone in there, so he put the radio on and set to work quickly, rolling up the rug and standing it in the porch, ready to take out to the garage for safe-keeping later. Laying out the dustsheets, he noticed for the first time the dark, worn wood on the arms of the old man's chair, and the red and green light falling on the carpet through the coloured glass panels in the tops of the windows.

– Joseph? Is that you, Joseph?

The voice was upstairs, muffled by distance, and it took him a couple of seconds to adjust: not alone. He turned down the radio.

– Yeah. Only me. I rang the bell earlier. I thought you weren't in.

No reply. Joseph wasn't sure what to do, and why the old man hadn't answered the door. He went out into the hallway, listened a moment and then called:

– I'll be making a start down here then.

But he stayed where he was, looking up the stairs to the empty landing.

– No. Come up, Joseph. Would you come up, please?

The old man's voice sounded further away than upstairs, and it didn't seem right to Joseph somehow. Halfway up to the landing, he saw the trapdoor to the attic was open, the old wooden ladder pulled down and sagging on its hinges. He thought, *Jesus*. And then: *fucking stupid*. Took the rest of the stairs two at a time, thinking David must have climbed into the loft and fallen, but when Joseph started up the ladder, the old man was above him, stooping over the hole in the gloom.

– I haven't been up here for years.

He was smiling.

– Found a few things to show you.

One of the bulbs had gone, but the other still cast its forty-watt glow at the far end by the water tank. Joseph moved slowly away from the square light of the trap-door, careful where he put his feet, waiting for his eyes to adjust. Lagged pipes and loft insulation, trunks and crates and cardboard boxes. In the middle was David, watching him, nodding.

– We can see well enough, can't we?

He pointed at the dead bulb.

– Didn't want to risk another journey down and up that

ladder again to get a spare from the kitchen. Isobel's knitting patterns.

He gestured to a box next to Joseph's leg, stuffed with magazines, their pages swollen with damp.

A trunk was open next to them, clothes, summer dresses, pastels and florals for a middle-aged woman. David lifted one of them out, held it up.

– I'd forgotten all of this.

The dress hung from his fingers but he was still smiling, and Joseph had to look away, down at the square of daylight next to him in the floor, and the landing below.

– Sorry. I didn't call you up for this. Thought you might be interested in my old service things.

The old man was making his way over to the water tank, head ducking the roof beams, one arm out to steady himself. He sat down on a trunk and pulled a small box up onto his knees. Joseph followed, hunched and careful, squatting down next to him under the dim bulb.

– I was looking for pictures of Isobel to show Alice. Found these. Our squadron.

Men in uniform on wet tarmac. Maybe a hundred or so: five or six rows of them in front of an aeroplane, the propellers on either side marking the edges of the frame. The men were arranged behind one another in tiers, the heads of the top row level with the wing.

– See if you can find me.

He passed the picture over and Joseph tried but they all
looked the same. Front row on chairs, hands on knees,
the men behind them standing, arms by their sides. All
stiff backs and cheerful faces.

– Fourth row down. Third from left.

David prompted, but he didn't seem offended. And then
Joseph thought the face did look like him: long with a
thin mouth smiling, but then so did the man next to
him. All with their caps on.

– That was Norfolk. This was Kenya.

The old man had a pile of small, white-framed snap-
shots in his hand. Passed them over to Joseph one by
one, explaining the views of forest and cloud taken from
his cockpit, mountains rising at the end of a wingtip.

– Those are the Aberdares. I have one of Mount Kenya
too.

Snow-capped, with another plane flying ahead: sun glare
on the metal, propellers blurred. And the last one was
of the forest canopy, far below, taken through the bomb
bay doors, Joseph could just see the edges of them,
hanging open. He handed the small pile back to David,
who looked through them again, quickly, nodding as he
slipped them one behind the other.

– I was a cadet, while the war was still going on. It was
what I looked forward to, all through the school day.
Morse code and aircraft recognition in the church hall

weekday evenings. I could recite names and wing spans, used to cycle over to the airfield at Northolt, halfway across London, to name them as they came in. Hurricanes and Spitfires. I'd check the wind direction, try to guess which way the pilot would land. They had a Polish squadron there, as I remember, with the highest Allied scores in the Battle of Britain. Wished it hadn't ended, the war. What a terrible thing to wish for.

He laughed and then glanced at Joseph, as if to make sure he was still there, still listening. The old man put the photos back in the box on his knees, told Joseph he'd been looking through his service papers when he heard the radio downstairs. David held a couple of letters out, which Joseph took from him, but he didn't read the typed pages because the old man was still talking. Telling him that he'd been called up, everyone was then, but he'd never have got an interesting job as a national serviceman, so he enlisted immediately.

— I'd have been out in under two years otherwise, and I already knew that wasn't long enough to learn anything. I was suggested for air crew, which pleased my father no end, I remember. Plus the fact that my training took me out to Rhodesia. It was something to be proud of then, a son in the Empire Training Scheme.

The old man took the letters back, didn't seem to mind or notice that Joseph hadn't read them, and he flicked through the remaining papers in the box while he was talking, but didn't take anything else out to show him.

— I remember looking it up before I left. I knew where Rhodesia was, of course, we were taught things like that at school back then. It was a habit I'd picked up as a boy, I listened to the radio in the evenings with my parents, followed the fighting on my father's atlas. The war made everything seem closer. I thought I had a picture in here, a postcard I bought in Salisbury.

David frowned and shut the box, glanced around the floor at his feet.

– I learned to fly Tiger Moths and Harvards out there. I'd only just finished my training. And then came Kenya and Isobel.

He looked at Joseph, blinking, and Joseph wasn't sure if he was meant to say something. The old man was jumping around in time, getting hard to follow. They sat quiet a minute or so and Joseph could feel the air moving in from under the eaves. There was a slit of sunlight and garden away to his left, and he could hear a passing car, birds in the garden. His ankles and knees were stiff from squatting.

– I've been going on, haven't I?
– No.
– I have.
– I don't mind.

David smiled, like he didn't believe him. Started searching in another box resting on the beam between them.

– I found a picture of Alice to show you. Somewhere.

It hadn't felt like a lie when Joseph said he didn't mind, but it was strange, squatting up here, between a bin liner of tablecloths and some empty suitcases, listening to another man's life. The old man sat up again:

– Here. Six, I think. Or seven. With her first glasses.

Joseph was glad to see Alice's face, and smiled at the small eyes, looking tired through the lenses, her uneven parting. He knew she wore contacts now, but he'd never thought she'd been a speccy girl.

– Her school reports are here too, old exercise books. Funny. Tent and things she put here last time she moved.

David pointed over towards the trapdoor, at two fruit crates, packed with books and papers. Joseph was tempted, but knew he couldn't really ask to look through them. Underneath the picture in his hand was another girl, but the photo was older.

– That's her mother, Sarah Margaret. Around the same age, perhaps a little younger.

David nodded at his daughter's picture.

– Peggy, little Peg, they called her. Her grandparents, up in Scotland. Not Isobel. I remember she told me: I don't call her that. Meaning, please don't call her that either.

Joseph went down first and then held the ladder steady. David came down slowly, switching the light off once he had his feet firmly planted on one of the upper rungs. When he was back on the landing, Joseph asked if he shouldn't close over the trapdoor for him.

– No, no. Leave it, leave it. Plenty up there to keep an old man occupied.

Pork pie, salad, boiled potatoes. David had made lunch when Joseph arrived the next day: jar of pickle and a pot of tea waiting at one end of the table with its cosy on.

– I tend to make the things that she did. This is a Tuesday meal.

The old man smiled, and Joseph sat down where the plate had been laid for him. He'd been at Stan's in the morning, sorting out an order for their next job, and bought a sandwich from the garage on his way over, still in his bag.

– Much better than what I'd have got myself. Thanks.

They ate together, talking about Joseph and Alice's trip to Scotland, and where they planned to go. They'd be spending most of their time on the Fife coast, around the East Neuk villages, where Alice's gran grew up, and David knew the area well, from visits to his in-laws, taking Sarah up to see her grandparents in the summer holidays. He said there was plenty of good walking and driving they could do, and he rummaged some maps out of a drawer in the sideboard to show Joseph.

– Take them with you. I should have given them to Alice last week, don't know why I didn't think of it.

They were OS, but very old, and worn at the folds. Joseph had already bought a new one, at the station after he saw Alice off, but he didn't refuse. Followed the coastal paths that David pointed out with his little finger, the roads might have changed a bit, but he could remember the routes to tell Alice about later.

The dining table was at the far end of the room that Joseph had been working on, pushed closer to the French windows than usual, and a bit crowded by the armchairs and the piano, which Joseph had moved down there, out of his way. The other half was covered in sheets, walls exposed up to the dado rail, strips of paper scraped off above it too. Joseph had thought he'd get it all done yesterday, but the time spent talking in the attic had taken a chunk out of the morning. Hadn't planned to come today originally. He was meant to see Arthur, have a game of snooker, only Ben was sick and Eve was working all day, so they said they'd have a drink later in the week instead. Joseph thought he could make use of the afternoon, catch up on the work here, and when he'd called David to say he was on his way over, the old man had told him he was going out after lunch so he'd have the place to himself. David didn't look in any hurry to get moving, though: folding up the maps for Joseph, saying he envied him a week up there, and that he had wonderful memories of that stretch of coast.

– Going through all those old photos yesterday. Made me remember how much I enjoyed being in Africa. Rhodesia especially, but Kenya too. Isobel didn't. It was all soured by her first marriage, I think. Or had been by the time I met her.

His lunch finished, knife and fork tidy, the old man was

looking out through the windows at his back garden, both hands resting in front of him on the table.

– Funny. I didn't think she was attractive at first, not really. I was getting better by that time, less tired, but there wasn't much I could do until I was fully recovered. This young woman became a diversion, I suppose.

Joseph put down his fork because it was hard to eat when the old man wasn't. David wasn't looking at him, but it still felt rude, chewing while he was meant to be listening. The old man said he used to watch Isobel leaving for work from his seat on the veranda, remembered her wide hat and gloves, her round shoulders. The Sumners' granddaughter stayed at the house for a weekend and Isobel taught her easy pieces on the baby grand in the drawing room. She spoke to the girl as they played and, from where David sat, he could hear Isobel's accent, but not what she said. When she wasn't working, she'd take the Sumners' car into town, and would come back around lunchtime with a pile of library books tucked under her arm.

– Once at breakfast, I asked whether I might take the car to the library with her. I told her it was deadly boring, being a convalescent. And I thought, rightly as it turned out, if I asked her in public, she wouldn't be able to refuse. I presumed I would need to make conversation, but once we were in the car she was rather candid.

David was smiling. About himself, it looked like: taken aback by the woman he went on to marry.

– While we were driving, she told me her husband had

fallen in love with someone else. *I suppose you've heard.*
She said it was an occupational hazard out there. Or
maybe just a hobby. That's how she put it. Told me other
people didn't seem to mind so much.

Joseph watched the old man talking and thought: he
should be telling Alice all this, not me. Her grandad's
eyes were still on the garden, and he was laughing at
himself.

– I couldn't look at her after she'd finished speaking. I
remember all the houses passing outside the car window
and I could name the mimosa and bougainvillea
growing in the gardens, but I didn't know how to
continue the conversation. It was the cynicism, I think.
And Isobel knew she'd shocked me. We didn't speak
much in the library, or on the way back to the house.
She wasn't at breakfast in the morning, but she came
and found me later when I was downstairs, reading. Said
she'd told me things I didn't need to know and she was
sorry. That surprised me too: I didn't think she had to
apologise.

Joseph could see the unfinished walls from where he
was sitting. He couldn't quite make out the clock, the
light from the window was reflecting on the dial, and
he didn't want to crane his head round, be that obvious,
but the afternoon was getting on. He was half-interested
in what David had to say, but only half. The pictures
and papers up in the attic had been more like it: Joseph
didn't know what had gone on in Kenya, thought he
wouldn't mind hearing about it. He liked the old guy,
but most of this was just too personal. Remembering
his dead wife. Saying how their library trips became
regular and longer, and they would go and drink Italian

coffee in one of the city centre tearooms afterwards, or walk through the park to stretch out their time away from the house.

– We met in public mostly, so our conversations had to stay reasonably formal. Isobel told me she'd had fun there, in Kenya, the first few months, while she was still working. Most of the girls she'd applied with in Scotland had gone to Salisbury, but she'd made new friends quickly in Nairobi. There were always nights out being organised, and clubs to get involved in, but that all stopped after she got married, gave up nursing. Life was very different, not at all what she'd expected. Sounded very dull, actually, the way she described it, for the wives at least. Endless coffee mornings and nothing to talk about except each other. It might have been different if they'd had children. Isobel used to give music lessons, private classes, for something to do as much as anything. She told me she was supposed to decide to stay with her husband. It's what both families wanted, and I believe he was willing. *But I'm afraid that's not likely*. I remember the tone of voice exactly. Resolved. I admired her for it, she had to face a great deal of disapproval, but Isobel didn't think the place was any good, Nairobi. The expat existence. She told me people would be watching us, of course. Speculating over their sheet music in our absence. Pink gins and loose tongues, that's what she said. They would have started long ago, and there was nothing we could do to stop them now.

The old man broke off for a moment, and it looked to Joseph as though he'd lost his place.

– It did bother me, if I'm honest. I'm sure our romance was tame by Happy Valley standards, but I was very aware of being a guest, for one thing. Not causing a scandal for the Sumners. I'd started to feel the curiosity, at those cocktail evenings. All eyes on us if we were there at the same time, hoping for a sensation. But she was beautiful to me by then, Isobel. I remember her in the park especially, under the flame trees, and the very British bandstand. In her white hat, with the wide brim. When we passed out of the shade, the holes in the weave let through bright spots of light. Like so many pin pricks of sun scattered across her cheeks.

The old man's fingers shifted across the tabletop, a small movement, involuntary, caught up in the memory, Joseph didn't think he was aware of it. David looked down at his teacup: undrunk, cold, he stirred it. He didn't speak again, his eyes unclouding, back in the room. Joseph thought it was probably over now, but he'd wait until the old man moved. They'd clear the table soon and then he could get on. Another couple of minutes sitting with him now wouldn't make much difference.

– Is he being alright to you, my Grandad?
– Made me lunch today.
– Did he?

Joseph could hear Alice smiling on the phone. She was having a fine time up at her mum's: they'd been away, the two of them, walking on Swaledale, staying up at the old farm. She told Joseph about it when he called. Just in from her grandad's and he was a bit tired, didn't listen to it all properly, just liked hearing her talk for a while. About a ridgeway she drove past on the way back to York, and how they should go there when it got warmer again, camping in the spring, maybe, if he had some time off then. Joseph sat on the edge of the bed and rolled a cigarette, receiver jammed in against his shoulder. He wanted to tease Alice about the school photo her grandad had shown him, specs and messy hair, see if he could make her laugh. But he thought about it a bit too long and then couldn't. She might want to know how he'd got to see it, the picture. Sitting up in the attic with David felt a bit difficult to explain down the phone, so he left it. Told her about the maps instead.

– Oh, I'd like to see those. My Gran would have used them too. Will you bring them with you?
– Yeah, course.

After she hung up, Joseph didn't know why he couldn't tell her. *Your Grandad was looking at old photos, showed me a couple.* But it was hard to feel that casual about it. He could see David sitting on the trunk in his neatly tied shoes. Polished leather, patterned with holes, narrow laces, well-kept soles. His trouser legs pulled up by his knees, the section of pale skin above the dark sock showing underneath, hairless and thin. Joseph knew he wouldn't be able to tell Alice about today either. Lunch and maps, yes, but not what David told him after. The old man never asked him to keep it to himself, but Joseph thought he didn't have to: it was all private, about his wife, that was obvious enough, and he'd tell Alice himself if he wanted her to know. It even annoyed Joseph a bit then. Being let in on someone's secrets. *When you haven't been asked.*

He thought about the old man and his tropical trees. All the schoolboy stuff David had told him yesterday too: deserts and mountains, bird's-eye, pilot's-eye views of snows and oceans, evenings by the radio with his dad's atlas open on his knees. His small head must have been full of it, Joseph thought. But maybe the old man was aware of that too. Hard to say with him and the way he spoke about things, sometimes. When he said his dad was proud of him going to Rhodesia, or how he enjoyed being in Africa, it felt to Joseph like he was careful, choosing his words. Passing comment, or at least waiting to see if Joseph was going to. His son-in-law would, maybe. Alice too, in her way. Joseph remembered her out on the patio that evening, blinking about the bare-foot servants. He thought her grandad must have noticed: *Alan would smile about that.* The old man acknowledged it himself, so she could keep quiet.

So maybe David was testing things out on him, but Joseph didn't know why. When they were in the attic, Joseph had thought David was waiting for him to ask. Questions about the air force, maybe. Or tell him something about when he was in the army, even. Join in the conversation, swapping tales of Osnabrück and South Armagh for Norfolk and Nairobi. But it didn't feel that way, not really. The old man talked, but always a bit like he was keeping his distance. Not expecting something in return in any case. And then this afternoon, it was all about Alice's gran anyway, being in Nairobi with her, nothing to do with why he was out in Kenya in the first place. Joseph wasn't even sure if David knew he'd been in the army, although it had occurred to him, up in the loft, that Alice might have told him.

But even if the old man didn't know, or wasn't waiting to be told, it was hard not to think about what it was like back then. Joseph couldn't stop himself making the comparison. The whole evening alone at home, after he'd said goodbye to Alice and hung up the phone. Didn't have photos to look at, but enough in his head, and the same thing kept coming back to him.

Contractor got killed. New RUC station being built and he was the plumber, meant to be going in to fit the toilets. Had a van load of cisterns, and they blew him up on his way there. IRA, INLA, one of them, some set of initials anyway, Joseph couldn't remember. It was Republicans, and their bomb probably wasn't meant to go off until the van was parked by the building.

Joseph's patrol got there about ten minutes after it happened, had to wait for bomb disposal, seal off the area. Tyre shreds all over, van doors, coat sleeves and what was left inside them. Took a while to work out there had been two in the van. Turned out it was his son who was with the plumber. Didn't usually work together, but he'd been on the dole a while and his dad was probably paying him a bit, or a favour for a favour. Joseph could remember laughing. About the body parts: too many of them. And about someone having to make a phone call to ask if the plumber had a mate. That and the toilets all over the road, had them all creased up, even the Corporal. The plastic balls that float, to make the water stop running. They were everywhere you looked: bright blue and yellow at the side of the road, in the hedgerows. *Ballcocks.* Someone said that's what they're called and then they were off again, pissing themselves over ballcocks and body parts. Townsend was puking. One of the other soldiers. Kneeling on the verge, bulking his breakfast up into the grass and laughing.

Joseph put up the new wallpaper at David's on Thursday. The old man made him a cup of tea when he arrived, but went out soon after he'd brought it in to him. Put his head round the door to say goodbye and then didn't come home until the room was finished, and Joseph was packing up in the garage.

– You've done a fine job.
– I put all the furniture back where I remembered.
– Yes. It all looks very good. Thank you.

It was drizzling a bit, so the old man stood just inside the garage doors, nodding while Joseph got his things together.

– I hope the weather's kinder to you up in Scotland.

Joseph smiled. He'd thought at first David might invite him into the house, but the old man was just saying goodbye. In his awkward way.

– I'll see what jobs I've got on when we get home, give you a ring. Get the rest done in a oner if I can.

Not in the mood for a cup of tea and a story. The old guy could see that. Probably why he spent the day out too: left Joseph to get on with it. All the stations were playing crap today, so he'd turned the radio off for a change. The old man's garden backed onto empty playing fields, and there was a golf course at the end of the street. No through traffic, no buses or people on the road outside, and it all felt very still. Just the odd train passing, or a plane overhead, a few birds singing. Joseph didn't stop for lunch, worked through the day and was glad of the quiet.

Over three years in the army and Joseph didn't think he was ever, not ever, by himself. A fly wank in the bogs once in a while, or a sly fag maybe, but nothing else, not even alone at night to go to sleep. Six in a room over in Armagh. Not like any base he'd known before, more like a bunker. It had been the village police station once, before the army came, but Joseph only knew it covered in barbed wire and reinforced concrete. Thinking back, it was like the place had no windows: nothing that would leave them open to incoming mortars. Everything done together, washing, eating, working, cleaning, TV, pool table, bar. Knew each other's smells and sounds better than their own. And all that talking: someone always mouthing off, always asking something, pissing themselves or whingeing all the bloody time. Joseph remembered walking corridors, trying hard to find a place where no one else was. Sat on the toilet and could hear the others cracking up about him, his slow bowels, but at least it was a small room just for him, for a while.

Always tired. Sixteen hours on, eight hours off and waking up all the time. Always too hot in his bunk, they kept the heating on constant, and Joseph woke at all hours, dry eyes and parched, tongue pasted to his teeth, like a hangover without the drinking. Learnt to sleep when you could. Was a relief when you were sent to get your head down, but you could kip anywhere after a while, anytime you were waiting. If your patrol was on standby, even on quick reaction, sitting there in all your kit at thirty seconds' notice, just close your eyes and you'd be dreaming. Mad things, twenty different stories and all in the space of seconds. People talking, noises outside your head making their way in: awake and asleep mixing together. A phone ringing somewhere in another room and in your dream you'd be patrolling, walking down the road and into a house to answer it. But there's no phone when you get there, just an Irish family in the front room watching telly, all getting up and heading for the door when they see you and your rifle. Only it's not them heading for the door, it's your patrol called out and moving, and so you're up and running too, outside sometimes before you were awake again.

Drumshitehole was what the outgoing soldiers called it. A main square and five roads off it. Three took you north and east, into fields and hills, the other two ran south into bandit country and west to the border. Down three streets, turn the corner and you were back where you started, everything still just the way you left it. Phone box, post box, chip shop. Joseph could remember how they joked about it, saying the Provos had left the shitehole to them, all fucked off over to England: Warrington, Bournemouth and the NatWest Tower all bombed the same year Joseph was in Ireland. A small place and it was quiet for weeks on end. More Protestants there than Crossmaglen, and it was nothing like the mad, bad days of the seventies, but they shouldn't be fooled, Jarvis said.

Ops room full of photos, known operatives, suspects. Sometimes felt like half the town was up there on the walls, even girls and grannies: no one you didn't need to be watching. B Company had ninety men to cover the place and the eighty square kilometres around it. A crossroads between the province and the republic.

– Smack bang in the IRA's fucking back garden, and that's not potatoes they're planting.

Joseph's Corporal again. He said the people spoke better down there, it wasn't like Belfast barking, but Joseph still got to hate the voices. Wound him up, even years later, hearing them again on Streatham High Street, or London buses. Prods would look at you while they were talking, that was the theory, how you could tell the difference. Joseph never thought that worked: everyone spoke at the back of their throats, out of their noses. Like they were talking past a mouthful of something they wanted to gob at you.

One of the sangars, where they did their guard duty. Big fuck-off cage of a place, metal fortress on a bog-standard street full of houses. All black steel and razor wire. You froze your balls off in there in winter, a sweat box in the summer weather. Nothing to do, just waiting and watching and sod-all happening. Old guy in the house next door had a garden. Big lawn with trees in it, flowerbeds round the edges. He was a pensioner, Joseph thought, because he was always out there, never working. Trousers ironed into creases and grey hair combed sideways, but you could still see his bald patch because you were always looking down on him. His grass was the thing Joseph remembered. Great black sangar and the watchtower on the hill behind it, mad spikey poles in the sky of the transmitters and receivers. And then this garden, just next to all that, this lawn like a big patch of velvet. Snooker-table green and perfect. Old man with a paunch and grey moustache, raking it clear of moss, aerating it with a fork. Beautiful and soft, rain keeping it lush.

The Troubles had been going on for years already. Over twenty, plus the hundreds before, which the army told them about and Joseph had forgotten most of before he even got on the ferry. He could still remember he was one of 18,000 British soldiers in the province. An extra battalion deployed; early nineties and the Irish were busy killing and maiming each other. Semtex, Armalite, Red Hand Commando. Nationalist, Loyalist, Paramilitary. Words Joseph knew from the telly and the papers, and then he was over there, and in the middle of it all.

Only knew about the IRA before. Got sent to Ireland with a whole new bowl of alphabet soup to swallow: UFF, UDA, UVF, UUP. One of them was a political party, but he could never remember. Riots in the cities, the summer he arrived, and the police attacked by Loyalists, which Joseph didn't understand at the time, because the RUC were Prods too, weren't they? Though you weren't supposed to say that.

Belfast was the only part you ever saw on the news: all burnt-out cars and huge murals on the gable ends, a long coil of razor wire they called a peace line and kerb stones painted sectarian colours. Red white and blue, green white and yellow. Or gold, they called it. Joseph never knew that Ireland would be beautiful. Days in Armagh when it didn't rain and you could see the high mountains away to the south. The country below was riddled with fields and grey stone barns. Lanes only just wide enough for two cars, hedgerows growing high along the sides, like green tunnels, twisting as they pelted down them, gaps in the branches letting flashes of day across the windscreen. Joseph remembered the wet ground out there, shivering grass and sunshine on his skin. Held the backs of his hands up under his nose to get the best of it, breathing that warm smell of them in. The only colours were brown and green and blue, but the shades were better than any he'd seen. Loved it then, being out on Ops. No one ever had to beast or bully him into getting moving, the tabbing miles on end that he'd hated in training. More soldiers killed there than anywhere else, but there were days when Joseph forgot all that, or it didn't seem to matter. Sleeping out and seeing the first light in the trees, hearing the sound of a stream before you got to it. Still days and sky, cold air, sparrowhawks flying. A few bright minutes by the lough: last white flare of sun on grey water before evening and the rain came on again. Feeling afterwards like his head had been cleaned out and his lungs been filled. Lying in his bunk and searching out the bruise on his arm where his rifle butt kept knocking; that great tired ache in his legs and shoulders; the strange calm that meant he was almost sleeping.

Joseph was there six months. Summer to winter. First part in Omagh, then down to the shitehole and all the Tullies and Ballies and Killies around it. That spring, a soldier from the outgoing company had been blown up at the border. Sniper near Forkhill got his fourth a few days after Joseph got there. Not someone he knew, from another company, but for days after he could feel it at the back of his neck, between his shoulders. Reminded of it anyway, every time he put his flak jacket on and his helmet. Not war but terror. Protection felt like an invitation over there: they were Green Army not special forces. Uniform target with a porcelain breastplate. Tail End Charlie, last man on patrol always walking backwards. A woman gave sweets to soldiers at Christmas: a two pound tin packed full of plastic explosive. They all pissed everywhere, against cars, trees, walls: like dogs, Joseph thought, marking out the province. On foot patrol, they found a body in the morning. Cold and just getting light, and there it was between the waste ground and the garages. Punishment beating, legs twisted under, lying among the dog shit and clumps of grass. Sometimes the whole place felt like that, all quiet and cruelty.

Eight

Joseph's train was late coming up, so their lunch in town ended up being a cup of tea in the platform café. They only had a short time together, but it was good all the same, Alice thought. Her mum, and Alan especially, seemed to like Joseph a lot. There was a cold week forecast and they joked together about Joseph having packed his tent, and whether he could use Alice as an excuse not to camp out. Alan's father had taken him camping when he was a kid, like Joseph's, and they agreed it was at least half about their dads wanting to get out of the house. Grab a few days' peace, away from the family. But it didn't always work out that way, of course, because they had to haul their sons along.

– Not that we didn't have our uses.

Alan remembered a hailstorm and a night in a hotel, and how the additional expense was blamed on him after they got home.

– He told Mum I'd been unhappy in the tent when the weather turned nasty. But the way I recall it, the hotel room was my Dad's idea.

Alice watched Joseph smiling, slipped her hand under his knee, under the table, and let it rest there, beneath the solid warmth of his leg. His hair was long again, curling over his ears. She'd been the last to cut it, a warm

Sunday morning in his kitchen with the radio on, a couple of months ago already, must be. A week away from him, and she'd surprised herself, thinking about those days, early on, when he'd stopped phoning, and they didn't see each other. They'd spoken almost every day while she was at her mum's, so she didn't know why. He'd given her no reason to worry over the phone, and most days it had been Joseph who'd done the calling, because dinner conversation usually went on for a while with her mum and Alan, and she'd lost track of the evenings. Alice thought, we still haven't known each other long. *Eight, nine months or something.* She was happy to see him.

They'd booked into a bed and breakfast their first night, and arrived just as it was getting dark. Joseph sneaked them a fish supper each up the stairs and then they got into one of the soft single beds together and stayed there. The curtains were thin, and there was sun in the room when Alice woke. Joseph had moved across to the other bed at some stage, probably when it got light, and it looked like he was still sleeping, his top pulled off, the sleeves knotted around his eyes.

They walked a lot, ate their lunches in empty tearooms or on windy beaches. It wasn't summer any more, but not cold enough to put them off. They followed her grandfather's coastal path the first day, and then kept on over the next few as well, moving from village to village, on foot and with the local buses. When it rained, they sheltered in shop doorways and under trees, and Alice liked this best: not moving, not doing, just still, the two of them. Good and tired, wet salt air blown into their faces, no need to say much about anything, Alice enjoyed all of being with Joseph that week: the twenty-four hours of it, the seven days long, and she let herself relax again. *We're doing fine.*

The evening skies were pale from their guesthouse windows, and they ate pub meals, sipping their pints amongst the other walkers. Alice listened to the locals, accents like her grandmother's: memories drawn out of her like teeth.

On their last day, Alice took Joseph to the village where Isobel was born. They'd planned it that way, to save it up, and Alice had been aware of it coming, through the week. She was unsure of what she felt when they were there and walking together through the rainy streets. Past the squat houses, the granite school building where her great-grandfather had taught. Along the riverbank, and under the high stone bridge from where you could see the beach already: sand and grey waves. Alice hadn't been there before, only heard about it. Her gran's childhood memories of fishermen and ceilidhs, her mum's of teenage boredom on holiday at her elderly grandparents'. Alice told Joseph about them while they stood under the bus shelter, waiting for the latest shower to ease off a little.

– It was dull for Gran here too. Maybe not when she was little, but later. She did well at school, she was expected to, probably, the schoolmaster's daughter. But a lot of the other expectations didn't sit so well with her. She hated learning the piano. Said it was all part of a pattern, even if she didn't really know it at the time. Music lessons and a suitable marriage. Children and a well-run house.

Alice watched the rain fall on the puddles in the road, and she told Joseph that her gran used to read books up at the piano sometimes, instead of practising: propped them open on the music stand. If she heard her mother coming, she'd pull the sheet music over them and start playing, always somewhere in the middle of a phrase, as though she'd been stuck, working out the fingering, and that's why the piano had been quiet.

– Gran told her music teacher that she didn't want to get married, and she was going to study medicine. I think she was fourteen then. Very earnest about it. Her teacher wasn't married and lived on her own, so Gran said she seemed like the right person to confide in. But the teacher reported back to Gran's parents, in front of Gran and Celie, her big sister, and they all laughed.

Joseph winced, and Alice said they weren't being unkind, not the way Gran had told it, just not taking her as seriously as she did herself, and she was mortified.

– Did she carry on her lessons?
– Yeah. But Gran said she did more reading than practising after that. She used to like telling that story, I reckon. Because she notched up two husbands, as it turned out. That was her punchline. Never went back to nursing either, looked after my Mum instead, and then me. Taught me piano. She enjoyed it. She was good at it too. Gave lessons to the kids down the road after we moved out.

Joseph stood close to her, listening, and Alice thought about her gran: the way she'd laughed about her teenage ambitions, as though she enjoyed remembering them. Hard to say now, if she'd minded that they were unfulfilled.

– Gran never told my Mum she should marry my Dad. It was his parents that were keen on that idea, I think. My Mum wasn't, and my Gran didn't try to persuade her. Thinking about herself at fourteen, probably.

Alice shifted a little. Now that she'd said it, this felt like an unsatisfactory explanation. Too neat a connection. She shook her head, self-conscious.

– I don't know, though. I'm just guessing, aren't I?

Joseph returned her smile. It was the most Alice had said all day, and it felt strange afterwards, the quiet under the shelter. Gusts of wind spattering drops onto the roof from the trees. Not raining any more. The timetable said the last bus was at three: too soon for Alice. They'd been in the village just under two hours, and there wasn't much left to see, but Joseph said he liked it, and that they should spend their last night there, even though it would mean getting up early for the only bus out in the morning.

– There was a B&B down at the harbour, had vacancies in the window. I'll shout you.

They'd paid for a night back at their first guesthouse already, were due to get a train out from there at lunchtime tomorrow. Alice looked at Joseph, the rain on his face and his smile, his nose and cheekbones pink from the wind.

– You don't mind?

He shrugged:

– No, this is a good place. A bit damp, but it's peaceful.

They stayed late in the pub next door, but Alice wasn't tired when she got into bed. Lay with her eyes open and saw not the ceiling, the wallpaper, just her grandmother's hands lifting off the piano keys, the corners of her mouth, teeth showing gold when she sang or smiled. Felt the loss of her: permanent, final. She dozed and then later she cried. Tried to be quiet about it, thought Joseph was sleeping in the other bed. But then he reached over in the dark and found the crook of her arm, rested his fingertips there. A bit later he took her hand and held it until she stopped crying, and longer. It wasn't what she'd expected, Joseph didn't come into her bed, but it was gentle, soothing somehow, and Alice was grateful to have him lying awake with her. They got up with the alarm for the first time in a week and dressed slowly, without speaking. Handing stray socks and jumpers across the beds to one another, packing and tidying. Sun just rising and they could see each other in the half-light, both puffy-eyed.

It was like his mind got stuck sometimes, turning everything over again to have a closer look. Not like he didn't
know it all already, but when he got that way, it was
hard to stop. Thought it was down to David this time.
Or down to himself for listening. Thought about the old
man a lot that week away with Alice: how he talked,
once he got started, just kept running on and getting
distracted. Joseph reckoned he knew how that felt: he'd
done enough of it over the years, not out loud like
David, but in his head. Thinking it might all add up to
something, maybe, all the remembering. Different parts
of it on different days, and the order of things kept
changing, but it was all the same memories and always
the same people in them.

September in Ireland, hot for about a week and the local
kids swam in the river. Sat on the banks in wet shorts,
skinny boys shivering. Sixteen-, seventeen-, eighteen-
year-olds, drinking cider out of plastic bottles. Smoking,
shouting, the hardest ones jumping off the old stone
bridge into the water. Cuts on their legs from the rocks
at the bottom, but no limping, no pain showing, at least
not while the girls were there on the opposite bank
watching. Back at the barracks, in their bunks and the
bar, the talk was all about how the girls surely had to
go swimming soon, and what the boys should be doing
to get them in there. But days passed, boys only, in and
out the water, stomachs pulled in from the cold and the

skin on their ribs shining blue-white in the unexpected sunshine. Out on Ops, they kept watch on them through binoculars: the boys showing off, charming and persuading, and the girls ignoring them. Joseph remembered being with Lee and Townsend on the hill above the village, always one of them ready for when the girls got their kit off.

The boys nicked some tractor inner tubes from one of the farmers and that was what did it. Genius, Townsend reckoned. Joseph was on stag, but he kept quiet and kept hold of the binoculars when the girls finally got off the banks. Still not showing much skin except leg: pale, wet limbs splayed, floating around on the black inflated rings, mouths wide. Joseph thought he could just hear them from where he was lying. Screaming and laughing, turning with the current, boys swimming out and splashing them, T-shirts and knickers soaked through and clinging so Joseph could see more by then, if he kept the binoculars still enough. Insects dancing in the long grass in front of him, sweat on his belly from the heat of the sun, from lying there for hours on his buckle, bored and uncomfortable. Breath held, pressed down onto the hillside, Joseph kept watching as long as he could, until the girls floated under the bridge and then he passed the binoculars on.

– You dirty fuck, why didn't you say nothing?

That was Lee. Who said guard duty was for wanking. Told Joseph all about his porn collection at home in boxes, in the attic at his mum's place. Always left a *Forum* or something stashed somewhere in the sangar, and if you were on after, you could spend half your time searching, take it away with you for later. Lee liked talking about it: called himself an addict, junkie for skin. Blamed the army, said they got him started, and that filth was all part of his training for the province. He told Joseph they showed him videos of riots and bombing with hard core cut in. Cunts and petrol bombs. Parades and fucking and burnt-out cars. Joseph didn't believe him, you sick bastard, laughed:

– How come I never got to see them?

Jarvis was out with them that day, heard Lee talking. Told Joseph to stop laughing, because it wasn't right to mock the afflicted. Said Lee's training video was just wishful thinking: too much time on his hands and not enough in his y-fronts to fill them.

They heard later that a few of the younger boys took a tube each and drifted off downstream, beyond the bridge and away from the town. Made it as far as the sea, miles away, down at Dundalk in the Republic, and when it got dark they hitched home again.

The farmer was furious about his inner tubes, dumped at the beach. His wife wanted him to go down to the police station and report them stolen, but there was no chance of that, because two of the boys were sons of someone who counted. An RUC officer told them about it, tight-lipped and livid.

– That's the way things work here. No such thing as due process. IRA makes its own laws. No one follows the ones we're here to be upholding.

Joseph knew it should have bothered him too, but he couldn't get worked up with the policeman: about the principle, maybe, but not about the boys and their inner tubes.

They saw them again a few days later, all up on ladders, painting the guttering on one of the farmer's outbuildings, and Townsend said they were witnessing the local version of justice in action.

– You've got to admire it, haven't you?

He was in the same brick, patrolling with Joseph most days, the whole time they were there. Townsend was Welsh, and kept a photo taped up on the wall by his pillow, of the hill behind his grandad's house in the Rhondda. Said he climbed it every time he got home on leave, and he liked having the picture there, to remind him what mattered. But you could never tell with him if he was serious. A wind-up merchant. Always watching you while he was talking, and always some part of him smiling: mouth, eyes, something about him. So whatever he said you'd have to be careful about joining in, just in case he turned it against you. Told Joseph his cousins used to torch the English holiday homes and quite right too, he'd have done it as well only his dad said he had to wait a couple of years until he was old enough to go with them.

– It was all over by that time. Wanker.

Not the most convincing story, Joseph thought. Especially the bit about his dad: sounded like a poor excuse for not joining in, if he'd wanted to.

– What the fuck you doing here then?
– Fuck knows. You?

Townsend sang 'Give Ireland Back to the Irish' in the NAAFI bar and got put on CO's orders. Drink in one hand, standing on a chair, loud, but still in tune. Hard to tell if he was pissed or just acting it. They were on two cans then, so he couldn't have been. Insisted he was only proving a point, settling a long-running bar room dispute: Macca could be as political as Lennon when the mood took him. Only Townsend was smiling again when he said it, and the Company Commander didn't take kindly. Two weeks on drill, forty minutes every morning being bawled at in the transport yard by the Provost Corporal, who told him to stay out of trouble, because he hated drill, too fucking boring.

Townsend reckoned most of the locals were happy enough with the way things were. Just like the law, they didn't really give a toss about the border: took the long view and figured it couldn't last. Plenty of money to be made while it was there, besides. Most of the time it wasn't guns getting smuggled, just pigs borrowed to double the subsidy from Brussels, or car boots full of fags and disposable nappies. The border was only marked every so often, so you had to keep your eyes open: for a line painted on a fence post, a symbol on a tree. Easy to cross and not know you'd done it, they ended up spending most of one patrol in the Republic. The Lieutenant heading up their multiple got a bollocking for that one. They didn't think they'd been spotted, but the local Gardai had put in a phone call to the Company Commander.

– What were you doing, playing Special Forces?

Joseph saw the blood vessels working under the Major's eyes, thinking about them upsetting relations with the

Irish government, making the company a laughing stock in front of the locals. It didn't turn into a diplomatic incident, but they did get a few cool smiles over the next few days.

– All Ireland, isn't it? Same woods, same fields, same rivers.

That was the woman who ran the post office, calling across the road to them, opening her shutters while they were out early, patrolling. Townsend said she was right, but not to her face, only to Joseph later on when they were mopping out the bogs. It was part of their punishment, not for crossing the border, but for laughing about it afterwards in earshot of the Major, and while Townsend was going on about drawing stupid lines in the earth and sky, Joseph thought he'd sooner be painting a barn than scrubbing out a pisshouse, any day.

Nine

Alice got her photos back from the developers, started sorting through them in the living room: pulling out the best ones to show her grandad on Sunday, laying out the panoramas on the coffee table to see if they worked.

– More or less. What do you think?

Martha was in and out of the room: in her pyjamas, but tidying the flat instead of going to bed. She nodded approval in passing, carrying empty mugs and glasses out into the kitchen. Keith was sitting in the chair next to Alice, tackling his accounts, long overdue, piles of receipts sliding off his knees, more spilling out of a bag at his feet. Glad of a distraction, he picked up the second pack of photos from the table and laughed about the weather.

– Looks like you had about half an hour of sunshine the whole time you were away.
– It wasn't that bad.
– No, but this is.

He held up one to show her: Alice grimacing on a beach, nose running, eyes teary in the wind. She laughed.

– It's for the bin.
– Show me.

Martha had come through from the kitchen again. She leaned over the back of Keith's chair, smiling as he flicked through the pictures.

– Joseph cuts a fine figure in a cagoule anyway.
– And I don't?
– You lack the military training. Takes years of practice to carry that look off.

Martha winked at Alice and then started gathering the papers Keith had strewn across the floor. He'd got to the beginning of the photos again, and put them back down on the table.

– I didn't know Joseph was in the army.

Martha interrupted his flow, holding out an invoice he had discarded, waiting. Keith took it from her, impassive, and then put it back on the floor after she'd turned away. Alice smiled at him, and he went on:

– My brother was too, after he finished university. What was Joseph's regiment?
– I don't know, actually. It was quite a while ago. I think it was infantry.
– Proper soldiering, Neil would say. He went for infantry even though he'd studied engineering, came home and joined our local regiment. Got frustrated in the end, though. They never sent him anywhere that counted, not in his mind anyway.

Martha came back with two more crumpled sheets for Keith, but when he just added them to the pile by his chair, she gave up on the mess and sat down.

– He was always off somewhere, far as I could tell. Whizzing about in Chinooks. Belize. I remember him going there, because you had to check the map to see where it was.

She kicked her boyfriend's feet and he smiled.

– Only because my Dad's atlas was old, it still said British Honduras. That was just training anyway. Jungle warfare. I've got an action man for a brother. He was forever training and never doing, that was a big part of the problem, I reckon. A platoon from his regiment went to Bosnia, part of the UN mission. Neil decided to leave after that: said it was too hard, always watching his men go without him.

Keith blinked, thinking about his brother. Alice was sitting on the floor by the coffee table, her flatmates were on chairs, on either side, talking to her, but across her somehow, and she wasn't sure how to join in. Martha said:

– Your mum was glad though, wasn't she? About Bosnia. She always was, when he didn't get to go somewhere. Used to call us to say how relieved she was, because she couldn't say it to him.

Keith nodded.

– Yeah, I remember. But he's the last of us kids, you know. By a few years. And the army takes you over, took him over, I don't think my Mum could get used to that. Or she didn't want to. Let go of her son to that extent.

He shifted, frowning a little.

– We went to school with army kids. I remember they looked out for each other, I liked that about them. The families moved a lot, so there were always new kids to look out for. I reckon it would have been easier if we'd been an army family, maybe, when Neil joined up. You might feel more part of it. You'd know what to expect, anyway. I mean, my Dad was in the army, but that was national service, like everyone back then, and it was before my Mum met him. He made army life sound tedious, if anything.

– Neil signed up for officer training, though. That was bound to be different.

– Yeah, but I think it surprised Mum that he wanted to do it. He didn't have to.

– Baby son has a mind of his own, shock horror?

Keith looked at his girlfriend, mild, amused.

– She worried about the guns and bombs, as you would. Didn't like it that he was trained to use them on other people either. It just didn't square with her idea of him. I was glad for my Mum when he gave in his notice. Got passed over for Major again. He told me they didn't want you getting complacent. Expecting promotion without putting in the effort. I think it gutted him.

Keith shrugged, looked over at Alice.

– It's a bizarre world, seen from the outside anyway. I'd be interested to hear what Joseph made of it. I'm sure Neil used to get off on the fact that we found it strange. Liked having to explain it to us. I still don't get all the dressing up and shunting around parade grounds in unison.

Alice smiled, because Keith was smiling at her.

– It used to scare me, actually, listening to him back then. He used to say he wanted to be tested. Validated. What a word.

Keith laughed, and then shook his head.

– Get it right and you get your troops out alive, get it wrong and they're in bits or in boxes. Or they see you as a liability and shoot you in the back. This is my little brother talking.

Alice watched him, still shaking his head, caught somewhere between incredulity and sneaking respect.

– He's a good, solid, diligent bloke, Neil. Lovely, to my mind. But he wanted to be something else, and they wouldn't let him, poor sod. He volunteered for every posting going, and then spent most of his time shuffling numbers around on spreadsheets and dealing with troublesome soldiers. Teenagers, most of them. Neil was like a cross between an accountant and a social worker. One of his boys was always getting caught half-cut in town, or driving while banned. He said you could take them to the most extraordinary, far-flung spot in the world, but all they cared about was whether they'd get lager there and porn on cable.

Alice turned back to the photos, started sorting through them again. She wasn't particularly enjoying the conversation. Keith was quiet for a minute or two, but she could feel him watching her, wanting her to look up again.

– Joseph was a squaddie, wasn't he?

– Yes.
– I'm sorry.

Keith was embarrassed. Alice blinked at him.

– Don't be. No need. Wasn't you that said it anyway.
– I know. I mean. I don't know.

He was smiling about himself now, back-pedalling and
failing, and the unnecessary apology left Alice irritated.
She looked through the last of the photos, mostly
pictures Joseph had taken, and mostly better than her
own. Lichen on stone walls, thick twists of seaweed,
careful about detail and framing: Alice started a small
pile to show him. Martha got up to go to bed and then
she was alone with Keith.

He didn't try to pick up talking again, and she was glad,
because the conversation had unsettled her. Not the
thought of Joseph drunk and watching porn in exotic
locations, it was the idea of Keith's family adjusting that
got to her: puzzling over the strange world inhabited by
one of their own. When Joseph told her he'd been in
the army, she'd made the same distinction as Keith's
mother, between doing national service and joining up
voluntarily. That was in those early weeks when it felt
like the more she found out, the more she liked him.
Alice couldn't get the army to fit with Joseph somehow,
and it had made her curious.

July weekend, sitting in his kitchen, Sunday papers
spread across the table, Drumcree and decommissioning
were both on the inside pages. Fewer marchers that
year, but still plenty of police there and plenty of
tension. Alice had watched Joseph skimming the head-

lines: he'd already lifted the page to turn it, but it was as though he couldn't let go of it, his eyes intent, settling on an article.

– Were you out there, then?

Joseph looked up briefly, then back down at the paper. Pictures of banners and sashes, bowler hats.

– Yeah. For a bit.

He turned the page, but found more of the same, and Alice persisted.

– What were you reading just then?
– About the IRA. The Garda know where they have most of their arms dumps now.
– Will they ever open them, do you think?
– I could tell you what the article said, if you want.

He didn't sound defensive, looking at her across the table, eyes clear and friendly enough, but the answer hadn't come immediately. Difficult to say if she was being told to drop it. Joseph was watching her, as though waiting for her to respond, but he wasn't exactly opening up the conversation: *if you want*. He flicked through to the back pages.

– The little bit I know is years old anyway.
– You'll still know more than me, though.

Joseph shrugged and Alice couldn't tell if he was irritated or what.

– Sorry. Do you get it a lot? People asking you about it?

– Not that much, no. Enough.

Joseph closed the newspaper, slid it away from himself across the table, and Alice thought he wasn't angry, but he was uneasy with the conversation, resisting, and it was strange to feel like she was pushing him, when she'd hardly asked him anything.

– It's just the obvious, isn't it? Ireland. If you've been in the army, people think you must have been there, one tour at least.
– Have you had people get angry with you?
– Sometimes. It's not that, though.

He shrugged.

– It's fair enough to ask, I reckon. Especially when something big hits the papers. Good Friday, Omagh, Bloody Sunday inquiry. You get so you expect it, but it doesn't mean I've got anything worth offering. Nothing you haven't heard before, just more information.

Joseph sat for a while, as though trying to decide whether to continue. She wanted him to go on and couldn't quite believe he would try to leave it at that, when they'd only just started talking. The window was open and Alice could hear kids, kicking a ball around outside, small voices shouting below them in the courtyard. She looked at Joseph across the table and thought he wasn't enjoying this at all, so she was surprised when he relented: told her he was working in Portugal when the Docklands bomb happened. Sitting in a bar that had English telly when he heard.

– Might even have been an Irish pub, but that's probably just memory laying it on.

He told her it was the day after, Saturday lunchtime, and most people in there were from home, a lot from London, so the place went quiet after the news came on.

– Windows shattered, office blinds flapping, sheets of paper flying all over the road. You'll remember what it was like. No one could believe it. IRA ceasefire over anyway, no doubt about that.

A few men in the pub knew him, and that he'd been in the army, and word got round the room fast. Joseph said he could feel them looking at him, expecting, kept his eyes on the screen. Remembered thinking he could say the IRA are animals. Or arseholes for breaking their word.

– Something easy like that, because then at least you've said something.

But Joseph said it wouldn't come out, and he told Alice it wouldn't have been good enough anyway, not for that crowd. Frank from Glasgow shouted from down the bar: said Joseph was only keeping his mouth shut because he knew putting soldiers over there made everything worse.

– A wind-up, could have been.

Meant to annoy him into talking, probably, but it didn't work.

– Everyone's a bit hyper, because of the news, and they all want you to kick something off, you know what they're thinking: he was over there, so he can't have nothing to say, can he? They're waiting, and you know you're making it worse for yourself, but there's still nothing coming.

The news went on, reporters, police and politicians, and Joseph said he tried but he couldn't find any words or thoughts that made any sense of what they were watching.

– I felt like a wanker. But why say something? For the sake of it? Enough of that goes on already.

Joseph told her Frank had started off an argument down his end of the bar by this time. One man said he agreed with the IRA's aims but not their methods, and got shouted down. He tried to keep talking through the beer mats aimed at him, and the noise went on like that for a good while longer, until someone else cut in, said he didn't know what all the bawling was about:

– Only two dead and one was a Paki, so he doesn't count.

Alice remembered how she had to sit back in her chair when he told her that part, and how Joseph smiled. As though he knew that would get a reaction from her.

– Just another wind-up, probably, but then who could tell?
– In very poor taste anyway.

Joseph nodded, said maybe so, but he'd been grateful for it at the time.

– It got a big enough laugh, and then nobody was too bothered any more, whose side anyone was on, or what I thought about Ireland.

Keith was sorting his receipts again when Alice started packing up her photos. He looked up and nodded to her, affable, his bungled apology and the cause of it already forgotten. Alice had wanted to join in the conversation earlier, but couldn't, and she'd found the whole thing embarrassing. Keith putting his foot in at the end had been the least of it: far worse was sitting there hoping they wouldn't ask her too many questions. How Joseph had come to join the army, what it had been like for him or why he'd left. All those things that Keith knew about his brother, and she'd expected to hear about Joseph too. If not in those early weeks with him, then at some stage at least.

Alice had told her grandfather that Joseph used to be in the services: she'd thought it might help him accept Joseph's offer to redecorate the house. But she hadn't told her mum and Alan yet, and she knew they might find the idea difficult. Alice had driven past Catterick Garrison with them, two weeks ago in Yorkshire, on their way out to the Dales. They'd made their usual comments about the MOD holding acres of prime walking land hostage: it was a family lament, but Alice had kept quiet. Joseph might agree with her mum and Alan, for all she knew. She had no idea. If she said he'd been in the army, they'd want to hear more about it. Bound to find it strange if she couldn't tell them, too many gaps she couldn't fill in for them.

Alice put the photos for Joseph in an envelope, ready to give him when he came round tomorrow. A day off to spend together, and she was looking forward to it, but she couldn't help thinking the Paki joke had worked for Joseph a second time around too, because she still didn't know anything really, other than that he'd been in Ireland. She could remember feeling he'd explained something at the time, but she wasn't so sure now. Looking back, it seemed more like don't-ask-me dressed up as a story. Alice didn't like to think about it that way because it was just too cynical: *and then at least you've said something.* A careful way of not revealing anything. Maybe this made her like the staring men in the bar, but Alice couldn't believe Joseph had nothing worth hearing.

It was over two weeks before Joseph went back to David's. He had three days clear to do the hallway and they arranged it all without speaking to each other directly. Joseph didn't plan it that way, but the old man was out both times he tried phoning, so Alice passed on his dates when she visited, and then Joseph was over at Eve's Sunday dinnertime when David called to confirm. He came home to a short message on his answerphone, which he listened to twice before deleting.

– Sixteenth and seventeenth I'll be out most of the day. Eighteenth I'd be happy to provide you with lunch.

He didn't see David at all the first two days. Let himself in and worked steadily, damp curls of wallpaper lifted by the scraper, layers falling away to reveal the grey-pink of the plaster: bare walls for David to find when he got home. Joseph got the papering table out on the second day, relieved to be covering them up again, getting the job over and done. Autumn now, and the sun was lower in the sky, moving around the house more than over, the way it had when Joseph was working here in the summer. Threw longer shadows in the front garden in the afternoon, and he worked with one eye on them, thinking time was getting on and he should get going. Joseph packed up quickly, locking everything back into the garage, untidy, and he felt like a coward, but he didn't want to see the old man. He left a note for David on the kitchen table, said his brother-in-law would be coming tomorrow, late morning, to help him hang the paper on the long wall from the landing to the down-stairs hall. Not to worry about lunch: they'd sort them-selves out with something from the high street, thanks all the same.

David was there in the morning, and Joseph couldn't decide if he was put out. Pruning the roses by the front path, he raised his secateurs and nodded while Joseph parked up, but the old man didn't show any sign of coming into the house when Joseph got to the door. Just gone eight, and it was a clear morning, but the front of the house was still in shadow, dull blue and cold with it. Joseph pulled up his shoulders.

– Thought I'd make it an early start. Booked up into November, so I'll need to get it all finished today.
– Right you are.

Friendly enough. Joseph let himself in and thought this was maybe just normal David behaviour: Alice always said her grandad was hard to call. The old man brought a mug of tea through to him after an hour or so, and made a bit of small talk about the state of the skirting boards, a bit scuffed and bashed near the front door. Joseph said it would be easy enough to do that one section and David listened, polite but not like it mattered that much to him, one way or the other. He kept on like that, cool and cheery, even after Arthur pitched up with Ben, which hadn't been part of the plan.

– You don't mind the nipper do you, Mr Bell? My girl-friend, Joey's sister, she's working today and I forgot.

Arthur stood in the porch, apologetic, tapping his big forehead with his knuckles. The old man had opened the door and Joseph was standing behind him in the hallway, so he couldn't see David's expression, just the hand he offered:

– No, indeed no. Thank you for coming.

Arthur hadn't been keen on the idea: he didn't get that many days off at the moment. Said he'd only papered his mum's spare room before, and the corners didn't bear looking at, but Joseph persuaded him. He'd be buying pints for a while after this, especially now he'd landed Arthur in trouble with Eve, but it still felt worth it: less chance of the old man talking with someone else around.

Ben shoved his little trucks up and down the hall and Arthur leant back against the banisters, listening while Joseph talked it through. He'd done up to the dado rail upstairs and down, so they just needed to paper above it now: start on the landing and work their way down to the hall. David watched them from the front door, keys and shopping bag in hand, waited until Joseph had finished and then said:

– I'll be back early afternoon.

There wasn't much morning left, but they set themselves up on the landing anyway. Ben got hungry and narky before they could get going properly with the papering, and he shouted when neither of them would listen to him, too busy pushing the paper up and down the wall, matching the pattern, to notice his upraised arms.

Joseph lifted him up onto his shoulders for the walk down the road to the chippy. Ben chatted and swayed while his uncle kept a firm grip on his calves: easy to make him happy. Joseph felt himself smiling too, properly, relaxing. Glad to have an uncomplicated conversation with Arthur in a café, away from the house for an hour or so. They made their way back along the suburban pavements. The town hall clock struck the half-hour and Ben was falling asleep, his mouth open, arms draped over his father's shoulders. Joseph took Arthur's car keys from him, got a blanket and the baby monitor out of the boot. They laid Ben down in the front room on the sofa, moved quietly up the stairs to carry on working.

David came home shortly after three, but he didn't call up to them. They heard his movements downstairs, amplified crackles on the baby monitor. He was in the kitchen first, unpacking the shopping, and Joseph, listening, heard packets and tins put into cupboards, feet walking into the living room, a chair pulled back from the dining table, and then newspaper pages unfolding and turning. A little later there was a young boy's cough and Arthur put his paste brush down mid-stroke, headed for the stairs.

– Hang on.

Joseph whispered, he held his hand up and Arthur stopped and listened with him. On the monitor, they heard Ben shifting on the sofa cushions, coughing again, and then David's voice, soft, in the background.

– Hello fella. Didn't see you there.

Joseph and Arthur ducked their heads in smiles, almost giggles, although it wasn't entirely clear what was funny. Listening to someone who doesn't know it, maybe. They held their breath, hands over their mouths. Ben's breathing was loud but steady, still sleepy, and he didn't seem upset by the strange room and the stranger speaking to him:

– Can I get you something? Something to drink or a biscuit perhaps?
– Biscuit.

Arthur rolled his eyes, mouthing please and heading downstairs.

– Righto.

The paste was drying on the sheet in front of him, but Joseph listened instead of working. To David rummaging for biscuits in the kitchen and Arthur's apologies.

– It's not a problem.
– Dad, the man said I could have one.
– I know, and that's very nice, but just one now, alright?

Joseph imagined the old man awkward, standing between them, and his mind's-eye picture embarrassed him. He folded up the sheet of wallpaper, dumped it, wasted, laid out another, started working again. The baby monitor went off and Arthur came upstairs with Ben and a tray: tea and biscuits from David for all of them. The boy was happy on the floor with his digger and chocolate digestives, while Arthur and Joseph worked their way down the stairs and along the hallway. They finished the papering with time to spare for tidying and sorting. Moving David's things from the garage back into the shed again, and Joseph's into his van. They didn't talk much, just had Ben nattering and bashing in the background. Arthur sang a bit under his breath while he worked, and Joseph was very aware in those afternoon hours of David alone in the next room.

All she asked was:

– How come you joined up? I've been wondering about it.

Joseph was driving them back to his place: early evening, and the roads were crawling with midweek traffic. It was a few days after he'd finished at her grandad's and they'd both knocked off early, met up at Stan and Clare's. Ended up spending a couple of hours in their kitchen, because Stan wanted to get some work done on his own house over the winter, and he asked Joseph to give him a price for the plastering and painting. The traffic was stop-start by the time they got going, took half an age just to get as far as the common, and Alice was quiet for most of it, before she brought up the army.

– How old were you? You've never said.

Joseph shrugged. They were stuck now, still a good ten minutes from home, longer at this rate. He said:

– Old enough to know better.

Townsend was sixteen when he signed up. *That's my excuse.*

No end to the cars ahead of them, so he turned off

early. More traffic on the side streets, they were stopped again, and Alice was watching him.

– Infantry Command Respect.

Joseph saluted, making fun of his younger self and the recruitment slogans, and he told Alice he remembered the posters from the pinboards at school, in the corridor outside the metalwork room.

– They put them up on all the bus stops too, on our estate. Around exam time usually, that's when they get their best recruits.

Alice smiled at his joke, but she was still waiting. The road was clearer again after the next junction and Joseph cut through the back streets, waiting to see if Alice would ask another question, but she didn't, she just let it go.

He hadn't been straight with her and she knew it. It bothered Joseph, and he kept thinking what he could have told her. It was true enough about the posters, but he'd laughed about them back then too, even when he was at school, how they always got covered in biro dicks and specs and had to be taken down. It was the same a year or two later with all the videos and leaflets the recruitment officer gave him: couldn't take any of that stuff too seriously, actors running about looking hard in cammo, loud music and speedboats. Never expected that from the army, he was never that stupid, and Joseph didn't feel right, fobbing Alice off with a story like that. She wanted to know and it was hard not to tell her something that counted.

Couldn't wait to leave school, he remembered telling his teacher, after he let off the fire extinguishers in the science block for a dare. She sat across the desk from him, shocked and frowning, and it was like she couldn't bring herself to believe it was him that did it, because he was quiet enough in class and never caused her trouble as a rule. Pissed him off, the way she looked at him, all let down: like he'd ever promised her anything. So Joseph swore at her, for good measure, and said he just wanted shot of the place, and all of them in it: get earning, get on with living. But then the novelty of that wore off quick enough. He liked his job alright, and his boss was a nice bloke, but it felt like pond life sometimes, stagnating. Work, pub, snooker club, all the usual streets and houses. A small life and he'd spent all of his in the same place, with the same people. Seemed like the most you could expect was the odd shag or a fruit machine that coughed up more than you fed it.

Lee said he'd joined up to get himself sorted. Jarvis reckoned the army had done everyone a favour:

– Bring us your great unwashed and sick in the head. Give us your borstal graduates, we take any old scum. Can't make men of them all, we're not miracle workers, but at least you know they've got an outlet.

But Lee's record started when he was thirteen and Joseph knew his didn't compare. Small-time thieving for cheap thrills and pin money.

– A good laugh, was it? Or couldn't you think of nothing better to do?

It hadn't impressed his dad. He knew the others who got collared with him too.

– What you doing with idiots like that anyway?

Gave him the third degree when he got back from the station, had refused to pick him up when he'd phoned.

– You're seventeen, Joey. Old enough to catch a bus on your own.

Took him out for a drink later, though. And a long talking-to. About how much he had going for him and why he shouldn't just chuck it all by acting stupid.

– I know it gets a bit boring now and again, but that's not so bad, is it? Not the worst thing that could happen to you, son.

Just a bit of half-arsed rebellion, too shameful to admit to, and Joseph knew it didn't add up to a reason for joining up either. Not enough of one to give Alice. His day in court never stopped him getting work. Plenty of jobs going round his way, maybe nothing too exciting, but plenty of other things he could have done instead of becoming a soldier. Joseph didn't know how to explain it to her. Signing up was just one of those things people talked about doing. Like living abroad or winning the lottery. Mates of his from school and work, late at night when they'd had a skinful, smoking too much and waxing lyrical.

– It'll get me out of this dump anyway.
– Army's for sad cases.
– Just because you couldn't handle it.

– Wankers giving you orders.
– Wankers is right. No birds. No decent ones anyway.
– Comfy shoe brigade.
– Get fit, get paid for it.
– Not enough.
– Not enough for taking a bullet.
– Better than hanging about with you cunts.
– Go on. Piss off then.

It was easy in the end. Couldn't believe he hadn't done it earlier. The recruiting office was on the high street and he just went down there one afternoon after he finished work. His dad read over all the papers with him, said he should take his time, that it was a big decision, but it didn't feel that way to Joseph: just the best he'd felt in ages. When he got his dates for basic training, it was like his whole life had got easier. Still getting up, going to work and coming home again. Still the same old same old but it didn't bother him. And it was like that again when he found out they'd been posted to Ireland. It was knowing he was going. That feeling: like something real was going to happen.

Joseph thought about telling Alice he'd hated it, because he had sometimes, especially out in Ireland. It got to all of them, the stress and the boredom, worst combination: led to poor concentration, zero motivation. Add the rain and cold, and days like that Joseph would be counting, counting, from the minute they started, clocking off time. Feeling everything slipping, seconds going by too slow and all gone slack inside. Uniform walking empty. No will, no muscle to put into the task at hand. Just wanting to get this patrol over and be back in his bunk. Still functioning, but brain and body shunted over to minimum.

Turned the volume on his radio down once. Stupid thing to do, fucking dangerous for everyone, but he just couldn't be arsed with the patrol that morning and all the orders. Slung his rifle and walked out across the stubble and on through a hedge, even after he'd heard the command to wait shouted behind him.

– What the bloody hell were you doing?

He was spoken to after by the Second Lieutenant heading up the multiple. Just out of Sandhurst and younger than Joseph: they'd all been giving him a hard time ever since he came. Joseph got the CO's face shoved up to his after they got back to the barracks too, and then a man-to-man attempt from the Lieutenant later on in the evening: he came and found Joseph having a cigarette out behind the cookhouse.

– I'm not getting one hundred per cent from you, am I?

He'd made a point of telling them he'd been to a comprehensive. Didn't sound like it, and Townsend had told him it couldn't have been nearly as comprehensive as his school was. Sir.

– Are you listening to me, Mason?
– Sir.
– Left us all open, your little display. Anyone watching would have been laughing.
– Sir.

Joseph knew what he meant: had wondered what the patrol looked like already, seen through a rifle sight.

– Very disappointing because I've read your file, so I know you to be a capable soldier.

The whole company had privileges withdrawn because of Joseph's fuck-up. The bar was locked and everyone was calling him a stupid cunt, so he'd come outside because he felt like one too. The rain had stopped, but Joseph could still hear it singing in the guttering: one ear on that, the other on the army psychology: praising and scolding. Disappointing. Just like being at school again. Except he was a grown man and getting ticked off made it hard to see the point in staying.

But Joseph couldn't tell Alice all that, just like he couldn't tell her he'd had no good reason for joining: it all sounded too much like he was making excuses. *Big mistake, not my fault, too young, I never wanted to be there in the first place.*

Plenty of times he'd wanted to chuck it, but he wouldn't have stuck his three years if it was that bad, would he? Moaning came with the territory: always somebody talking about leaving, or slagging off the army. You could tell when Lee was losing it, because he'd start banging on about how the IRA had all the best suppliers: arms coming in on fishing boats from America and Gadaffi. He'd keep hauling out the same old chestnuts. Given the choice, would you have an Armalite or an SA80?

– The IRA buy quality and we get this piss-poor excuse for a weapon.

Joseph wasn't like Lee, never felt he had axes to be grinding. Not like Jarvis either, who said he slept and ate and shat the regiment. Jarvis didn't mind them complaining, as long as they didn't do it out on patrol. He said soldiers who moaned were better at doing what they were told:

– Give you an inch, I can get a mile out of you after, and you won't really mind.

Most of the blokes he knew in the army were happy enough to be there, and Joseph thought he should count himself among them. A capable soldier. Even when he was piss-wet through and knackered. Out in the November wet and dark and feeling hungry; fields and roads coming up to the border; Townsend tapping on the passenger's window; the man by the car was reaching again, so Joseph shouldered his rifle.

It was all part of the same thing, and he just couldn't have Alice knowing. She was asking now and he knew it shouldn't surprise him. Wanted to be straight with her, but he didn't think he could be.

Joseph left early again, said he had a job on north of the river, and Alice lay in his bed for a long time after, until she was late for work and had no excuse to give them. *I don't know what's going on with my boyfriend.* She knew that wouldn't really cut it. Clare would be on this morning, and Alice thought she might talk to her about Joseph at lunchtime, but couldn't think what she would say: it wasn't anything concrete. She thought of him in the car, avoiding her questions. Nothing hostile about him, but he was resisting, and it made her uneasy.

Soldiers and Northern Ireland. Alice kept trying to push them away, all those associations. Teenage boy shot in the back while he was driving away: not a terrorist, a joyrider, but they baked him a cake all the same, the soldier who did it, threw him a party back at the barracks to celebrate. Another four, another time, stabbed a man with a screwdriver, because it was the end of their tour and they were still alive and they wanted to do over a local before they went home. Disconnected incidents. Fragments, only half-remembered from the news, from years-old conversations in front of the radio and TV.

Alice was aware of getting ahead of herself, making too much of yesterday's failed conversation: she had no idea why Joseph had been so cagey, might even have had his mind on other things entirely, he was working a lot just now, and tired with it. But then, that was just the problem with not knowing, wasn't it? Left you too much space for speculation.

British forces, welcomed by Catholics when they first arrived, but quickly hated: dawn raids, bedrooms turned over, humiliation. Bessbrook was built by Quakers, but now the biggest army base in Ireland took up half the town. Alan must have told her that one, or her mum, it was the kind of detail they'd pick up on. Stephen Restorick was a name she remembered. Because he was the last British soldier to be killed there. Shot at long range while he was talking to a woman, a civilian. She was a Catholic and she stayed with him while he died, because his mum couldn't be there.

What would Joseph say? That's just the obvious? Alice could accept that much: maybe these bits and pieces did just reflect her ignorance. Or at least her choice of daily paper. But he was the best person to put that right for her, surely? He could tell her. What would he do if she pushed him, just kept on insisting? Even thinking about that was frightening: she'd gone too far before, and her dad had stopped writing. It was too easily done, that kind of damage, and too complete. But it didn't have to be that way with Joseph, did it? The cup of tea he'd made for her skinned over on the box that served as a bedside table.

Joseph didn't have much furniture, said he could never get round to it. His flat was mostly floorboards and crates, with a couple of nice things he'd picked up from skips and on jobs. He'd told Alice it drove his sister mad: he'd been there four years and she said it still looked like he was squatting. It wasn't so important to Joseph, Alice knew that, and she liked the fact he didn't care about owning much. A comfortable mattress, a few good albums on vinyl, but walking around his rooms that morning, she was tempted to agree with Eve: it did all seem very temporary. *Irrational. You've got no reason to think he'll be going, have you?* Alice washed and dressed. She was alone in the flat and thought for a while she could go looking. *No. Pathetic.* Whatever it was, she wasn't going to find it in his sock drawer or his kitchen cabinets.

Alice worked with a woman from Glasgow: Siona was a few years older, had lived all over, left home and Scotland when she was sixteen. She'd taught Alice 'The Fields of Athenry' at a hospital party once. Her dad was a Celtic supporter, her whole family, and he'd taken Siona to the football every weekend, even before she started school. Her mum drew the line at Old Firm games, but her brothers told her about them: Red Hand of Ulster on one set of terraces, tricolours and rebel songs on the other. Siona said she'd always known the words, and on which side she belonged. Told Alice about the Orange marches through the city centre too: could feel the drums in your belly, even when they were streets away. And about the blades that got pulled on the side roads after matches, away from the stadium and the mounted police, where the crowds got thinner. *Best to stick with your own.* Siona had been glad to get away from it: *that mentality. Imagine being caught up in Belfast or Portadown, where that shite really matters.*

On Sunday, Alice visited her grandfather as usual. Crossword and tea, and then she helped him do some autumn tidying in the back garden. Raked the leaves

into black bags for rotting, stacked up twigs and dry
stems ready for burning. When the light started to go,
they retreated into his kitchen. Her grandad talked frosts
and pests while the kettle was boiling: a nothing conversation that Alice joined in with, standing next to the
radiator, but the cold of the day stayed in her face and
fingers. This was nothing like the conversations they'd
had in the summer: her grandfather was back to his old
arm's-length habits, and Alice didn't like it.

He asked after Joseph, interested, the way he always did
now, and it irritated her.

– He's fine, working hard before things slow down over
the winter.

Alice shrugged out the platitudes. Through the door, she
could see the new wallpaper in the hallway, thought of
all the hours and days Joseph had spent here. The job
was finished, but he'd even talked about coming again,
touching up the woodwork, which didn't look to her
like it needed doing.

It was cold outside and starting to spot when she left.
Her grandfather waited in the porch while she unlocked
her bike, and then he came to the gate as always, but
she didn't give him a kiss, just waved, backing away,
saying she'd call and see him in a fortnight. Alice cycled
to the station, angry with them both, her grandfather
and Joseph, but she was also ashamed at her own behaviour. Sulking about the two men and the time they spent
together. Neither of them was giving anything. She
pushed hard against the pedals.

His dad's birthday fell on a Saturday, and his mum was cooking lunch. She dropped hints on the phone about inviting Alice along, and Joseph was glad when he asked her, could see she was pleased.

– Who else will be there?
– Just Eve and Art. And Ben.

Alice was pulling on her waterproofs in his hallway, ready for a wet morning's cycle to work.

– Yeah, alright then. Yeah.

She stopped to answer, smiling at him from behind her jacket collar, and Joseph thought the invitation could be a way of making up to her, maybe. For the way he'd been with her lately: on his guard, and he didn't want to be. Picking up extra jobs, though he didn't need the money at the moment, just kept saying yes to them, working all hours and he'd hardly seen her this past week or two. He kissed her before she went out the door.

Alice had met Eve and Arthur before, but only once and accidentally. She'd arrived at the flat as they were leaving one afternoon, and they'd all stood out on the walkway shaking hands and smiling, Ben hiding behind Eve's legs and Alice crouching down to say hello and everyone laughing because he was so shy with her.

Joseph stood out there now, looking down at the courtyard. Watched Alice cycle through the puddles and out
onto the road. She wasn't stupid, wouldn't stand this
treatment long, he knew that, and it made him nervous.
She was happy about meeting his parents, but she'd also
want some proper answers to her questions.

Joseph's mum had a new blouse on when they got there,
a spot of lippy too, for Alice's benefit probably. He smiled
about it with his mum in the kitchen, getting cups of
tea ready for everyone, and she swiped at his knees with
a dishcloth for making fun, but she wasn't angry.

– Go and sit down, smartarse, I'll bring the tray in.

Ben was sticking close to Eve again, watching Alice the
whole time, but not going near. Alice tried kneeling
down by the tank engines on the rug for a while, but
he wasn't having any of it. She did better with Joseph's
mum, sitting next to her over lunch, talking to her about
what she could do for her back, the nagging pains of
twenty-odd years spent bending over people's haircuts.
Joseph watched them across the table, tucking in their
chins and dropping their shoulders, thinking about what
Alice had said about her job, how you could get to know
people looking after their tendons and joints, that was
the best part, if you got that trust. His mum was
following Alice's lead, straightening her spine, and letting
her arms hang loose by her sides.

Joseph's dad was first at the door after the washing up
was done. Standing with his coat on and his snooker cue,
waiting while they all said goodbye to Joseph's mum. Alice
was slow about her buttons and said it didn't seem right:

– First you cook for us, and now we're leaving you here
and going to the pub.
– Don't be silly, love.

Joseph's mum waved her off, pleased to be made a fuss
of. Ben was sleeping upstairs, and she said someone had
to listen out for him. Joseph knew Alice was doing
everything right for his mum, but she was pissing Eve
off in the process. He could see his sister trying to keep
it polite, and failing:

– We'll take it in turns. It's what we always do.
– Oh right, okay.

Alice blinked, awkward, and Joseph was glad when his
mum smiled at her again.

– I'll be fine, put my feet up. Do some of your exer-
cises first.

It was wet outside and the estate was quiet, just a couple
of boys on bikes with their hoods pulled up. The rain
came on harder again while they were walking, so they
cut through the alley past the shops, which got them to
the side entrance of the snooker club. There was a reception on in the function room and a sign pointed the
wedding guests round to the main door on the road,
the paper damp and flapping. Joseph's dad stood aside
for Alice and they all followed her inside.

Music leaked through the walls from the party, but there
were only a few in the main bar, and one game on round
the corner where the snooker tables were. Joseph played
his dad, because that's what they always did on birthdays,
and Arthur set up one of the other tables with Alice while

Eve got the drinks in. They weren't playing a proper game: Arthur was just explaining how the scoring worked and setting up shots so Alice could get used to holding a cue. It wasn't done on a Saturday really, taking up a table like that, but the club wasn't as busy as usual, probably because of the party next door, and no one was complaining. Alice was on form too, and Joseph had to admire her: new place, new people, and after the bad start with Eve and everything, she wasn't letting it get to her, and not taking herself too seriously either. In a room full of would-have-been-professionals, and creasing up when she couldn't get the white up the length of the table. Never made it as far as the pink, came to rest a good couple of feet from the cushion. Hard to tell what she'd been aiming for, the yellow would have been easier. It was good to see her like that, his dad and Arthur laughing with her, and Eve as well. Even the old sod who'd come in after them and was waiting for a game cracked a smile.

Joseph's dad had a comfortable win and stayed on the table to play the next man. Their first drinks were nearly finished, so Joseph took a turn up at the bar, but there was nobody serving. A bloke came in from the function room carrying pints, nodded to Joseph and then back at the door he'd just come through:

– They're all in there. Never put enough staff on today.

He looked familiar, but Joseph couldn't place him: one of his mum and dad's neighbours maybe. He'd recognised Joseph too: not at first, but after he'd passed him, gave him a longer, second look over his shoulder. Still no one behind the bar, so Joseph signalled to Arthur that he was going into the big room.

It was hot in there and full of people. Pork pies cut into quarters and pints served in plastic glasses. A few wedding guests were dancing, not pissed enough yet and a bit embarrassed, sharing fags and trying to pretend they were only talking while they shuffled to the muffled disco on the cracked lino. Someone had closed the curtains to get the right atmosphere going, only there weren't enough to cover all the windows and Joseph could see that it was still light outside. A sign on the wall said free bar for half an hour and the queue was three deep. Everyone was getting pints and chasers and when he finally got served, the drinks Joseph ordered for his dad and Arthur came with shots he never asked for. Too many glasses for the tiny tray the barmaid brought him. Joseph didn't think about it for long, just downed them.

His dad was over by the fruit machines when Joseph came back with the drinks. He had a small crowd gathered around him, shaking hands and back-slapping the birthday boy, and they turned and acknowledged Joseph as he was passing: men he'd known all his life, mates of his dad's from work, dads of his friends from school. Joseph looked back when he got to the tables, but the bloke from earlier wasn't among them.

Eve and Alice were sitting together now. Space enough for at least one person between them on the bench, and it looked like Alice was making most of the conversation, but they carried on talking after Joseph pulled a chair up with them, so he didn't like to interrupt. Just sat back and watched Arthur playing the old sod from earlier. He listened to the karaoke from the other room, 'Hi Ho Silver Lining' and then 'I Will Survive', felt the warmth in his throat making its way down to his guts, the chasers getting to work.

The place was filling up, smelled of wet coats and fag smoke. Arthur lost his game but Joseph's dad was going strong. All the tables were busy and more people waiting, the nodding bloke from earlier among them: he was standing by the far wall and kept looking over, Joseph was sure of it. He watched Eve to see if she'd noticed, maybe she knew who he was. But Eve was still talking to Alice, and Arthur was in the next room up at the bar, so Joseph read the names chalked on the board to see if one of them matched: Michael, Martin, Trevor. Nothing coming back.

Arthur put his tray full of drinks down on the table, said the women next door had a line dance going:

– Slapping thighs, all wobbling chins and arses.

He shook his head and Eve laughed, told him not to be so rude: they were probably friends of hers from school. Alice smiled her thanks for the pint he'd bought her.

– Reckon this is one too many.

She raised her glass to Joseph, then pressed it against her cheeks, grinning, a bit pink-faced: alcohol or nerves, most likely both. She'd been chatting to Eve on and off for a while, all quite friendly, so maybe it was relief. The party next door was getting louder, and some joker had put the jukebox on to try and drown it out. Joseph's dad was still playing and the bloke was still by the far wall, watching, a couple of mates with him now, and they had their heads leant in close and talking. Joseph had met one of them before, he couldn't remember

when exactly, but it was definitely at Malky's. After he
left the army, and before he went to Portugal: not a good
time to have known him. Joseph tried to stop looking,
keep his mind on how things were going with Alice
and his sister. Arthur was talking about going back to
the house: Ben would be up by now, and it was about
time Joseph's mum came out. Eve said she'd finish her
drink and follow on, and Joseph thought maybe he and
Alice should call a cab and go home. Getting dark out
now, his bladder was full, the table covered in empty
glasses. He leaned over them to Alice:

– How long do you want to stay?
– I'd like to buy a drink for your Mum when she comes.
– I'll get it just now. One for my Dad too and then
we'll get off, eh?
– Okay.

He hadn't talked to her all afternoon, wondered what
sort of a time she'd been having. Both been drinking
for hours, wine at lunch and then however many pints
in here. Joseph stacked the glasses. Arthur was gone, his
mum would be here soon, and they were serving up at
the bar again now, so he stood up to get the drinks in.
Steering himself between the tables towards the toilets
first. Had to walk past the bloke to get there, hadn't
thought it through before he started. Too late to change
his course because the bloke had seen him now, step-
ping away from the wall.

– You alright?

Not a friendly question. Joseph tried to keep his head
down and keep moving, but he couldn't get far. *Stupid.*
Wall and bar stools and too many people. Shouldn't have

come this way. Bloke between him and the door and
Joseph had to stop.

— Malky's psycho pal, aren't you?

Still a couple of feet away, but that was too close. In
range of feet and fists, and Joseph didn't want anything
to start: not today, not now with Alice there behind him.
They were laughing at him, the bloke and his mates,
and the men around them were turning to see what it
was all about.

— You come to have another go?
— No.
— Leave him alone, Trev, it's his Dad's birthday.

Joseph didn't look to see who that was. Someone behind
him, another familiar voice. Someone else moved aside
and Joseph pushed his way through the gap. Past Trevor's
laughing, angry face and into the bogs.

No one followed. Quieter in there, it smelt of spliff and
piss, and two little boys in wedding suits were over by the
sinks. Bored with the party, they were running the taps,
stuffing the plug holes with paper towels, first basin in the
row already flowing over. Joseph went into the cubicle and
locked the door, still no one following, but he still couldn't
piss, thinking how much of that Alice might have seen,
his dad too. He'd have been used to that kind of thing a
few years back. Never said anything about it to Joseph,
but it stung to think about all the sly nods and elbows in
the bar. *Tommy Mason's boy, he's lost it, headcase.* Joseph knew
half the people in there would have a story about him,
only most of them liked his dad too much to tell.

Trev. Trevor. Joseph still couldn't remember, but it was some kind of trouble from back then, must have been. Gave him a kicking once, or got one himself, most likely. A half-memory of pain in his ribs and fingers, but he had plenty of them, couldn't be sure if that was the right one. Nothing he'd want Alice to hear about, anyway.

She watched him come back across the room to the table, her face still red, but worried now, not laughing. Trevor was gone, and Joseph's dad and Eve were at the table. Both stood up when they saw him, and both of them wanted to ask, but not with Alice there, and she could tell. Joseph didn't want her embarrassed like that, but he had no explanation, nothing he could say that would cover the situation.

– I'll go and get that drink for your Mum.

She got up and Joseph left it a minute before he followed her. They stood together up at the bar and Alice said:

– You okay?
– Yeah. You?

She nodded. He couldn't tell what she was thinking. She said the barmaid had called a cab for them.

Joseph's mum came and Eve went home. She kissed Joseph goodbye, and told Alice it had been nice to meet her, properly this time. The doors to the function room were flung wide open, wedding guests and regulars spilling over, winner stays on the tables, and the groom was beating all comers. The taxi was a long time coming, and Joseph and Alice stayed up at the bar, waiting, his mum and dad with them, watching the spectacle. Girls running about in gangs with balloons tied round their fingers; boys keeping busy swiping drinks off tables; men smoking and women dancing, jigging clumps of colourful blouses. The father of the bride put on a slow number and then talked all over it. Stood on the dance-floor hogging the microphone, remembering his wedding day and crooning out of tune with the chorus. Alice was watching the old man and smiling and Joseph put his arms around her. Couldn't really hear what she was saying, just that she thought it was funny. Felt the hum of her voice, face pressed against his shoulder. Held her too long or too hard or something, because Alice shifted, uncomfortable, and he had to let go.

Ten

Three days without a phone call. It had been Alice's choice. Sitting in Joseph's kitchen, the night they'd been to the snooker club. Sobering up by then, asking him and still getting nothing.

– I think I had a fight with him. I don't know. Years ago. Seven or eight maybe.

That's all he'd been able to tell her, and Alice didn't know if she could believe him, that he didn't remember. It didn't feel like a lie, not the way Joseph had said it, but it still didn't make sense to her. Nothing much had happened in the bar that evening, an exchange of words, but it felt like there was much more to it.

– Seems like a long time for someone to stay angry.

She couldn't forget the way Joseph's father and sister had reacted either: they were so protective, Alice could understand that part, but then they hadn't asked him anything about it. Whatever it was, they must have known already, that was the only way to explain it. But Alice still didn't know why Joseph couldn't tell her, sitting across the table from her, wordless: another gap he was just going to leave wide open. She felt as though she was still too drunk or too tired to make the right connections, couldn't find the right questions.

– What was it about? The fight you had?

Alice had tried again, and then Joseph put his hands over his face. She didn't know what that meant. Humiliating being asked, perhaps, when he really didn't remember. Or he just didn't want to tell her. It wasn't only the fight, of course. The longer they sat there, the more she saw it as confirmation: there was too much she didn't know, that Joseph hadn't told her.

So then she'd decided. It wasn't final, that wasn't what she wanted, but she couldn't have those hands in front of his face either.

– It's not fair.

She was being humiliated now and she told Joseph that's how it felt.

– Not just now, or last night.

It happened whenever she asked him something and he shut her out.

– Feels like all the time now.

Joseph had listened to it all. Dry-eyed and quiet. Alice couldn't cry either, not even later, when she'd wanted to. Cycling home while it was getting light, drifting on the empty road, feeling sick with lack of sleep and what she'd just done. Shocked at how little he'd said, how little reaction she'd got. Joseph hadn't even asked her how long she wanted. Alice didn't know. It felt as though he'd been waiting for her to say something like this, the whole night they spent sitting in his kitchen.

She could remember reading about someone a while back, a young Irishman who lived in the North but worked in another town, a couple of miles away in the Republic. He had to cross the border every morning and evening, and Alice didn't know what had made the police or the army suspicious of him at first. The article she'd read was an interview with his brother: he said they were from a Nationalist family, but the way he described it, the young man had done nothing, other than maybe go through the checkpoint at the edge of their estate too often. His car would be taken apart, and he'd have to remove his coat and shoes in the road, his lunchbox would be searched with bare fingers, and he was told he'd be late for work. He made complaints, through his union first, then his priest and finally the press, and the intimidation got worse. They stood on his throat at one point, the soldiers who stopped him, and another patrol told his father they had a bullet waiting for his son. He was killed walking to the football ground one afternoon. The army claimed the shot was an accidental discharge, the soldier was cleaning his rifle. Alice remembered how incredulous his brother was at this story, and that no one had ever faced charges. The interview had been part of a series, to mark the anniversary of the Good Friday Agreement, one illustration of the human cost of the Troubles. She couldn't connect events like those with Joseph, but she was aware of testing them out against him somehow. Going through what she could remember, searching and comparing. *When would that have been? No, he wasn't there then.* It made her angry: didn't know what she was doing, scaring herself or looking for reassurance. It was ridiculous. *Thirty years, tens of thousands of soldiers.* Wasn't likely she'd have heard about Joseph on the radio.

In Heathrow, a few years back, when Alice was going through customs, a group of young men in front of her were all pulled aside, all of them with Irish accents. They hadn't seemed surprised, it was as though they were used to it. The queue moved along, no one else was stopped, and Alice passed them as they were emptying their pockets. For all that they were happening in the same country, the Troubles had been distant from her: there for so long they'd just become part of the background, maybe. Telephoned warnings, wrongful convictions, strangely dubbed voices on the news, sealed postboxes in central London, no more lockers at any of the stations. She'd been interested, appalled sometimes, but never felt it involved her until now.

Alice had a patient once from Manchester: Irene, Reenie, who'd gone shopping with her daughters the day the IRA bombed the Arndale Centre. Showed Alice the scars, visible through her tights: three long cuts in her thigh where some shards of glass had lodged. Deep enough for stitches, but she told Alice she couldn't remember it hurting at the time. Said she spent the whole ambulance journey crying about her girls, even though the paramedic kept reassuring her. She could see them, unharmed, there in the ambulance with her, but just couldn't trust her eyes. *Only three and four at the time.* Alice treated her a couple of years later, when Reenie was pregnant with her third child, a boy this time. She liked to talk, said she was lonely after moving down to London, and told Alice a few times about the blast. How it felt like being hit by a plank, smack on her back, and then all the glass flew out, way beyond the police cordon. The shock of that was still obvious to Alice when Reenie talked, or lifted the hem of her maternity dress to look again at the scars. But Irene had been a bystander, not a participant, only involved by accident. So despite the marks, it hadn't come as close to Alice somehow, not the way it was with Joseph. Always more of it, relentless. She could feel herself pulling away, and she didn't like that.

Four days, another, the weekend. Alice went swimming on Saturday afternoon, stayed in and watched a video with Martha. She called her grandad and said she could come over early tomorrow.

– Before lunch, do some work in the garden again. Dig over that patch at the back we cleared.

– It can wait. It's a good thought, but I'm quite tired.

He sounded it too. Alice tried Joseph after that but hung up when she got the machine. She hadn't seen so much of him lately but he'd rarely left it more than twenty-four hours without saying hello. Difficult to go for days like this, and it was hard not to think about that week he'd cut her off last summer. Not to look at the past month or two as some kind of withdrawal. More gradual, but he'd been removing himself nonetheless, she was sure.

It hadn't happened yet. But she wasn't going to stay with him unless he came up with something. He'd sat there with her, all those hours into the morning, and he couldn't remember what he'd thought, when they first started seeing each other. That it wouldn't come up? No questions asked? Should have just left it that first time, that week, early in the summer when he couldn't see her, that would have been better than this: too soon to do so much harm.

Pointless thinking. Joseph knew that. He didn't want it to be over, but the whole week after she left, he felt like he was getting ready. Up every morning and working, home every night, late sometimes, but still no message from her.

Clive called him on Thursday: Joseph was in the van, on his way back to the flat. The job Clive was meant to be doing had been postponed, so he was thinking of going down to Brighton to get some work done on his house.

– Bathroom's just about ready for plastering, and the small bedroom, if you're not busy. Short notice, but I could drive you down there in the morning, back up on Monday, first thing.

Joseph said he was sorry, he had too much on, needed

to stay at home. He didn't want to be miles away if Alice phoned. But after he'd spent another evening waiting, he called Clive back and said he would come. Didn't think about Stan until the morning. Just gone seven and Clive was due in about ten minutes, so Joseph called in sick. He'd never done that before, in over three years working for him, and it took Stan a few seconds to catch up, surprised, or maybe just not awake yet. He believed him anyway, and that made Joseph feel worse. He saw Clive's headlights coming into the courtyard, but he hung around the flat, delaying. Thinking he could still go to work, leave it a couple of hours, say he went back to bed and then he felt better. Couldn't believe he hadn't thought. *Shouldn't be doing this.* It was all getting away from him, and Joseph knew he shouldn't let it. Clive beeped again and Joseph locked up and took his bag downstairs.

Clare asked after Joseph at work on Monday. She was surprised Alice didn't know he was ill. The morning clinic was full, and Alice had been glad of it, but then Clare arrived at lunchtime with her news: Joseph hadn't been at work at the end of last week or this morning either. She'd brought coffees with her from the canteen, and they stood awkward in the doorway together after Alice said she hadn't seen him for a few days.

– Oh, right.

Clare looked at her, checking, Alice shook her head. Too many people coming in and out to go into details. Clare covered the silence by telling her that Stan was juggling three jobs at the moment: a bit risky, but there would be a few slack months after, and they'd need the money then.

– It's our fault really, taking on too much. I thought you might be able to tell us when to expect him back.
– Sorry.

No answer when she phoned, but that didn't mean much. Alice didn't leave a message, didn't want to feel like she was being screened. She cycled over to Joseph's instead, when the clinic was over. Early evening and his van was in the courtyard, so she locked her bike to the railings and went upstairs. No answer when she knocked.

If he was sick, maybe he was sleeping. She pressed her hands up to the rippled glass in the door, but she couldn't see anything inside. Didn't feel like he was there. Too still somehow. The light in the big room was on, and it fell into the hall through the open doorway, but then she knew Joseph often left a light on when he went out: two of the flats below had been broken into earlier in the year. Alice called his name through the letterbox, twice, and she waited, but there was still no response.

She was relieved to get back on her bicycle, away from the dark of the walkway and the quiet her voice left behind. Angry too: Alice didn't think he was ill. She didn't know what he was doing. Making himself unreachable.

She left it another day, but then Clare was off work on Wednesday, and their manager said she was using up her annual leave to sort out some mess for Stan. Alice went round to see her at lunchtime, after she'd finished her shift. Thought if Clare had heard something, she would have phoned, but the mess had to be caused by Joseph.

Clare made her tea, and didn't seem surprised to see her. Said she hadn't heard from Joseph, without prompting, and it didn't sound like she was expecting any news from Alice. They sat down in the kitchen and the phone started ringing, but Clare didn't get up, she just nodded.

– He's meant to be plastering a loft for us in Forest Hill at the moment. We're already late finishing that job, and the woman's been calling me every half an hour, just about. Says she'll withhold payment until it's done. I don't blame her. Can't stop her either, but it'll leave us well short and there's a stack of invoices waiting.

Clare pointed through the open door into the living room, at her desk in the corner, behind the kids' Lego: her computer was on, the phone was still ringing, a box file of bills lying open beside it. She said they had to get another plasterer in last Friday, had to pay him well over the odds too, because he knew they hadn't any choice. Alice didn't know what to say, so she said nothing. The phone stopped and then Clare sat for a moment before she said:

– Not your fault, I know.

Alice thought about leaving. This wasn't making it any easier to go and talk to Joseph. It was nearly time to pick up the boys from school: she saw her friend's eyes wander to the kitchen clock, calculate the minutes left for talking.

– I picked a bad time to come round.
– It's alright. Listen, Alice. Maybe you know all this already. When Stan was ringing round for a new plasterer, he had a couple of blokes bad-mouthing Joseph to him.

The phone started again in the other room, but Clare ignored it.

– He had it once before too, years ago, but it was from someone Stan never got on with either, so he didn't take much notice. Thought if Joseph had let the bloke down, he probably had a reason.

Clare blinked at her. Alice knew her friend wanted her

to say it was alright, that Joseph had told her about all this before, because then she wouldn't have to. The phone kept going and Alice thought about lying, how it might be easier: that way she wouldn't have to listen to the rest of what Clare had to say either.

– What did Joseph do to him?
– Same as us. He used to do this a lot, by all accounts. Had a bit of a reputation for going missing on jobs a while back.

Clare stopped again, but Alice knew there was more coming.

– He also used to pick fights. That's what this one guy said. Put his electrician in A and E. Fetched himself a beating from a couple of the team in the end. The guy reckoned he'd had it coming. Said he wouldn't go near him again, and Stan would be wise if he didn't either.

Alice knew it was her turn to say something.

– So what's Stan going to do?

Clare was looking at her: not the question she'd expected, but she let Alice steer the conversation away from her and Joseph.

– He doesn't know. He doesn't want to drop him, especially without talking to him first. But we can't afford to mess our clients around, can we? If we start losing jobs, then so do other people.

Clare shrugged. She looked tired.

– Last night, Stan said Joseph sorted himself out before, he can do it again. But he was swearing at Joseph's answerphone this morning, so you tell me.

The phone stopped and she went next door, pulled the plug out of the wall. When she came back, she said:

– We talked about it. Me and Stan. We were thinking. If you didn't know it already, then you probably should. I'm sorry.

Alice thought Clare was expecting tears. She was too, had been waiting for them for days.

– I want to but I can't.

She pulled her coat on, pressed the sleeves hard against her eyes.

– I don't know what any of this is about. That's the hard part.
– Having to hear it all third hand would make me cry.

Clare put her arms around her, like she wanted to help her to tears, and Alice thought of all the reasons she had: Joseph threw punches and she didn't know why, messed people about so much they wanted him out of their lives. She might feel the same way before long, that was the worst of it. But Alice couldn't cry about that, because that was too much like willing it to happen.

Alice went to work on Thursday as usual, Friday morning too, but she didn't stay in the canteen for her lunch break. Went to the café across the road and called her mum.

– Of course you can come.

Next week was autumn half-term, so she had no classes, and she said Alice could stay as long as she wanted. Back at work, Alice went through her appointments. Clare would be back at the start of next week, and she told Alice on the phone that she didn't mind covering for her when she could.

– Get some time off, book yourself onto a train. I would.

Alan met her at the station Friday evening, because her mum had to stay on for a meeting at school. She was at home when they got there, the table laid, kitchen windows fogged, the garden beyond them dark. It was late by now, but they'd waited for Alice before eating. Alan had cooked for them earlier, and he served and poured, but then took his own plate and glass upstairs, with a kiss for both their heads as he was leaving.

– Did you tell him to make himself scarce?

Alice's mother didn't answer, except to smile at her across

the table. Now that she had someone there with time and patience to talk it over, Alice didn't know if she wanted to start. She hadn't told her mum anything on the phone, just that she wanted to come. It might have been easier to be at her grandad's this weekend, digging and drinking tea, no need for conversation. Alice said:

– I should phone Grandad. Didn't sound right when we last spoke.
– I was thinking about that, actually.

Her mum put her fork down.

– I talked to him a while back about coming down this half-term. We never made any firm plans, but maybe we could drive down together next week? Depending on how long you wanted to stay, of course. It's just that I'd like to see him.

She said he'd called her yesterday evening, which was unheard of.

– He didn't even have anything much to tell me. I spent the whole phone call waiting for the pretext.

She laughed.

– Maybe he was angling for a visit, I don't know. He said you offered to spend the whole day with him last Sunday.

– I did.
– And he was an old fool for turning you down.
– He said that?

Her mum nodded, smiling. Alice thought it tickled her mother that she was so surprised. All those visits when Gran did the talking, Grandad coming in and out of the room, going about his business. It had always annoyed Alice, even though she was used to it, they all were, and they just let him behave that way. She'd often thought her family made too many allowances, especially on the rare occasions she brought a friend or a boyfriend with her: the extra pair of eyes making her realise how rude her grandad seemed. As though he had no interest in other people. So it was strange to think he'd regretted declining her visit. But then Gran was gone, nearly a year now, and the house was finished, so he didn't have Joseph for company either. Alice's mum smiled at her.

– I promised him a couple of plants. They're in the garden up at the farm. Better to take them down than send them. I'll take you walking over the weekend, shall I? We can go and see him together after we get back.

Joseph was away almost a week in the end. Left Clive in Brighton on Sunday: he'd finished the rooms and told him he wanted to get back up to London early. Went to the station, but only as far as Lewes on the train. Walked and hitched from there, east to the High Weald and south again to the coast, with the wad of notes Clive had paid him in his jacket. Too cold to be sleeping out, he wasn't going to do that, but he didn't want to go home just yet. Found a caravan park, closed, out of season, but the man up at the farmhouse let him rent one for a few days when he said he'd pay cash. Joseph hauled a full gas cylinder back down the hill with the keys. He bought enough food for three days at the Spar in the village. Reminded him of years back: traipsing along the verges in the evening dark with the carrier bags knocking against his legs and all the cars rushing past. All those other times he'd done this. Joseph promised himself it wasn't like that now: he wasn't going to let it get that way again.

Over a week now since he'd heard from her. He didn't know what Alice was going to do, when she was going to tell him. Leave him to work it out for himself, maybe. Joseph didn't think he had any right to be angry.

Two messages the next afternoon on his mobile, both from his dad. Joseph had been out walking most of the day, and only picked them up when he got back to the caravan. His dad didn't say so, but Clive must have called him: Joseph thought he'd been careful over the weekend, not to give his dad's mate any reason to worry, but he must have been showing it. *Just give us a ring would you, son?* Just like the messages he always used to get, so maybe Clive thought he was acting the same as he did back then. Joseph called home and said he was doing alright.

– Honest, Dad. I'll be back by the end of the week. Just a few days away.
– Where are you? You want me to come and drive you?
– It's okay, I can get to Hastings easy enough from here and catch a train. They're every half-hour or something, I checked.

Joseph told him the name of the farm too, and the number of the caravan park, and having an address seemed to reassure his dad. Not disappearing, just retreating.

Three days, quiet and hours for thinking. Plenty to be sorry about. The way it was ending with Alice mostly. That he couldn't find a way to stop it. Didn't like the way he'd left it with her grandad either: stacked everything tidy in the shed and swept the floor in the garage, but he couldn't be alone with him, and Joseph thought the old man had been aware of it, avoided him because of it. Made Joseph cringe now, thinking how obvious he must have made it.

The days were warm and blowy, and the fields around rough with stubble. Joseph felt the wind coming in over them when he woke, pushing against the high sides of the caravan. He thought about the days he'd spent with

Alice near here, the week with her in Scotland, the plans she'd had to show him Yorkshire: Fremington Edge and the moors beyond. Bleak to some eyes, but not hers: high places, kite-flying places she'd said. After breakfast, he cut straight across the wind and stubble on his way down to the shore. He found a beach he knew from before: small, encircled, the high, solid mound of sand skimmed smooth and perfect. A cove tucked into the headland. Same as the last time he'd been here, years ago, the spring before Portugal maybe, when he was getting better. He must have been working again by that time, because he'd driven out of London in the van: left early and caught the low tide, walked the miles-long sands and scrambled over the rocky foot of the head-land. The small beach was a surprise, in the lee of the wind. It was cut off later, covered by the high water. He remembered walking above it, standing and watching as the sea came in. Still used to come down to the coast a lot that spring, but he wasn't desperate any more, just looking to be by himself. He'd worked out that much by then: *take yourself off before you do any damage*. He still didn't like it, being that way, disappearing on people, especially his family, but he knew it was better than staying. Helped a lot to know he could get a grip on it too. Stopped taking jobs when he wasn't up to working, got good at avoiding: anyone he'd had trouble with, crowds and queues of people, confrontation. Walked away from raised voices, even if they had nothing to do with him. Two women shouting at the bus stop, Joseph went on to the next; Eve and Arthur working out how to cover their loan repayments, he took himself off round the block. He shut down when he had to. Didn't know when it was he'd stopped. When he didn't need to any more.

Joseph sat on the sand, out in the middle. When the waves returned, he found the path up through the rocks. The woods above were just about bare already, and it was light up there. The sun got in everywhere when it came out of the clouds, lit up the trunks, moss on the stones, and the thick, damp mat of leaves on the ground. The last strip of beach was still showing below him, and the scuffed line of his retreating tracks. Places to show Alice. *Try and get her to come down here. Before she makes a decision.*

Eleven

When the phone woke Alice on Saturday morning, it occurred to her that Joseph knew her mum's number. He'd called her here a few times before, and she sat up, half-asleep and hopeful. But she hadn't told anyone she was coming up here, not even Martha, and then she heard Alan discussing departmental budgets in the hallway, trying not to be irritable with whoever it was that had phoned so early on a weekend.

They discussed walks over breakfast: Alan had figures to check, and couldn't come with them, but he joined in with suggestions.

– You could do the seven fields and go over the foot-bridge by the waterfall. The river should be full now, you'll get a good show.

Alan and her mum had got to know each other on walks with mutual friends. Used to drive out of London most weekends back then, and sometimes persuaded Alice to come with them. They'd leave before the traffic built up and drive home in the evening after a pub meal. Usually, they stuck to footpaths, but they liked to trespass too, particularly her mother: she said people kept the best places hidden and that wasn't fair. Alice was a teenager then, and scornful of her mother's rebellious streak, but she still remembered an old walled garden they took her to. The lean-to greenhouses fallen in and beds overgrown but beautiful. Tall, yellow weeds and blue thistles, a fig and a pear tree still bearing last year's fruit. The estate was big enough to hold two houses, the one the kitchen garden used to serve had subsided, and the family had rebuilt on better ground on the other side of their land. The fields were ploughed when Alice was there, pheasants strutting the furrows, and the high grass banks were riddled with rabbit warrens. Her mum and Alan went back a few months later and discovered they had gamekeepers too. There were new 'Keep Out' signs erected, which they ignored as usual, but then the shooting started, before they got to the garden. They didn't know what to do, so they just sat tight in a thicket and waited until it was safe to sneak out again.

Alan said:

– The high track would be a good one for Sunday. I could drive up in the morning and meet you at that pub, just before you get to the village. The one that brews its own ales.
– We'll call you tonight. Have to see what the weather gets up to.

Alice's mum was non-committal, but if Alan was put out, he didn't show it. Alice thought her mum would have discussed it with him already, set time aside to spend alone with her. She packed a lunch for them both, a flask and a bar of chocolate while Alice washed up. She knew her mum was waiting: she still hadn't given a reason for her visit, hoped she wouldn't need to. Wanted to talk to Joseph again first, not just about him to other people. The morning was mild and the sky had started clearing by the time they were dressed and ready. They drove up to the Dales and talked about Gran instead of

Joseph. Alice said they'd found the house where she was born, while they were up in Scotland.

– Would Gran have gone back there after her divorce?
– She did. Damp coats and chilly little houses must have been strange after Nairobi. I couldn't tell you how long it was, a month or two perhaps. Just until the papers had come through from the lawyer.
– But would she have stayed there, I mean? If she hadn't got married again.
– I expect she'd have had to, yes.

Her mother parked near the start of a favourite walk: a marked path, little acorns on posts at regular intervals. They stood together, leaning against the bonnet, with the sun on their backs, and Alice could feel the wind buffeting the car while she laced her boots.

– I think Mum dreaded it too, the disapproval. Not so much her parents', although that would have played its part. Papa Young, your great-grandfather, he served in the Great War, and always said he was glad to have daughters, because they would never have to fight. But then Aunt Celie married a soldier. There was a war on again by then, and most young men were enlisted, so I suppose it was either that or be a spinster. He was killed in Italy. Celie wore black for years, even when I knew her. I'm sure Papa didn't want that for his youngest girl too. In any case, Gran said he only gave his approval after Dad handed in his notice.

Her mother smiled.

– He was staunch too. Wouldn't brook comments from the villagers. The schoolmaster defending his dissolute daughter. I love that idea. And she refused to wear sack-cloth and ashes, which wouldn't have helped her case with the local gossips. Mum told me once that remarriage didn't make her divorce any more palatable to their neighbours. But at least she knew she wasn't stuck there.

– Do you think that's why she married Grandad? One of the reasons?

Her mother looked at Alice, curious, teasing.

– Are you wondering what possessed her to marry such a curmudgeon?
– I didn't say that.
– No, I did. And I've wondered it too. I checked once, my birthday against their marriage certificate. It's nearer eight than nine months, so she might have been pregnant already, but I doubt she'd have known it. And they'd planned it all already, of course, the wedding. They started their life together in married quarters somewhere in Lincolnshire, while Dad served out his notice.

Her mother smiled.

– I think that haste might have looked a bit unseemly. Suspicious. I'm glad they were in a hurry. They wanted to be together. He wasn't a curmudgeon then. From what Mum told me he was shy, a bit gauche even. A young man who fell in love with her. I like to think of him like that.

Alice did too. It made sense of his awkwardness, and why he'd left most of the talking to Gran: easier to think of him as shy than not interested. But then she always found it easier to feel tender about him at a distance.

They walked in silence for a while until the track they were following dipped a little, and they were out of the wind again. Her mum said:

— He's definitely got worse as he's got older. I've come up with so many explanations over the years, lost count. Loneliness. He was never good at making friends, didn't socialise at work any more than he had to. It's strange to think like this now, but his marriage would have set him apart from people. Maybe that stuck with him somehow. I thought it was retirement too, that adjustment. I don't know how much that's got to do with it. I do remember playing with him. Out in the garden. Throwing and catching. Along the rose border. Pink and blowsy. We used to deadhead them together when he came home in the evenings, to keep them flowering. I'd have been about five then.

Playing wasn't something Alice could see her grandfather doing, and she thought her mum knew that. She often took his part this way. Alice remembered talking to her about when she got pregnant and that she'd never worried what Grandad would say, only Gran. Neither of them suggested she should give the baby up, much less have an abortion, but Alice knew her mum had rows with Gran about it. *Have you thought this through, because you need to?* While they were still busy having words, Grandad went to the Post Office and opened an account. He paid into it every week until Alice's mum started working, but didn't say anything until he handed over the passbook. It was their holiday fund: took them to Skye and Pembrokeshire and Dorset, lasted them five years, and her mum and Alan still used the camping stove she'd bought back then. *Has trouble showing it, but he's always loved us.* Her mum never wanted Alice to doubt that. They stopped at a stile, at the top of a rise, and stood a moment to get their breath back.

– Mum left Kenya before Dad did. He was ill for a while, I think, but he did some flying again afterwards.

The sun was low in the sky, and Alice's mum had to shield her eyes when she turned to talk to her.

– He didn't tell Mum about this for years. Never told me. She did.

She dropped her hand, blinded, lifted it again, went on.

– They used to bomb in a line, two or three planes at a time. Dad's was the last that day, so he would have been able to see the others ahead of him. The spotter from the police, and the other Lincolns.

She was talking too fast, had to stop and take a breath, slow down again.

– The second plane was over the target when one of their bombs went off, too early. It was the first one they'd dropped, that was always the largest, and it went off outside the plane, but it hadn't fallen far enough yet. The explosion triggered all the other, smaller bombs they dropped after it. Worked its way up through them, one by one, up and up until it got to the Lincoln. The bottom of the plane was still open, the bomb-bay, so there was nothing to stop the shrapnel. Dad said it ripped its way through everything.

Alice's mother squinted at her.

– Sympathetic detonation, it's called. I can hear him explaining that to Mum, can't you? He said it might have been atmospheric pressure set the bombs off. That's jargon for accident. Or it could have been because they were faulty. Doesn't really matter, does it? They did their damage. Sent shards of themselves tearing up as far as the cockpit. Right through the flight engineer's seat. He bled to death. Before they could get him help back on the ground. I think that's the part that matters. I don't know if Dad could see them by that stage, but the radio transmission was left open, so he heard everything.

Alice walked next to her mother for a while. She tried, but she couldn't imagine it. The winter grass underfoot was pale and flat and the sun made it hard to look anywhere but down. Her mother wiped her eyes. The path turned and led them towards a line of trees, and Alice waited until they'd drawn level before asking:

– Have you told Alan any of this?
– No.
– Not even after that row they had, him and Grandad?
– No. I thought about it. Of course I did. But then I thought it might make Alan feel worse. Too much too late. If I was going to tell him, it should have been before. For Dad's sake as much as his. Could have avoided the whole thing.
– Why didn't you tell him before? And me?

Alice's mother shrugged.

– I promised Mum.

She walked on, but more slowly.

– I'm not sure he wanted us to know either. She might be the only person he's told.

Her mum blinked at Alice, eyes small, although the sun was behind the branches now.

– He never stayed in touch with his squadron, and he knew they had reunions. Every few years he'd get a letter about them. I used to think we might have a conversation about it, at some point.

She looked ahead again.

– I'm glad he talked to Mum.

Back at the flat on Friday evening, Joseph dug out his maps to mark up the best places on them for Alice, and found David's maps among them. He'd given the old man his keys back, but he still had those: an excuse to go round there, it was blatant, but in the morning, Joseph put them in his bag. David was probably expecting to get them back off Alice at some stage, not a special delivery with her boyfriend attached, if that's what he was. Joseph wasn't sure if he was going to apologise to David, or what for exactly. Avoiding him, maybe, or for being so obvious about it. But how do you say that? He'd just go round there, offer to take care of the skirting in the hallway or something. Have a cup of tea, get things back on a good foot with the old man anyway.

It was early, but he knew David would be up. Joseph had started work on the upstairs bedroom around this time one morning, to fit the last coat of paint around another job he'd had on in the same part of town, and the old man had just finished his breakfast when he'd got there, already dressed and shaved. It was the same this time: Joseph could see the kitchen light through the stained-glass panel in the top of the door when he rang the bell. Then the shadow of the old man passing in front of it, coming to answer. He didn't open the door immediately, and Joseph imagined him stooping to look through the spyhole. He stood back a bit, so the porch light would be on him, but David still put the chain on.

The sliver of face was angry, fearful. Joseph wondered if Alice had said something to him.

– It's me. It's Joseph.
– Oh.

The door closed and opened again, wide, relieved.

– I'm sorry. I wasn't expecting. Did we arrange something? I must have forgotten.

The old man was pleased to see him. He was walking ahead of Joseph down the corridor back to the kitchen, offering tea and smiling, but still confused about him being there. *Alice can't have told him.* Joseph said:

– I was on my way past.

And it sounded like a lie. He got the maps out, put them on the side by the bread bin.

– I just wanted to give you these back.
– Oh.

The old man was pouring fresh water into the pot. He looked at the maps and then at Joseph, who still had his jacket on.

– But you'll stay for a cup?

They sat at the dining table together, the old man's breakfast plate pushed away, cups of tea sitting on their saucers between them. Joseph told him about the holiday, which villages they'd been to, and the routes they took between them, although it was weeks ago now, and he knew Alice would have done this already, shown her grandad the photos. David didn't seem to mind. He listened to it all, watching Joseph's face, attentive, and when he'd finished talking, the old man said:

– I think I owe you an apology.

He blinked, waiting for a response. Joseph hadn't thought this would happen, and it threw him. David stopped a moment longer, awkward, and then continued.

– I'm sorry for running on the way I have.

He smoothed his tie against his chest.

– It's where I met my wife. Kenya, I mean.

The old man broke off again, uncomfortable. His mouth forming the words before they came out.

– I used to talk about it with her.

David didn't look at him, and Joseph was glad.

– I always had her to talk to before, and I've been missing that.

An effort to say it. Joseph nodded. Thought the old man would see the movement, even if he couldn't see his face.

He stripped the skirting boards in the hallway. David had only pointed out one damaged section to him, but

Joseph did the lot, working through till lunchtime. Left them ready for sanding, told the old man he'd bring some paint with him tomorrow.

He knew David would start talking again: it was like he'd given him permission, and Joseph thought he was ready to get it over with now. Wasn't surprised when the old man sat down on the stairs in the morning and watched him cutting sandpaper to size. Ten, fifteen minutes, longer: Joseph had cleaned off three feet of skirting board before he said anything.

– It was an unreal existence, in many ways. Dawn, we'd be out flying over the forests, the Aberdares. Back again before folk in Nairobi had finished their breakfasts.

The old man sat stiff-necked, self-conscious, and Joseph was careful, quiet, getting on with the sanding, not wanting to interrupt or draw attention.

– The rest of the day was difficult to fill, I remember that. We had briefings, we had to fly up to Aden occasionally for parts and bombs, but there was an awful lot of idle time. One fellow in the squadron, he couldn't get used to it. His son was born shortly before we left for Kenya, and I know it frustrated him terribly, being so far away with nothing to do. I remember he spent the days painting, out by the hangars, where you got the best view of the hills. Watercolours to show his wife. Quite accomplished. A portfolio full of them by the time we left.

David watched Joseph working again for a while, told him the name of the airfield, Eastleigh, and described the low buildings and corrugated iron roofs, said it was nothing like what he'd been used to in Britain. The single runway was only metalled at each end, with hard, red earth in the middle.

– Murram they call it. Dusty in the dry weather, muddy in the wet.

He said they shared the military side of the airfield with another squadron and their Harvards, and there was a civilian part too, where the commercial flights landed. Only a handful a day, so there was only one small terminal building, little more than a customs office and lounge. David told Joseph they'd often go over there and drink coffee after they got back from a raid.

– That only added to the sense of unreality. Sitting with stewardesses and businessmen, hitching flights over to Lake Victoria or up to Aden if we had weekend rest. We'd walk round the rim of the volcano there, and swim out at the NAAFI facility at Steamer Point. Sleep on the veranda at Khormaksar if the camp was full. I enjoyed that, the warm nights.

Joseph had worked his way past the stairs, past the old man, and he had to turn his back to him now, to sand the long edge of the hallway, but David didn't seem to mind.

– You have to understand this was hugely exciting. To be twenty-three and flying across Africa to go swimming. At a time when few people took planes anywhere, long before package holidays and so on. I had to fly down to Mombasa once, took us past Kilimanjaro on the return leg. One of the most magnificent things I'll ever see. I knew that too, while it was happening. That's just what it felt like. The most enormous privilege.

He was quiet then, but it wasn't like he was waiting. Joseph didn't think he had to do or say anything: remembered listening to the old man in the summer, how he paused like that on and off while he was talking, but always picked up again if you let him. Joseph finished sanding, and started brushing everything free of dust, but then the quiet went on too long and he had to stop, because it had him unnerved.

David wasn't facing him when he looked up. Still sitting at the bottom of the stairs, eyes still fixed on a point somewhere beyond the open door of the living room. He said:

— For years afterwards, when I thought about Kenya it was to remember falling in love. The Sumners' house and garden. Being ill too, that weakness, the long recovery, but that was all bound up with Isobel anyway.

He shifted a little, but carried on with his careful explanation.

— All of what I've just described sounds so harmless, doesn't it? The Mau Mau shot a Kikuyu chief in the mouth. That's what prompted the Emergency. They hijacked his car and murdered him. He was a government official, of course, and the Mau Mau despised them. Men in the Home Guard, Africans who worked for the state, 'Tai Tai', that's what they called them, because of their European dress. They hacked a Kikuyu politician to death with pangas, on the marketplace out in the African quarter, because he was a moderate, he spoke out against them. One farmer, a white man this time, his wife and young son, they were butchered like that, by their own workers. Cut the legs off another farmer's herd. Didn't kill them outright, you see, left that for the farmer to do. Not only financially ruined, but he had to finish off his own livestock too. Doubly cruel.

He stopped a moment, then he nodded.

– I never saw any of that. I didn't see what our forces did on the ground either, the army. Or the Kenyan police. Any of the detention camps. Thousands passed through them. Thousands died. I know many were hanged. Many more were beaten, starved. Women and non-combatants among them. But I've only read accounts.

The old man frowned.

– Impossible to reconcile. Do you see? My memories with what I learnt later. I've tried, but what I see are mountains and forests and lakes, and the woman I went on to marry. Strange to say it: we were there to combat an insurgency, but most of the time it felt like being on an exercise, bombing on a vast practice range, if I'm honest. Even when we flew low for the strafing, the trees were so dense, we really couldn't see much, just the canopy. The ground, and whatever our bombs finally hit, our bullets, that was somewhere much further below.

He blinked, kept looking straight ahead, but Joseph thought he was aware of being watched.

– Seems like nothing when you compare it with Hiroshima, with napalm in Vietnam, the firestorms in Dresden. And I've read enough afterwards to know that we didn't do much damage. Not by military estimations.

We didn't have enough bombs to do the job properly, for one thing, and those we had were often old. A mix of instantaneous and long-delay fuses, they were unreliable, leaky, many failed to explode. Most people agree, in fact, that we were responsible for very few enemy deaths. The air contribution was mainly in supply. Keeping the ground forces serviced with food, munitions. Some go so far as to say it was a costly waste of time us being there at all, the bombers.

David was silent a moment, his eyes narrowed.

– But I wonder whether I repeat these things to console myself. I've read about monkeys, their fur scorched, down to the flesh. Craters, thirty feet deep, trees splintered and torn up by the roots. Elephant and rhino with holes ripped in their ears, deep gashes in their flanks. I remember a rumour while we were there, something in the region of two hundred Mau Mau dead or wounded after one series of raids. That figure was discredited. Still, I can't believe we never hit a human being. In twenty months of air operations, that would seem deluded.

The old man's voice was low, controlled.

– The Mau Mau used the terrain to their advantage, they had supply lines coming in from the Kikuyu reserves, a great deal of support from their people, gave our ground forces a great deal of trouble. But I'd still have to describe it as an unequal battle. They had no flak, no anti-aircraft defenses, unless you count the forest. I don't. I can't.

A small movement, his head, or maybe just his eyes. Quick, but Joseph had seen it: as if David had wanted to look over at him, but thought better of it again. He went on:

– I know what kind of damage the bombs we used can do, when they explode.

Another short pause.

– If they don't kill, they can deafen and blind and burn, and plenty would have detonated, after all, it stands to reason.

The old man passed a hand across his face: an involuntary gesture.

– What should I say about all this? I have never known what it is that I should say.

He broke off, adjusted his hands on his lap, but when he started speaking again, there was no change in his voice.

– My son-in-law tells me it was brutal. How can I deny that? I've heard myself talking, in this house all these years. I can hear how brutal it sounds.

The old man stayed where he was, but Joseph knew he'd finished. Pot of undercoat by his feet, he opened it, and stirred the paint. Calm and deliberate, only that wasn't how he felt. There were two more pots over by the door, but he couldn't see the brushes from where he was sitting. Brought them in from the van this morning, must still be at the other end of the hall, where he'd started. He'd have to walk past the old man to get them, but then he'd be the first to move, disturb the quiet in the hallway, so he waited.

Minutes had gone by already. David was still sitting on the stairs, hands folded in his lap, shoulders curled around him. He looked small and old and it made Joseph angry.

– Is that you done now?

It came out cold, and the old man looked up at him.

– Because I'll get on with my work if you are.

His pale eyes were hurt behind his glasses. Joseph hadn't come here to be cruel to him, but it was like he couldn't stop himself. It turned his stomach. He hadn't been shouting, but his voice was loud, and the old man was only a few feet away from him. David blinked, but he didn't say anything, just sat there watching him. Looking at Joseph, like he was thinking. He used to talk about it with his wife, that's what the old man had told him. Joseph pictured them both, sitting here in these rooms, years and years of talking and trying to work it out. Couldn't see what it amounted to.

– You feel bad about what you've done. My heart bleeds. I believe you. So you can let me get on.

The brushes were in the porch, but Joseph still couldn't move. Not with those eyes watching him like that. All upset and waiting, like they were expecting something from him.

After what felt like a long time, the old man stood up and walked past him: into the kitchen first and then out into his garden.

Joseph saw it happen, even before he'd started. Paint hurled across walls and banisters. Undercoat, heavy and stinking. Thick, oily mess of it under his shoes, slipping on the dustsheets. The floor turned slick and grey and he was already looking for the next tin to throw. Something else, anything to create more damage, and wherever he moved Joseph left marks: footprints, palms and fingers coated, paint oozing up his arms. Last pot he got through a window, smashed it. The top of the door all spikes of glass. Dripping white, he couldn't see through any of it now except the hole: above head height and showing autumn sky.

The old man must have heard it all but he never came back. Joseph stood at the door with the shock of what he'd done. Cold, outside air filling the hallway. Paint flung across the floor and walls and the windows and seeping into the carpet.

Twelve

Joseph tried writing lists. While he was still in the army, and again after. To get things down on paper. Once they were there, he could maybe try to organise them later.

The dead man: that was always the first thing, even though it was one of the last things to happen. He always had to write that down, get it out of the way and then on with the rest of it, split under different headings.

What he could hear. The car engines, both of them running. The Escort ticking over and then mis-timing, like it's going to give out any second, not enough revs to keep it going. The kids in the back seat, crying, sounded more like little dogs than children. Rain too. On the road, in puddles, rattling on the car bonnets. Had been on and off all morning. Joseph remembered it coming down his neck, and that the fronts of his thighs were cold and sodden. What else? Breathing: his own, coming fast, caught under his helmet, and then there was the shouting. Blokes' voices: loud, and close. Sometimes Joseph thought his must have been one of them, because his throat was sore with it after, only he didn't remember what he'd been yelling.

What he could feel. Wet and sick. Rain got into his boots. Maybe it was sweat. Helmet too heavy to be holding his head up. Loose guts below, tight feeling in his throat like a cord pulled and knotted.

What he could see. Car headlights up on the verge, grey-green branches and dark sky behind. Like night coming except it was afternoon. Joseph remembered torches too. Middle of the day but dark enough to need them on the checkpoint, with red cones pulled on top while they were stopping the cars. More torches after the man was down, but those lights were white, jumping circles, three or maybe four of them, moving like they were running, and then they were all over and under the Astra, checking. Shining in through the windscreen at the other man, the passenger, still in there, all white face and terrified, squinting in the torch beams.

The exhaust pipe: Joseph could see the fumes coming out of it, red in the tail lights, and white too, so the car must have been jammed in reverse. Not moving, though, just the engine running. But there were two cars, so which one was it? Back windscreen, steamed up, small faces behind it, smudging, small heads moving. That went with the small dogs sound on the other list, but Joseph stopped himself there, because he was meant to be just writing things, not trying to tie them together.

He started finding things he'd written that he didn't remember. Tore up his lists or burnt them. They came out different every time he tried and so he stopped trusting the pieces after a while, and then his ability to slot them together. *Maybe you twist things to suit. I think I do. Or you turn things against you. Might do that too.*

The man was older than Joseph when he shot him. Not much, a year or two maybe, still early twenties. Joseph got older than him every year now, and he hated the way his head did that: searched out that detail and held it up to hurt him.

He panicked just after it happened. Stood up from the road thinking he'd shot someone's dad. Kids in the back, woman in the front, and he was thinking: *what fucking car did the man get out of?* Escort? He never saw. Kids crying, making that small dog noise and maybe that's why. *That's their dad.* Looking at the man, curled up on the road with his jeans on. *That woman in the front seat, she's his wife.*

Joseph was lying on the road too, after it happened, between the cars. But he couldn't remember how he got down there. On his back, so maybe the rifle had kicked him. But his shoulder didn't hurt, no bruise above his eye from the sight, and there would have been if he'd fired that badly. He must have been on the ground a while because the backs of his legs were soaked, and he could remember standing up too, because Jarvis helped him, but the rest of it had just gone, in all the years it hadn't come up again. *Shot through with holes, everything.*

How far away was he when I shot him? Five metres. Ten. Fifteen. Couldn't have been far because Joseph had detail: the man's jacket was undone, his beard was a real one not just unshaven, the Astra had rust spots all along the driver's-side panel, next to where the man was standing. The car door was open and he was talking to the Lieutenant, and the Lieutenant was writing when he should have been looking.

But it wasn't always that way: other times, Joseph saw all of it at once, the way he could never have really, because he was only over by the Escort and that was much too close. The man standing at a distance, the two cars, the full width of the road, and from this angle, Joseph could see who the man was looking at too: Townsend. Up on the verge. Knocking on the window, on the passenger's side, but the passenger wasn't moving, only the man standing in the road, and he was reaching behind him. That was before Joseph shot him, but how long? He couldn't say now.

Years ago. But Joseph didn't think time had much to do with it. His memory was already slow to respond the morning after. Soon as he woke he felt it, there was something about yesterday. But then there were long seconds in bed before he could say what was wrong, and what it had to do with him.

A week after it happened, Joseph was sent to see the chaplain. They sat in an office together and talked about thou shalt not kill and why God had made that commandment. The chaplain said if it was done to protect others, He might not look at it unkindly. At the time Joseph thanked him, but it never gave him much comfort. Too convenient. *Rules you can bend give you nothing to lean on.*

Things he could smell was another list he used to write. Wet road, wet clothes, hot tyres and exhaust fumes, but fresh air too. He hadn't dreamt about that day yet, never had a nightmare, but he woke up with those smells around him sometimes, couldn't get away from them.

In the sheets, so he'd get up, but then they followed him: on his face, in his hair. It was the rain on the ground and the exhaust fumes, but mostly that fresh air. Cold smell, like windows left open in winter.

Joseph went to see Jarvis about three years after they got back. He was in a bad way then, staying at Eve and Arthur's, kipping on their sofa, and he took off without telling them. Thought he had maybe a day and a night before they got too worried. Hitched east, along the Essex roads and all their red brick and pebble-dash, endless junctions. Jarvis was still with the regiment: a good soldier and the army was good to him. Told Joseph he'd made sergeant when they spoke on the phone, and Joseph remembered Townsend had kept a book on that, but the odds were too short to be worth it: too certain.

Jarvis had been posted at home since their tour ended, and Joseph knew he lived out, on a new-build estate in the town, with his wife, their children. She hated being an army wife, couldn't stand the hauling from post to pillar and living in married quarters. She didn't much like Joseph turning up there either. Understandable, he thought, while he stood in their hallway and listened to them arguing. The door to the front room was closed, but he could still hear what she was shouting and he didn't blame her. You turn up and you can't remember their kids' names and you look like a wino.

Jarvis cleared it with her, got Joseph a couple of cans to drink and made bacon sandwiches. They stood in the kitchen while his wife took the kids round to the neighbours'. More of them than Joseph remembered, and the oldest girl looked like a teenager already. The washing machine filled and turned while Jarvis grilled the bacon, and Joseph thought about how his Corporal had liked it in Ireland, his first tour anyway. Up in Tyrone, two years, and he'd had his family with him then. Always said he'd sooner be back there than in the shitehole. Their first daughter started school in Tyrone, and Jarvis reckoned it was the best education: reading writing arithmetic. Said she was well ahead of the other kids when they got back to England.

They ate and Jarvis said he did basic training now so he wasn't away so much, his family wasn't shifted around. The girls would have exams to do soon enough, so it was better to be settled. His wife was happier too, didn't give him a such hard time any more, not like she used to. The house wasn't a bit like the ones you get from the army and Jarvis said she'd wanted it that way: sick of the standard sheets and the cutlery.

– What's going on with you then?

Joseph hadn't thought of a way to start.

– Don't know. Can't really get it together at the moment.
– Looks like it. Full moon, is it?

Too thin and fewer teeth than the last time Jarvis saw him, Joseph was aware of how rough he must look, and was glad of the cigarette offered, something to do, because he didn't have any banter.

– You were one of my lot I'd back-squad you.

Jarvis was smiling.

– Different out there, is it?

Joseph nodded, shrugged.

– Told you that when you were leaving, didn't I? Does your head in to be outside. You ever wanted back in?

He shook his head.

– So what's going on then? To what do I owe the pleasure?

Nearly an hour had gone by already and Jarvis was tapping his thumbs, lightly, on the table. Maybe not aware of it, but Joseph was. Of the crumbs on the plates and the washing machine emptying and spinning. The evening passing and nothing said yet, nothing settled.

– Think I'm having trouble with my memory.
– Oh yeah?

Joseph wasn't sure if he wanted to go on, only Jarvis was doing that tapping again.

– You ever get that feeling? That you've done something but you can't remember it properly?
– What kind of something? Drinking?
– No. Something wrong.
– You in trouble?
– No. I'm talking about before. When we were over there.

His old Corporal looked at Joseph a long couple of seconds before answering.

– You going to get all Brits Out on me?
– No. No. Not that.

It wasn't going well. Jarvis sat up straighter.

– Come on then. I'm not a bloody mind-reader.
– Don't know. I can't get it straight. You know? I just thought. You were there. I just thought I'd come and see you or something.

He wasn't making sense, but Jarvis was still listening.

– You talking about when you did that bloke?
– Yeah.
– Well, go on then.

He was listening, but he wasn't going to make it easy. Joseph tried again.

– I don't know what went wrong that day.
– Nothing.
– But we stopped people loads, all the time.
– Yeah?
– We got them arrested and charged.
– So?
– Why didn't we get him arrested?
– No. Hang on. You've lost me.

Jarvis was smiling again, but frowning too. Like he couldn't believe what Joseph was saying, and Joseph thought he'd hardly started and he'd lost him already. Dry mouth and no lager left in the can, couldn't be asking for another. Stupid heart going now and Jarvis was looking at him, waiting.

– I just can't remember it straight. I keep thinking if I did it right, I don't know, fucking procedure. I don't even know if he was armed sometimes when I'm thinking about it.

Joseph laughed, but it came out strange and Jarvis didn't join in.

– He had a gun.

Just a statement. No argument. Jarvis was there: Joseph thought he had to remember that, next time doubt took over again.

– Gobshite in the passenger seat was sitting on a pistol too.

Joseph hadn't forgotten: he hadn't seen it either, but he'd read the report, that ballistics had traced it back to a kneecapping in 1987.

– He was a Provo, Mason. A terrorist.

Joseph lifted the empty can and put it back down. Jarvis went on:

– He was a member of the fucking Irish Republican Army. Army. They train just like us. They call it a war.
– I know. I know.
– What were you going to do? Talk to him nicely about giving up his bad ways?

Joseph didn't know what to say then. Maybe that he wasn't wearing a uniform, the bloke, the terrorist, but that sounded pathetic. Like some trick his own head played on him: the man looked like anyone you'd see on the street or in the pub or the park and you wouldn't think to be shooting. Jarvis was leaning back in his chair now, fingers spread out on his thighs, looking at him, and Joseph felt like he was putting his head on show. All the mad thoughts in it, all tangled and strange and it made him want to cry, seeing what a state it was in.

– I just remember the rain and the cars, you know, and one of them had that woman in, and her kids were howling.
– What you on about?
– I'm just saying.
– What?
– I just want to say what happened.
– I was there. You don't need to. Cars and kids don't have nothing to do with it. Bastard Fenian had a gun on your mate and you stopped him.

Joseph waited, but there was nothing else, not even the washing machine turning now. He wanted to hear more, and he wanted Jarvis to tell him: start before the cars came and go all the way through it, but Jarvis was just sitting with his arms crossed, looking at him, holding his eyes, and Joseph realised he was staring. Must have looked like he was demanding an answer, and then he remembered what their Quartermaster Sergeant used to say about people who ask questions. Family, friends, people who corner you at the bar and want to know how you deal with it. You might have to kill someone. Don't you ever think about that? *Civilian eyes*. They look at you with them, waiting to see who'll blink first. Always think they'll be the ones to break you: get through to that human being they just know is trapped in there, somewhere. Your fucking bleeding heart. Joseph used to laugh when he said it: he knew that look. The way they'll ask you roundabout questions when what they really want to know is if you've done it. And what was it like? Even the pacifists. Fascinated. Sergeant said if you keep quiet they'll always presume you have. Think the army is all running around and shooting, wouldn't cross their minds that you might be a cook or mechanic or something. Keep it zipped and they'll never know how boring you really are.

– Maybe it didn't have to happen, though? What about if I shot him in the arm, you know?
– Yeah, right. Winged him. Like you had all the fucking time in the world.

Jarvis smiled, a small, tight movement.

– Or should you have gone for the legs, you think? Shin bones. Like they do?
– I just mean, maybe I could have stopped him some other way. No need for him to die, was there?
– I don't know what the fuck you're talking about. He had a gun on your mate.

Jarvis was closing him down. Hadn't he come to hear this? A gun, a bit of certainty from someone who knew, but it wasn't working. Joseph thought he might shout, didn't want to, didn't know what Jarvis would do if he started. He waited and he was relieved when Jarvis didn't say anything for a while, just let everything settle. Pulled out a pack of cigarettes, got up quietly, lit one on the gas ring and laid the pack open on the table for Joseph, ashtray between them and the greasy plates cleared away.

– You did what you were trained to do. Job well done, I say. It was him or Townsend. You hadn't done it, you'd be sitting here now telling me how you wish you fucking had. Bawling your eyes out, thinking about your mate and all the bloody Welsh hills he can't be climbing now. Sorry Mrs Townsend but I got terrible confused and let your son take a bullet. Gifted the Provos another one of ours. That's what I joined the army for.

He passed his cigarette over so Joseph could light his on the end.

– You've got yourself stuck, Mason. You're just looking at it all wrong. Letting your memory try it on.

Jarvis rubbed his chin, watched Joseph watching him.

– Way I see it: you were on a tour of duty, just doing what needs to be done.

Joseph knew he'd been looking at his old Corporal like a civilian now. Recognised the way he couldn't accept his answers: he understood the words but they just didn't mean enough. He'd been expecting something to change after Jarvis finished speaking, something to ease back into its rightful place. That's why they always look at you that way, same reason he was looking at Jarvis now: waiting for that click, the relief when something starts to make sense. Different set of rules, different world he was in then. Is that what it was?

– You always were a specimen, Mason. I remember that. Odds-on for a choker. Too quiet or something, weren't you? Didn't surprise me you left us.

Bastard. Jarvis was smiling again, putting the boot in. Joseph had no comeback, and Jarvis knew that. What could he do? Even if he did start, Jarvis would finish him easy. Probably why he let him in here in the first place, had him sized up as harmless on the doorstep, and now he was just letting him know.

– You think about things like this, Jarvis?
– Course I do.
– And?
– See what thought did?

Joseph watched him clean out the ashtray, clear away the empty cans. In his kitchen that smelled of food and clean clothes. Wedding ring, and kids' paintings taped to the walls. Joseph thought if you had all that, maybe it wouldn't be so hard. A wife and a houseful of kids. No doubts: Jarvis had too much else to be taking care of. Seemed too simple to Joseph, but what did he know about it? He was a specimen, always had been. Three hours they'd been sitting there, longer, and then Jarvis told him he couldn't be staying.

– Kids'll be needing their beds. I'll get you a towel. Disposables are upstairs in the cabinet.

He told Joseph to get in the shower, get shaved and then he'd put him on a bus.

– You got money on you?

Joseph shrugged. Jarvis picked up his wallet and his car keys.

– Doesn't feel like it, I can see that, but you're lucky.

No one chasing you through the courts. I've got a mate up on civil charges. Didn't even kill, got his man so he can't walk now, can't work. Family wants him convicted, wants compensation. That's stress for you.

Joseph wondered if he knew the bloke, but he didn't ask: didn't want to know.

– No one's saying you did wrong. Are they? The reports gave you the all clear, so it's just you. You're the only one. Useless thinking. Put it away. Get on with the rest.

Jarvis was the one who picked Joseph up from the road, and he was with him again, a few weeks later: back in England, at their home barracks and in the pipe range together to zero their weapons, ready for a training exercise that afternoon. The Corporal started before him, but when it came to Joseph's turn to shoot, he couldn't.

He'd carried the same rifle on every patrol in Armagh, cleaned it every day, did everything as normal, only he'd never fired it again. So maybe that was it. Or it could have been something about the sound the training rifle made when he lifted it. Smell of the oil, the cool rubber feel of the cheek piece up against his face. Different place, different country, different bloody weapon, but something he did was the same, some movement his body remembered. Back out in the rain and the cold. Dark and the shouting and the kids and the cars. Like it was happening now, not weeks ago.

A few seconds. Not long, but it was hard to get himself straight again after. Sweating so much it got into his eyes. Shaking, so Jarvis had to come over and take his rifle. Not like shivering, much stronger, more like a fit and it was frightening. Started somewhere in his guts, pulling hard and tight under his ribs, backs of his legs like water, and he thought he was slipping, going over. Jarvis saw it all, made him sit down against the wall, pushed his head down hard, between his knees, and held it there. Joseph tried to get up again after a few minutes but his Corporal wouldn't let him.

– Puke-pale you are, Mason.

Not going anywhere until his blood was running properly again. He sat down next to him.

– No one to see you here anyway.

Jarvis had stayed with him then, and he waited with him for the bus too, even though it was late, and their conversation was over. He stood on the forecourt, watching while the coach pulled out, the only person standing there on the concrete.

Thirteen

Alice's legs ached under the table. Eight miles yesterday, another ten today. It was Monday evening, and Alan was up at the farm with them. He'd bought lamb for dinner: his speciality, with rosemary from the garden, and a good red, which Alice helped herself to more of. Her mum and Alan rarely drank more than a glass or two with a meal. They didn't look at Alice when she filled her glass for a third time, or at each other, and that maddened her. It had been noted, and would probably be talked about later, after she'd gone to bed. *She hasn't said a word about Joseph since she arrived.*

Alice had tried to walk herself tired over the weekend, persuaded her mum to do the full curve of the ridgeway that afternoon instead of cutting back across the valley to the farm. They walked the last mile in the dark, the small, white shapes of the sheep disappearing into the grey of the hillside. The track was narrow and Alice walked ahead, thinking about her grandfather. Couldn't get away from his loneliness. Couldn't help but think about Joseph too, and what her grandad might have told him. Alice was sure now: that's what had been happening, over the summer, after they came back from Scotland. She didn't know if it hurt her. She knew it would her mother.

Alice tried to picture them. Sitting in the living room together, or maybe at the dining room table, but she couldn't get the idea to work, and it frustrated her. Couldn't imagine them talking like that to each other.

Too hard to think about Joseph. Alice sat in the kitchen, at the far end of the table by the stove, shared the last of the wine into their three glasses, wondering if there might be another bottle in one of the cupboards. London tomorrow. Alan and her mum were discussing the week ahead in low voices, and Alice thought about her grandparents, because that came without trying. She wondered how long her grandmother had waited. If it took months or years before Grandad said anything. How it felt, to have to wait like that, if it had been frightening. Whether there was more: things he'd never told her, and if she'd ever tried to guess at them.

Alice and her mother set off early next morning, and shared the drive down to London. Her mum did the first leg, and then they swapped at a service station. Alice caught sight of herself in the mirror as she walked into the toilets: white face, tight shoulders. She'd been aware of lying for a long time last night, eyes open in the dark, but she did wake up, just before six, so although it didn't feel that way, she must have got some sleep.

When she came out, her mum was at the payphones: calling her grandad to let him know when to expect them. It was a brief exchange, and she hung up, frowning. Alice recognised the look, or the feeling behind it, had experienced it often enough during her own phone calls with her grandad.

– Is he alright about us coming?

Her mother shrugged, nodded. Alice had helped her dig the promised plants out of the garden after breakfast, spindly and leafless, they didn't look like much, but her mum had been quietly excited, told her they just needed time to get established. Alice could see them in the rear-view mirror as she drove back out to the motorway, in a box on the back seat, clods of earth and twig wrapped in plastic bags.

– What I told you this weekend, about your Grandad. I'm not saying that's why he's the way he is. But it might explain why Kenya's difficult for him at least.

They were about half an hour out of London before they started talking. Alice could feel her mum looking at her and she nodded.

– I haven't asked him, don't worry. I mean, I did start in the summer, but we only talked about Gran.
– I'm not saying you shouldn't, Alice.

She could remember her mother telling her to be careful before.

– Might be good for us all, if he could talk to you. I doubt he'd ever speak to me about it. Alan says that's his fault, but I don't know. I've always found it hard, Dad and Kenya, and I'm sure he knows that.

Grandad used to buy them all red poppies for Remembrance Day, and Alice could remember her mum wearing a white poppy alongside. She'd given one to Alice once too, when she was small, and explained that it was right to help people hurt in wars, but there shouldn't be another. Alice had inspected her reflection in the hallway mirror, waiting for everyone else to put on their scarves and hats, and she'd liked the way the two flowers looked on her collar. She wondered now, if the idea had come from Papa Young, her great-grand-father: the pacifist whose sons-in-law were both in the military. Alice's grandparents certainly didn't wear both, because she could also remember the hissed argument between her mum and Gran, that same November day, out on the path after they'd left the house. When they got to the gate, first the white and then the red flower had been removed from Alice's coat: *until you're old enough to decide for yourself.* Her mum had stopped wearing poppies too, at some stage, Alice couldn't say when, and she turned to ask her why, but her mother started talking first.

– There were huge police raids in Nairobi, the African quarter. This was before Dad was posted there. Anyone and everyone suspected of dealings with the Mau Mau got arrested. A lot of innocent people.

She shook her head.

– Mum remembered all the rumours afterwards, about servants not turning up for work. She had friends with Kikuyu housemaids and she said it chilled her, thinking they'd had Mau Mau in their homes. No good kuke like a dead kuke, that's what people said. Even some who wouldn't have dreamt of it before the Emergency. Mum told me meeting Dad was like gaining a bit of perspective. He didn't get caught up in the hysteria, and not all the security forces were like that. He was meant to carry a revolver, whenever he came off the airfield into town. Others would make a bit of a show of their webbing holsters, but Dad said a gun was just a cumbersome nuisance where it wasn't needed. Mum couldn't believe how casual he was, but there was never any real danger to them in Nairobi. Just too much talk of oathing ceremonies and witchcraft. Mau Mau drinking each other's blood, that sort of nonsense. Hardly any Europeans were killed during the Emergency. Most of the time the Mau Mau targeted Africans, mostly other Kikuyu.

Her mother was quiet for a while, and then she turned to face Alice, twisting against the seatbelt.

– Alan found a picture once, in an article about Kenya, and he photocopied it for me. It was of a pilot, from the police reserve I think, a white Kenyan. He'd painted little brown figures on the side of his plane, with spears and shields. Recorded his kills. Mum always said I shouldn't confuse Dad with the authorities, or the white settlers. But he bombed the forests. The people in them. I still don't find that easy.

She sat back again.

– He's been through all the entries in Hansard, every debate they had about Kenya in the Commons. Objections were raised to British forces being sent in, the way the Emergency was handled. Mum told me about that. About all the books he's read on the subject too. He can't really be accused of burying his head in the sand. Or Mum for that matter, I know she read them as well.

Alice thought about her grandmother, sitting on her piano stool, her favoured reading chair. Lid down on the keys, book propped open in front of her, elbows resting on either side. Grandad would often read with her, but in the easy chair next to the piano, and he'd tease her sometimes, for sitting like that, in the mild way people do who've teased each other for years about habits they know will never change. *I can concentrate better up here.* Alice wondered if that's where she'd read Grandad's books too, to give them her best attention, and then she thought how quiet her grandmother had been during that argument with Alan, all those years ago. Alice could see them all, sitting at the dining room table, her mum and Alan frowning, asking, insisting, her grandfather overtaken, stubbornly asserting his position. Her gran had been there too, but silent, her eyes on her husband. Alice searched her face in her mind's-eye picture, looking for a sign of what she'd thought of the argument, where she stood. Gran had often taken his part in debates with Alice's mum, but not that time. Gran had been upset for him, Alice could picture the slight frown, the rapid blinking, but she hadn't intervened. Alice thought her gran had read the same books, and she'd lived in Kenya too, for almost six years: of course she would have come to her own conclusions. Alice couldn't imagine her grandparents arguing, but they must have discussed what they'd read and experienced, and it would have been strange had they always agreed. That would make sense of her grandmother's expression: concerned, but holding something in reserve.

– I don't think Dad regrets the empire.

Alice glanced over at her mother.

– I doubt if he thinks about what he did in Kenya in those terms at all. I mean, if you asked him, he'd probably say British rule had had its day. Something along those lines. That's why the situation in Kenya arose. India had already gone, just a matter of time for all the others. He might even concede that the system was unjust, aspects of it at least, but I don't think it troubles his conscience.

She looked straight ahead while she was talking, her expression difficult to read.

– I don't know what that makes him. Blinkered, maybe. A product of his times. He's not going to feel responsible, in any case. However much I might wish it.

She shook her head a little, and Alice thought she was impatient, but with herself as much as with her father.

He was at the window when they pulled up at the house. Started a little, when he saw them: caught waiting. He waved to them and Alice thought he'd probably laid the table already, and filled the kettle. Her mother went in first, with the plants, and Alice followed on after she'd taken her things out of the boot. They were in the kitchen when Alice got to the porch. They'd left the front door open for her, and she could see them standing together at the window, both looking out at the garden, discussing the best position for the plants.

– Sheltered in any case.
– Yes, and shade is fine, they like that.

Alice stood her rucksack and boots in the porch and listened to the familiar voices at the other end of the hall. Debating, agreeing. No trace of awkwardness between them. It smelled of paint in the porch and Alice was confused: that was all finished weeks ago, surely?

She must have stood there a while, because her mum came back out into the hallway to see where she'd got to.

— It's brewed, love. Aren't you coming in?

Alice waited for her mother to notice. The new glass in the top of the door. The wallpaper, so carefully chosen and now painted over. The skirting boards had been done too, which meant Joseph had almost certainly been here. But it didn't explain the other changes, or why her grandfather wasn't drawing their attention to them. He'd been so proud of all the new work before.

He was in the hallway too now, at the far end, dishcloth in hand. Late morning, but the day still hadn't got light and she couldn't see him properly. He was watching her, though, Alice was sure. Standing behind her mother and waiting.

The man in the snooker club, the disappearing, sitting in Clare's kitchen, listening to things she didn't want to know about Joseph. Shattered glass and everything that went with it: Alice didn't want to believe he'd done that here.

She moved past her mother down the hall and when she got to her grandad, she took his arm. Stiff at first, but he let her, and Alice found herself scanning his face and hands for signs of harm. Saw fine broken veins, soft folds of skin beneath his eyes, and their milky blue, blinking at her, uncertain, as though he were asking her not to say anything. Alice couldn't understand what that look meant, didn't know what had gone on here between him and Joseph, but there must have been something. She was still holding on to him, too hard, and when she let go, he caught her hand: a clumsy, dry palm folded briefly around her own.

When was the last time she'd cried in front of him? Must have been a little girl.

Fourteen

No phone calls, no visits from Alice. Not even to shout at him, and Joseph thought she might just leave it like that: no way to get things back now, he didn't need her to explain.

Her grandad returned the cheque he'd sent. Joseph knew what it was, soon as he saw the envelope. It had been a pathetic thing to do really. Pathetic gesture. But if David thought so, he was too kind to say it. There was a letter with the cheque: street and date written top right, kind regards at the bottom, a few polite lines between. Not necessary. The repairs were carried out quickly. In any case not substantial. Everything was downplayed: *nothing owed or due now, everything over.* The old man said Alice had given him the address, but there was no word from her with the letter.

Can't be set right: Joseph thought that was understood. It shamed him, that David had to put his house back in order, and he didn't like to think what Alice had seen or heard when she went round there. What she'd thought of him.

He couldn't get rid of that day in the hallway, it just stayed in his head all the time. Like he'd been twenty-two again and raw, a year out of the army. Hadn't thought it could happen again like that, not after so long. The old man had just sat there watching him, waiting for him to explain, and that's all it had taken to tip him: just those eyes on him.

David had had his wife, an ear to pour himself into, someone who knew, that was how he must have done it. But Joseph had been alright too, for years: from before he went to Portugal, up until now. *Just this past few months*. Too many questions on their way from Alice, and all the things the old man told him. Joseph thought he didn't need reminding like that: he knew what he'd done. Jarvis said it was the right thing, but that didn't make any difference. It was just the fact of it: the man on the road was always there, didn't matter how you looked at it, and Joseph was still the one who killed him. He didn't need to go over it, not the way David wanted to. Never knew him while his wife was alive, but from what Alice said about her grandad, having her there and listening didn't stop him being an awkward bastard. *Maybe you can't stop that, not completely*: Joseph didn't want to judge him for it, God knows he didn't have a leg to stand on there. But he still couldn't understand the old man going over the same, hard ground all the time. Why did he want to do that to himself?

He didn't get Alice either. Why did she have to keep on at it, make it the one thing that counts? *If I'm going to know you, there's this one thing I have to know*. Joseph didn't think it had to work that way.

The closest he'd ever come to telling was with a girl-friend once, and he thought about her again, in the days after he got the old man's letter and there was nothing from Alice. He didn't like it at first: it felt disloyal to be thinking about someone else. She was called Julie, but then Joseph didn't think he was remembering her so much: it was more about the way it had happened, and why he'd come nearer that time than he had with Alice.

She was his ex by then, a year it had lasted with her, give or take. He'd moved into her flat over the winter: a few clothes left there first, a toothbrush, CDs, and then his friends started phoning him at her place. They never really talked about what was going on between them, but Joseph started paying half the rent in March. He told her he loved her, because he did. His mum was pleased and he thought Julie was as well.

In the summer she told him she didn't like it. That he was so quiet sometimes. She said it bothered her that he went days, weeks it felt like, without talking. Breakfasts together, dinners eaten, whole evenings spent on the sofa and no how are you love, what's been happening, did you see, no nothing.

– Like you're not there. Or I may as well not be.

They were out the back of the pub on the benches when she said that, and it was a bright evening, sunset behind the estate, yellow in the trees. Pints on the table and a bag of crisps split open between them. Julie cried and it threw him: they'd never had a row before, and he wasn't sure that's what they were doing now, or what was happening. Her make-up ran and Joseph went inside for some toilet roll, chest tight and head gone blank, he didn't know what to be thinking. Said he was sorry when he came out and he put his arms around her.

Didn't know what he was sorry for, not really. Shocked him, never thought she was unhappy, didn't know he was like that.

Joseph had met her a few months after he left the army. She started coming to the snooker club, the sister of a girlfriend of someone he'd been to school with. Her family didn't live on the estate, but she grew up in the high flats, just a few streets away, and Joseph knew her cousins too, worked with one of them before he joined up. He slept with her a few times and that was good, and then he started looking forward to her being there, mostly it was Thursday nights. She was seeing someone else, Malky told him, and then a week or two later he said she wasn't any more. Julie never said anything, it just worked out that way: no discussion, no embarrassing asking, just time passing and then they were a couple.

Joseph was living at his mum and dad's then, and he'd started paying back what Eve had lent him. His parents went out together on Friday nights and Julie came to see him, stayed over whole weekends after a while. Joseph would go out with his dad and play a few games of snooker, and Julie would stay in and watch Saturday telly with his mum. Packet of biscuits open, their feet pulled up into the easy chairs, he'd hear them chatting as he went out the door and down the road.

Joseph came home with bottles of lager, and after his mum and dad had gone to bed Julie would pull her knickers off, smiling, and they'd lie down on the sofa. Or sometimes it'd be the kitchen, or sometimes she wanted the cold tiles in the back bathroom. Her feet wedged up against the washing machine and her eyes closing, lashes

flickering: small tits, pink-red nipples, soft belly, hard arms
and legs all pushing and pulling. Her mouth was the best
thing, thin lips, wet teeth, cool tongue. They'd share a fag
and a bottle and then that mouth would be smiling again,
pressing and nipping him on.

She worked for the gas board and their office was on
the industrial estate. Rented a flat ten minutes up the
road from his mum and dad's place. If he went there
after work she'd take his painting clothes off at the door
and run him a bath. She'd scrub his arms and hands,
and then they'd get into bed, and afterwards Julie lay
between his legs and talked to him. About things she
read in the paper, what her boss said, who her sister
went out with the day before. Her hair spread across his
chest and he loved it, listening to her but not listening
while the evening passed and she was talking. Joseph
thought this was getting settled, thought they were
happy. Didn't know it was starting, even then.

— I never know what to do when you're like that, Joey.
What am I supposed to do?

The sun had gone down and they were still outside, first
pints finished, more bought, the spilled tops of them
spreading out across the table. He loved her and put his
fingers in the wet and drew lines while she called him
moody, said it was impossible sometimes to know what
he was thinking, and it drove her mad being the one
who had to do the asking all the time. He said he didn't
know what she meant and she said:

— See, see? That's exactly it. I'm asking you, I'm asking
you now and you're not telling nothing.

They argued a lot that summer. Still sleeping together, and that was still good, but then she stopped wanting that in the autumn.

– Just a substitute. Fucking for talking. No good having one without the other.

And he hated it when she said things like that because it wasn't the way he felt about it, about her. Nowhere near. Not something he did to fill in the gaps, it was just what he wanted to do to her, with her. It was what he thought about when he thought about her, which felt like most of the time. Days at work he'd want to be crying, remembering how she used to unzip her skirt and be looking at him, smiling.

Julie asked him to leave and he didn't, so then she told him to go. He got a room at a mate's place to tide him over and he'd still see her sometimes at the pub, or the snooker club. Once or twice she slept with him again, but they always ended up crying. And then she started seeing someone else: Malky told him. Joseph saw them together a few weeks later and embarrassed her, shouting. In the middle of her street on a Saturday morning and all the neighbours standing at their windows, watching.

What was he supposed to tell her? What did she want? Joseph remembered being on edge the whole time, after she started asking. They grew up in the same place, knew all the same people, he thought there was only one thing he'd never told her, and he was sure she wouldn't want to hear that, not really. It wasn't just the problem of where to start, or how to explain. There was just no way of telling what she would do or feel or think after he said it, after she knew. Not likely to be the end of it, was it? Wouldn't solve anything. Just the beginning of a whole new set of problems.

Joseph went round to her flat again, about a year later. He'd been gone a few months, and he could see from her face she'd heard from someone: that he was losing it these days and living back at his mum and dad's, sponging off his sister. Julie was alone and when he said he wanted to talk to her, he saw the way she rolled her eyes and he thought he'd do it now, give her a proper shock and she'd be sorry for asking. He sat down in her kitchen that had been his once too, and then he started to tell her about the road block and checking the cars through. About who else was there that day, the other men in the multiple. It was all coming out, all the words, and she was listening, and he really thought he might say it, and even thinking that made him start crying.

Julie was crying too, standing there across the room from him with her fingers wiping at her eyes, even though he'd told her nothing yet, hadn't even got halfway through.

It was too much then. Gone from being nothing to too much in seconds.

But Joseph kept on talking: he'd started now, it was too late, and so he finished his story. But that's all it was, because the way he told her, it was Townsend who fired the rifle, and he was just one of the men who saw him do it.

– What you crying for?
– Because you are.

But Joseph wasn't any more, he just felt worn out. Julie didn't want him to go but he left anyway, because he thought she might take her clothes off or say she was sorry or something and he didn't want any of that to be happening. Thought it'd be just like the last time he saw her: bed first and then more crying.

Tears and remorse. Joseph thought that's what Julie had wanted. Couldn't give them to her, and he was glad he hadn't. He was sorry for the way he'd treated her, but he didn't want to howl in front of her about what he'd done in Ireland. *Why? Cry long enough and loud enough and you'll be a better person for it? Better than the man you were, when you dropped the bombs or fired the bullet?* Joseph didn't believe in that. *Just a way to get yourself off the hook.* Didn't think it worked either. *Look at David: years of it, over and over, until you're an old man and you're still no closer to an easy conscience.*

He hadn't planned to lie to Julie. He'd gone there to frighten her maybe. Tell her and then ask her, what the fuck do we do now then, now I've done the talking? But he wasn't proud of the way he'd reacted that day, and he didn't want to do that with Alice. Had no wish to scare her, didn't want any shouting either, no anger, never wanted to get angry with her. He just didn't want to tell her.

All the questions Alice asked her grandad, and him too now. That's what she wanted, or thought she did maybe: for him to squeeze it all out, every last guilty drop. Prove it to me, just how sorry you are. Should have asked her gran, the old girl could have told her: there's no end to it, it's just self-pity, and it just goes on and on.

You think about it and think about it, you do nothing else.
Only remember, and then you let yourself stop. Not overnight
and never completely, but that was the way it happened,
and Joseph couldn't see that as wrong.

If it's not going to help. If you're never going to change it.
Why touch the sore part any more than you have to?

Alice didn't know how to describe it. Whether she was angry or frightened, or both. All her grandfather would say was not to be hard on Joseph, nothing more. It didn't seem to matter how often she or her mother asked him what Joseph had done and why.

Her mum called her, every couple of days, and in every conversation, Alice said the same thing.

– I can't just do nothing.

She worked and cycled and shopped and cleaned and cooked. Couldn't phone him or go and see him. Her mouth felt stopped up, throat blocked. She was hurt: cut out. *Useless too. Weak, just wasting time.* She had no idea what Joseph was thinking or feeling, where he was or if he was alright. Alice knew she was out of her depth. She washed her face and brushed her teeth and thought over and again how she couldn't just leave it, not like this.

– I don't know what to do.

Her mum suggested his parents, going to talk to them, but Alice still wasn't sure. She thought Eve would be better: Joseph saw more of her, she might be able to tell Alice more, but it still took her days to make the decision. Eve had always been wary of her, and if she was honest, Alice was afraid how she might react. Didn't know what Joseph might have told her about the past weeks. She wasn't in the phone book under Mason and Alice didn't know her address, but she knew the name of her business, Joseph had talked about it a few times, and so she looked it up in the Yellow Pages.

– He's alright. Getting there.

Eve wasn't very forthcoming at first.

– He's living at ours mostly, but he goes home a bit too. Stays overnight.
– Your mum and dad's house?
– No, his flat.

Alice didn't want to hang up, just give up on Eve, but she didn't want to talk like this, on the phone: too easy for Joseph's sister to keep fending her off. Almost as prac- tised as Joseph was. She was surprised when Eve agreed to see her. Two days later, at lunchtime, the office was in a railway arch, not far from the hospital. Eve ran stalls on markets and Alice knew she didn't have a shop, but had never thought where she might work from before. She wheeled her bike along the concrete path that led off the road, through the high gates, past the car wash and the lock-ups, and found Eve hosing down the floor. Torn leaves and pollen swimming in the gutters outside the big double doors. It was a cold day, and not much warmer inside. Eve apologised for that: it was the first thing she said, told Alice she had to keep it cold in there because of the flowers. She was thick with layers, long woollen socks pulled up to cover her legs, old mittens with the fingers and thumbs chopped off. Eve smiled.

– You won't want me to take your coat.

In the far corner there was a sink and a fridge and a
kettle. Eve filled it up and rinsed two mugs, kept her
back turned and Alice thought she was taking her time.
A long table stood against the wall on her left, and at
the near end were two folding chairs: open and ready,
it looked like. Alice leaned her bike up against the doors
and sat down.

The room was vast, the ceiling high above their heads:
curved brick and damp, whitewash peeling. The whole
place smelt green with sap, although Alice couldn't see
many flowers. The floor to the right of her was a mass
of black buckets of different sizes, all half-filled with
water, ready for whatever came back from the markets
this evening. Four large arrangements sat at the other
end of the table, waiting for Eve to finish up and
deliver them. She'd told Alice she had to leave by two
at the latest, and Alice thought that gave her less than
an hour.

– I think Joseph needs help.

Such a banal thing to say, so obvious. Worse because she
was speaking to his sister's back.

– What do you think we're doing?

Eve replied without turning, stirring milk into the mugs,
putting the carton back into the fridge.

It stung, being spoken to like that, but Alice let it pass.
Keep going. On past experience, she thought she should
have been prepared. The one time Eve had been different

with her was at the snooker club. When Joseph was away
for what felt like ages, buying a round in the other room,
and Alice had finished her game with Arthur. She hadn't
known what to do with herself until Eve came over and
sat next to her. She'd asked Alice about work, and after
her grandad, and it was small talk really, but Eve knew
all the details, even Grandad's name. Alice had presumed
Eve wasn't interested in her, but it was clear then that
she'd been interested enough to find out a bit from
Joseph. Alice had been aware too that Eve had come
over to make her feel comfortable, and she'd liked her
for it. *She can't have invited me here just to be rude.*

Eve turned round slowly, carrying the mugs across the
room. She set them down on the table before she spoke
again.

– He'll find his own way.

The other chair was in front of her, but Eve stayed on
her feet. Her arms were folded, but it looked more like
she was cold than on the defensive. Her tone was
different too, and Alice thought she was trying. Eve said:

– He managed it before.
– But won't the same thing just happen again? If he
doesn't get some kind of support. Professional, I mean.

Eve looked at her. Alice didn't stop.

– Isn't that harder for Joseph? To have to start again,
every time. For you too. Everyone.

No response.

– I'm sure you and Arthur are doing a lot for him. I don't want to offend you.
– None taken.

Eve was matter of fact, but it seemed genuine. She went on:

– It's just we've been over all this with him before, you know?

Eve shifted her weight, and Alice wished she would sit down. Too hard to have this conversation already, and it was as though Eve wanted to keep three paces between them.

– I thought the same when it started, I wanted to get him help. Professional, quick as possible. I knew that people who leave the army have trouble sometimes, end up homeless and everything. I phoned all the right organisations. Art got leaflets out of the library. I thought that's what Joey needed: he had to make the adjustment and we could find the right people for him to go to.

Eve smiled a little, and Alice thought she might be making fun of herself: that she could have presumed it would be so simple.

– I know he's not alright. Doesn't take a genius, does it? I've talked to so many people about Joey, I can't count. There was this one place I visited, I wanted him to go. You get individual treatment, but they have a group too, therapy. They meet every week, and people go as long as they need. A lot of them are ex-service, but you don't have to be, just need to get your doctor to refer

you. They had a waiting list, months if you were lucky, but it sounded good. Worth it. He'd been gone for a while and when Art went and got him, Joey promised me he'd talk to the doctor about it, but I don't think he did.
– You never asked?

Eve blinked at her.

– Yes. Course I did. I made the appointments for him at the surgery. Got shouted at enough times about it, or he just blanked me out. What am I going to do? Strap him into the car and drive him there like I do Ben?

Alice thought maybe she should have. Eve said:

– He's the one has to live with it. Not for me to decide how he does it.

Alice felt herself shifting forward. *With what?* She saw Eve retreat: too obvious, what she was about to ask. She wouldn't get an answer that way. Alice started again:

– Joseph's spent a lot of time with my grandfather over the last few months. Grandad was in the services too, in the RAF. I'm sure they've spoken to each other, but I don't know what about. My Grandad won't say. I thought you might be able to tell me.
– Sorry.

Eve shook her head. Alice didn't know what that meant. That she didn't want to say, or Joseph had told her not to. Maybe he knew Alice would come asking.

– He smashed a window at my Grandad's house. Trashed the hallway. I'm pretty certain of that. And I know he's done worse.

Eve nodded, she held Alice's gaze, but she still wouldn't speak.

– I'd like to know why. I'm sure you can understand that. And I want it to stop. For Joseph too.
– I can't tell you because I don't know.

A calm statement. It took Alice a while to take in. Eve said:

– I'm sorry.

Alice didn't know whether to believe her. She'd come here to find out, or at least to make a start, but she wasn't even going to be able to do that. Alice said:

– I tried asking him.

Eve nodded again, but it was irritable this time. Alice thought she had to carry on, try to get something out of her. She didn't know what she could do if this didn't go anywhere, and she wanted Eve to know how painful it was too, being shut out.

– He wouldn't answer the door last time I went round.
– Didn't you want some time away from him?

Alice stopped.

– This all started before that, Eve. I'm not responsible for what's happened.

She wasn't, logic told her so. She'd been over and over that ground herself, but Alice heard her denial come out too strong, and she was embarrassed by it. Eve looked away.

– No. That's what Joey says too.

She put her mug on the table first, and then she sat down opposite Alice, rubbed her face. Fingers over her eyes, her nails blue-pink with the cold. Alice waited, struck that Joseph had been defending her, arguing with his sister and taking her side. He was self-willed, Alice knew that, and so maybe Eve was telling the truth: she didn't know what Joseph had been holding back, and she couldn't tell Alice why because Joseph wouldn't speak to her either. Eve said:

– Just a second. Sorry.

She was pale, wearing eyeliner, but it looked like yesterday's. Alice wondered if Joseph was at her house now, and whether Arthur was with him, what he was doing, and if Eve had those same thoughts all the time now. Eve put her hands in her lap, and then she asked:

– He's never said anything to you?

Alice shook her head. Eve sat a moment and then she leaned forward a little.

– You say you want it to stop. Of course you do, we all do. But you want to know if he did something wrong too, don't you? While he was in Ireland.

Eve looked at her, she was speaking quietly.

—You know about some of the things soldiers have done there, and you were hoping I could tell you Joseph isn't one of them.

— No. I wasn't. I'm trying not to presume anything.

It wasn't pleasant, the way Eve had recognised what she was frightened of hearing. Maybe his sister had had the same fears: she would have been familiar with the same news stories. Eve looked at Alice and shrugged, as if to say Joseph hadn't told her. She couldn't provide reassurance or confirmation. Alice nodded, and then Eve said:

— I never liked Joseph being in the army. He knows that. I could understand it, if that's the way you feel too. Because of the things soldiers have to do sometimes. I wouldn't blame you. We're never going to like it, but what we think doesn't matter, that's not the point.

She stopped for a moment, and Alice watched her face. Of course Eve was right: whatever it was that Joseph didn't want to tell them, it didn't have to be criminal to be troubling, he could have been following the rules of engagement. Alice wasn't sure that made her feel any better. Perhaps it wasn't meant to.

— The way I see it. He was in the army. Chances are, he's done something or seen something done. What kind of person comes away from that with peace of mind?

Eve seemed to weigh them equally, these possibilities: Joseph as witness or perpetrator, either or. Alice couldn't believe that's how she really felt. She knew which of the two she found easier to bear, couldn't imagine it would be so different for his sister.

Eve was watching her now, frowning.

– Why do you have to know? You talk like you've got a right to know or something.

She wasn't being unfriendly.

– You want to know. But that's different.

Eve looked away again after that, her eyes on the table, thumbnail tracing the rough grain of the wood.

– Even if he did get treatment. Even if that helped. He still might never say. Only to a psychologist, or a group. I don't think that would be enough for you, would it?

Alice wanted to deny it, but Eve was talking so quietly, not accusing. And it was true, so it would have been pointless to contradict her.

Alice spent a long time thinking over the conversation. *He's never said anything?* For all she insisted, Eve was still curious. Alice remembered her expression, once Eve was sure Joseph hadn't told Alice either: the way she'd nodded, satisfied, somehow. Or maybe that was unkind. It would have hurt, probably, if she had known more than Eve, his own sister. Alice could understand that.

You want to know, but that's different. Joseph didn't have to tell her, Eve was adamant. Even though it seemed like she was the one who took him in each time, put up with the fighting, the going missing. He didn't owe her any explanation. It was almost admirable, Alice thought, to allow someone so much latitude: must take a lot of tolerance. If he could cope with it, then Eve would too. Perhaps Joseph didn't give her any choice, but Alice still couldn't understand it: how Eve could put herself aside like that, and all her questions, the misgivings she must have had.

Alice left later than they'd arranged: it was well after two by the time they'd finished talking, but Eve didn't hurry her out. She walked with Alice as far as the road and then she said:

– Much worse for him than it is for any of us, you know?

Later, Alice thought maybe that was how Eve did it: she put her brother's behaviour down to a guilty conscience. Alice could even follow her logic, although it made her uncomfortable: Eve could accept his absences and anger if they were his penance. It meant Joseph was in some way culpable, of course, not just a witness. What he did may have been sanctioned, but he still thought himself responsible. He had to live with it, and Eve wasn't going to interfere.

It seemed bleak to Alice, lonely for Joseph, and it was unfair, surely, to make such an assumption. She thought of her grandfather, the bombs exploding up into the plane, and the engineer bleeding to death on the too-long flight back to Nairobi. Joseph might have seen any number of terrible things while he was in the province, legitimate or otherwise, and not only done by soldiers. He had no physical scars: Alice caught herself, looking for marks on the body she remembered. Wasn't it still possible that he'd been harmed? Eve didn't seem to allow room for that.

But then Joseph wasn't telling, and Alice knew how hard that was to live with. His sister had gone looking for what she needed, and Alice couldn't blame her. She could see the consolation in what Eve had found too. *What kind of a person comes away with peace of mind?* Far better to know he feels something than nothing.

Fifteen

Before Joseph moved back to the flat, he painted the walls. Eve came to see him on the last day, to admire his work, brought an indian with her, a late Sunday lunch, with a can of lager each to toast the job. She stood the bag in the kitchen and went through the flat with him first. The sun was already going down, so Joseph turned on the lights. Still bare bulbs in every room, and the floorboards still needed varnish, but he was getting there.

Eve dished up while Joseph washed his brushes, and then they ate in the kitchen, looking out over the courtyard. His neighbours had fairy lights in their windows, snowspray and tinsel. His fourth Christmas there and some of the decorations were familiar by now. He and Eve drank their beers and talked about what to buy Arthur and their dad, and all the time Joseph watched his sister and wondered. What she'd been thinking these past weeks, while he was staying back at her place. If she'd ever wanted to know, the way Alice did. Joseph had thought it might happen this time, Eve might ask him what was going on and why, but here she was, eating curry with him and talking about Christmas.

She'd always kept her door open and never seemed to need an explanation: Joseph was grateful to his sister for that. Hard to talk to anyone about it, and Eve made it easy not to. It had worked for him before. Might do again. Except that Alice wouldn't have him back, not on those terms.

Weeks went by, most of the winter. Martha got pregnant, and after many rows with Keith, she told Alice one morning they'd decided to keep the baby.

– Good.
– Really?

They were both sitting at the kitchen table, both meant to be leaving for work, but they'd taken to having an extra cup of tea together lately. The windows were steamed up against the morning, and Alice thought Martha was pleased, even though her flatmate was doing her best to sound otherwise.

– There's one bad thing about it. Apart from Keith I mean.
– You're giving me notice, aren't you?
– I am. Sorry.
– That's okay. I've started looking.

Her grandmother's will had come through in January, and it made a mortgage just about possible. Instead of visiting her grandfather at weekends, Alice had been looking at flats with him. He'd drive, because they could never get round more than one or two on public transport, and then they'd find a café or a garden centre to browse through between appointments. It was strange at first, the idea of buying so near to where she'd grown up, but Alice couldn't afford anything closer to work, and then she got to like the prospect of living a few streets away from her grandad again. He started scanning the property pages of the local papers, and sent his recommendations, red-ringed, through the post.

– I can separate the wheat from the chaff for you at least.

He tended towards ground floor, with a garden, and space enough for the piano. Her grandmother had left it to her, but Alice had thought it should stay at her grandad's: removing it would leave such a hole in the living room they'd shared. It pleased her that he insisted she should have it, wouldn't listen to arguments against. On a Saturday afternoon, over mugs of tea in a greasy spoon together, waiting for an estate agent to show up, he suggested hiring specialist removers and contacting her grandmother's tuner for advice.

– You can play for me when I visit.
– I'm nowhere near as good as Gran.
– You'll have to practise.

Said in the same dry tone she remembered from when he'd got to know Joseph, and she'd seen what her grandfather could be like, when he enjoyed someone's company. Perhaps he'd been like that with Gran too, when the rest of the family wasn't around. This tone came out more often in their conversations now: still new to her, but Alice liked being teased every once in a while by her grandad.

They sorted through Gran's papers together. Alice took two days' holiday at the end of February and they slowly emptied the drawers of her grandmother's desk onto the dining room table. Dental records and bank statements, her divorce papers, the order of service from her father's funeral. Scraps of ribbon and folded wrapping paper, stored for re-use, spare notelets and envelopes, a pocket calendar from 1962 with friends' and family birthdays marked. Her grandfather said he wanted to keep that.

– I'll try and remember to use it too.

He'd brought two boxes down from the attic when Alice arrived the second morning. Mostly personal letters, and nothing he wanted to throw away: he'd been through them already, but he showed them to Alice anyway. In small piles, ordered by date, and neatly tied with string. Alice recognised her grandfather's handiwork: she knew the birthday cake parcels her gran had sent were always tied by him. Beautiful, and it felt like sabotage to use scissors, but the knots were impossible. He left Alice with the letters and went to put on the kettle.

The postmarks ran across the decades. Most were from the fifties, with Kenyan as well as British stamps: her grandparents' love letters. Fewer of them later, but they continued well into the nineties, and Alice wondered that they'd been apart long enough during those years to warrant sending letters. While Gran was up in York maybe, or visiting Aunt Celie, and Grandad stayed in London: a week away at most, but they'd still found things to write. Her grandfather had sorted them into pairs, wherever he could, and for almost every letter, there was a reply.

– I wanted you to know where they are.

Her grandfather was back in the room. He smiled at her, hesitant:

– You can read them, but you might have to wait until I'm gone, I'm afraid.

He set a cup down beside her, and went to drink his by the window. He knew she was disappointed, Alice could see that: to have to defer the untying and opening, the reading. They stayed like that for long minutes, the width of the room between them, and then Alice slotted the letters back into their box. Reluctant but careful, in order of date, just as her grandfather had done. Conscious he was unlikely to be with her the next time she saw them.

They'd started a list the day before, subscriptions to cancel, charities to contact, standing orders to stop or transfer, and they went through this together, dividing the tasks between them. Many were already months overdue: Alice was ashamed not to have offered her grandfather help earlier, and that she hadn't thought he might need her to. It was lunchtime before they'd finished. Alice had cycled past the deli on her way over, and she went into the kitchen to put everything onto plates for them. Her grandfather had cleared a space on the table when she returned with the tray, and he'd also laid two envelopes in front of her chair.

– These are for now. If you'd like them.

They were addressed to her grandparents, both of the letters, but the handwriting was unfamiliar. Dated a few weeks apart, in 1972, a couple of months before she was born.

– I don't have the letters we sent them, of course, but they may have kept them.

Alice turned the first envelope over and recognised the return address: her father's parents. She'd written to him there, the first letter, and he'd told her they had sent it on. Her grandfather left his plate untouched while she read the handwritten pages. Both full of concern for her mother and what life with a child but no husband would hold for her. In both they also expressed their regret that their son did not want to stay in contact. *We still hope he will change his mind.* The second letter referred to a meeting, and confirmed the date, with directions from the A-road that passed their village.

– You went to see them?
– Yes.
– You and Gran?
– Yes.
– Why didn't anyone ever tell me?

Her grandfather looked at her, shocked. She hadn't shouted, but she had raised her voice. It was the first time Alice had felt angry with him in months. Not since Joseph had smashed the window. She'd only felt protective. But then he said:

– I presumed Isobel. I thought. I'm not sure now.

He looked at the letters, frowning. Old eyes flickering.

– You should have known. Of course you should. I'm sorry.

He was squinting a little. Alice said:

– What did you talk about?
– Practicalities. The different options.

He looked at her, almost embarrassed.

– I mean marriage, adoption. Financial considerations.

Then he smiled a little.

– Not that we had much influence, of course. Our children were both stubborn. A good thing Sarah was.

Gran had known that she'd started writing to her father.
Alice thought about all her grandparents' letters and was
certain Gran would have told him.

– He stopped writing to me. Almost two years ago now.
– Yes. We did think. We assumed something must have
happened.

Alice thought her grandad was reddening.

– I liked them, your other grandparents. I've often
wondered. That they never knew you. I'm sure they
would have liked to.

Alice remembered the letter she'd sent her father, the
first one, and that his reply had come so quickly. They
must have forwarded it immediately, the same day
perhaps. Did they think it was from her? Addressed by
hand. They can't have got many letters for their son, not
thirty-odd years since he left home.

The first Alice heard of Joseph again was when she went round to see Clare. It was sometime early in March, not long after Stan's birthday, and Alice brought round a bottle for Clare to pass on to him. Their extension still wasn't finished, but the kitchen cabinets had finally arrived and the walls were plastered too. Clare saw her looking at them and then apologised.

– Joseph. He insisted.

Alice nodded. Thought about how Joseph had insisted on doing her grandad's house too. *I wouldn't want paying.* Maybe he'd seen it as a way to make up, for disappearing on her, the first time. She said:

– You don't have to be sorry.
– No. I know. Stan wants to give him another go.

Clare still sounded apologetic, but Alice surprised herself by feeling pleased. The regret came after she left, slowed her limbs and her breath, and was much more familiar. Later, she described how those autumn weeks had felt, on the phone to her mother:

– As though he wanted me to split up with him. Be the one to give up. I thought he was willing me to do it. Even before that business at Grandad's.

Alice sometimes thought she'd complied too easily: remembered how cowardly it had felt, not to include a message in the letter her grandfather had written him. But her mother said it wasn't her fault it had ended. The way she saw it, the break would have come anyway.

– I mean, I don't really know Joseph. I liked him when he came up here, and Dad seems determined to defend him. But he was shutting you out, even before the autumn. You can't expect to be with someone and do that to them, not in my book. Not if you want them to be happy with you, anyway.

It made Alice feel better, talking to her mother, but after she'd hung up, she wasn't sure she agreed.

There was an old conversation with Clare, one they'd had often over the years. About Stan, and how he'd so wanted to get away from Poland. *All the things that never happened, and the things that were done wrong.* That's how he put it, and it was all he would say. It used to frustrate Clare, that he wouldn't tell her more, and yet when friends or family came over from Wroslaw, and the wine came out, that's all they talked about. Hours and hours, whole nights, in a broken-up mixture of Polish and English, so it was difficult to follow.

– I make the most of those evenings, get what I can. It's still frustrating. But Stan has to talk about it with them, you know? He has to, and I think he hates it. He's always jumpy for days after they've gone. Has a really short fuse. He can forget about it with me and the kids. I might not like it, but he does.

It wasn't the same: Stan was running from an economic situation that had become unbearable, parents who were too bitter about the past, and the changes that hadn't made enough of a difference to their lives. It didn't compare, but Alice thought she was still trying to imagine a way she could let Joseph have his silence.

She went to Stan and Clare's party: a late birthday do, and a sort of warming for their new rooms. The place was crowded with people she hadn't seen in ages, and there was so much to catch up on, it took her the best part of an hour to make her way across the party to where Clare was standing. For months now, Alice had been avoiding places she thought Joseph might be, and she was relieved when Clare said he'd been and gone already, much earlier in the evening. But it also made her wonder when it was going to stop. They had friends and places in common. She didn't want to pretend she'd never known him.

Her grandparents' letters were back in the attic. She saw the box again when she went to sort through the things she'd left at her grandfather's, ready for moving. Her grandad had cleared the attic over the winter, and said her books and camping stuff were getting dusty in their uncovered crate. He'd left an old suitcase under the eaves for her to put them in, if she wanted. Years since the last time she was up here, only two trunks and four or five small boxes left, grouped together by the trap door, and the letters were second from bottom. Alice had heard some of what must be in them already: the things her mother had told her, the explosions, the crew member lost. But since she'd seen the letters, she thought there must have been more. All those years and pages he'd written, the conversations he'd had with Joseph. Alice tried again to imagine them talking, and couldn't: thought she was still afraid of what she might end up hearing. She'd preferred Ireland at a safer distance. Perhaps Gran had felt the same way about Kenya. Sitting there, Alice didn't feel impatient for her grandfather's letters any longer: more curious now to read her grandmother's responses.

She must have wanted to leave it behind: her first marriage, expat Nairobi, the unhappy years there, but she couldn't. She'd have had to leave Grandad too, and Alice knew Gran would never have done that. Alice had been so critical of their relationship. The way her grandmother allowed him to retreat behind her conversation, tolerated his rudeness as though she were blind to it. She didn't believe her gran was so thick-skinned: it must have upset her too. Alice had loved them, but never wanted a marriage like theirs: a partner whose behaviour you'd have to cover for. Still didn't. But she was aware now that something more had been passing between them, in all that time.

Something gentle, undeclared, about how they were with each other, but you could never intrude. Alice remembered the hush in their house on summer afternoons. No radios or water fights on the back lawn, or loud celebrations at the end of the working week, the way it was when she visited her friends after school. She used to put it down to them being old, easily tired, but now she thought their weekends were for being a couple. Their time, in the garden and kitchen: they would sit together, hands held, eyes closed, hot Saturdays after lunch in the shade on the patio. Alice was never told or reprimanded: there was no need, she just didn't get in the way. Lifted her bicycle out of the shed as quietly as possible, and carried it round the side of the house.

She thought about it often, that day they'd driven down from York: her mother's anger, standing in the hallway, trying to understand what had happened, and her grandfather's quiet refusal to blame Joseph or venture an explanation. They'd stood together, she and her grandad, even after her mother had given up asking and appealing, and went outside instead to dig in the plants she'd brought for his garden. He seemed so calm. Alice thought maybe he was relieved to have got it all over with: the repairs and the inevitable scene when she and her mother saw them. She'd stopped crying and could remember feeling glad of him, his quiet company and his small, clumsy gestures. And how sad he'd looked later, when she said she didn't think Joseph wanted to see her any more.

Sixteen

It was much easier than Joseph thought it would be.

Summer again, but no hot days yet. He'd been down in Brighton, finishing Clive's house, and he came home to a message from Alice, the first in months. She left a number, a new one, said she'd moved. He phoned her back the same evening and she asked if she could come round one day after work. Familiar and unfamiliar, that voice, and no edges to it. She said she'd left some things behind. A jacket and a hairbrush, a bike pump and the spare key to her lock. He knew where they all were: he'd left them where she had. Went round his flat collecting them into a box, chose a small one he reckoned would fit on the back of her bike. Put the map in there too, at the bottom, with the small beach and the wood above it marked.

They sat on the chairs in the big room the day she came, something they'd never done when they were together. Always sat in the kitchen then, because it was the only room he'd got anywhere near finished. Alice gave him the news about Martha's baby, due in a few weeks, and then she shifted a bit in her chair before telling him she was going to see her grandparents at the weekend.

– My Dad's parents. I asked them up to London last time, and they've returned the invitation. My Dad knows about it. He won't be there, but we've started writing again. I think so anyway, a couple of letters.

Joseph thought: one way got blocked so she found another. Alice was smiling, and it was hard not to smile with her. She lifted her hands to her face. He knew those fingers, that skirt and T-shirt, old trainers and bare legs.

She never said anything about the colour on his walls, or the furniture, although he saw her looking, and she didn't bat an eye when he asked after her grandad either, just said he was up north at the moment, visiting her mum and step-dad.

– A long weekend. They've lined up a garden to visit every day. All over Yorkshire. Poor Alan.

She laughed. And then:

– My mum's got this idea of us going to Africa. To Kenya. See the places Gran lived, I think the hospital she worked in might still be there. Mum's talked about it on and off over the winter. I don't know how far she's really got with planning it or anything.

Alice rubbed at a smear of oil on her shin.

– She'd love my Grandad to come with us, basically. Show us the places they got to know each other. He says he's too old now, but she reckons she'll wait a year, let him come round to the idea. I'm not sure he will, though.

She smiled at him and Joseph remembered something Jarvis had said. About another Corporal he'd served with, a bit older than him. He'd been in Ireland, early in the seventies, and after he'd finished his twenty-two years, he went back there. Got himself a job selling advertising on beermats, with a company car and a hospitality budget. Drove around the province from pub to pub, and after he'd got through his business with the land-lord, he always stayed for a couple and tried getting into conversation with the locals. Sounded like the worst idea to Joseph. But Jarvis said he went to all areas, loyalist and nationalist. Always told them he used to be in the army. *Didn't get into as many fights as you might think.*

Alice was still sitting, but pulling her bag and jacket onto her lap, and the box, and it occurred to Joseph that she'd been gathering her things together for some time. He stood up, to let her go, and then she smiled. Alice went ahead of him down the hall, and she nodded goodbye after he'd opened the door, backing the first few paces down towards the stairwell.

Joseph stepped out onto the walkway and looked over the side, waiting for her to get to the bottom of the stairs. It was a bright day, and the air was warm on his face, but the concrete still felt cold through his socks. The courtyard below him was full of sun, only the stair-well door was in shadow. Alice came out and he thought she might look up. She crossed the courtyard, into the sun, a brief flare of red, and then she was gone.

Acknowledgements

Toby Eady and all at Orme Court. My editors Dan Frank and Ravi Mirchandani. Dr Claire Fyvie and colleagues at the Rivers Centre in Edinburgh, and especially Richard, Michael, Stuart, William, Mark and Pauline for letting me sit in, and being patient with all my questions. Dr Robert Hunter at Gartnaval Hospital in Glasgow, Angela Preston at the Arndale Resource Centre in Drumchapel, and Jayne Herriot for all her time. The Imperial War Museum film archive. The Royal Military Academy at Sandhurst. The RAF Museum at Hendon. The 49 Squadron Association, and particularly Stewart Kaye and Stewart Henderson, for photos, articles and long conversations. Willy Maley, Adam Piette, Paddy Lyons, Kate McLoughlin, Paul Welsh and Caroline Knight for all the reading. Gretchen Seiffert. The Arts and Humanities Research Council and the University of Glasgow.

Special thanks to DW for reinforcing the corners.

Although some of the events described in the novel are based on fact, this is a work of fiction, and the characters are of my own invention. I am enormously grateful for the help I have received from those listed above. Any mistakes that remain are my own.